MORE PRAISE

"*Murder Strikes a Pose*, by Tracy Weber, is a delightful debut novel featuring Kate Davidson, a caring but feisty yoga teacher … Namaste to Weber and her fresh, new heroine!"

—Penny Warner, *How to Dine on Killer Wine*

"[T]his charming debut mystery … pieces together a skillful collage of mystery, yoga, and plenty of dog stories against the unique backdrop of Seattle characters and neighborhoods. The delightful start of a promising new series. I couldn't put it down!"

—Waverly Fitzgerald, author of *Dial C for Chihuahua*

"Three woofs for Tracy Weber's first Downward Dog Mystery, *Murder Strikes a Pose*. Great characters, keep-you-guessing plot, plenty of laughs, and dogs—what more could we want? Ah, yes—the next book!"

—Sheila Webster Boneham, author of *Drop Dead on Recall*

MURDER
STRIKES A POSE

MURDER
STRIKES A POSE

A Downward Dog Mystery

TRACY WEBER

MIDNIGHT INK
WOODBURY, MINNESOTA

FIRST EDITION
First Printing, 2014

Book design by Donna Burch
Cover design by Kevin R. Brown
Cover illustration by Nicole Alesi/Deborah Wolfe Ltd.
Edited by Connie Hill

Midnight Ink, an imprint of Llewellyn Worldwide Ltd.

This is a work of fiction. Names, characters, places, and incidents are either the product of the author's imagination or are used fictitiously, and any resemblance to actual persons, living or dead, business establishments, events, or locales is entirely coincidental.

Library of Congress Cataloging-in-Publication Data

Weber, Tracy, 1964–
  Murder strikes a pose : a downward dog mystery / Tracy Weber. — First edition.
    pages cm
  ISBN 978-0-7387-3968-7
1. Women—Fiction. 2. Homeless men—Crimes against—Fiction. 3. Yoga—Fiction. 4. Seattle (Wash.) I. Title.
  PS3623.E3953M87   2014
  813'.6—dc23   2013030623

Midnight Ink
Llewellyn Worldwide Ltd.
2143 Wooddale Drive
Woodbury, MN 55125-2989
www.midnightinkbooks.com

Printed in the United States of America

ACKNOWLEDGMENTS

Writing a book is like raising a child. It takes a village.

My village contains a huge network of supporters who encouraged me long before I believed this novel would ever come to fruition. I'm sure I've forgotten to mention many of you, but that doesn't mean your assistance is any less appreciated.

To my yoga students, particularly those in my yoga teacher training programs: Thank you for having faith in me and patiently listening to my never-ending litany of writing updates and Tasha-dog stories. Without your encouragement, I never would have persevered through the challenging process of getting published.

Joan, Claire, Larra, Mary, and Frankie, thank you for reading my early drafts and giving me insightful feedback that made the work stronger. Marta Tanrikulu, without your editing support, the book would never have been publishable. I recommend your services to other writers every chance I get. Margaret Bail, my fabulous agent, thank you for taking a chance on a newbie author and working at lightning speed to make her dream come true. And to Terri Bischoff, Midnight Ink editor extraordinaire, a special thank you for seeing the potential in this book.

Last, but never least, a huge thank you to my husband Marc for the support he has given me, both in writing and in running my yoga studio. Marc is also the fabulous developer who created my studio and author websites. Being married to a small business owner is tough—to a writer, even tougher. Marc had the challenging destiny of marrying both. Thank you, Marc, for being you. I always appreciate you, even if I don't say it enough.

Namaste (The light in me acknowledges the light in each of you.)

ONE

I LAID MY BODY on the cool wood floor, covered up with a blanket, and prepared to die.

Metaphorically, that is.

Corpse Pose's ten-minute rest always soothed my stressed-out nerves, and for once I didn't feel guilty about the indulgence. My to-do list was blank, Serenity Yoga's phone was silent, and I had a whole blissful hour between clients to do my favorite activity: practice yoga.

Even my eclectic Greenwood neighborhood seemed uncharacteristically quiet, lulled by Seattle's rare afternoon sun. The residents of the apartments above the yoga studio were off at their day jobs; the alcohol-addicted patrons of the block's two dive bars slept off their Jim Beam breakfasts; the soccer moms shopping at next door's upscale PhinneyWood Market purchased the day's supplies in unusual silence.

I wiggled my toes under a Mexican blanket, covered my eyes with a blue satin eye pillow, and inhaled deeply. The ooey-gooey smell of Mocha Mia's chocolate caramel cake wafted from across the street and filled my nostrils with sweet toffee-scented bliss—my all-time favorite aromatherapy.

Paradise. Simply paradise.

I released my weight into the earth and silently coached myself, exactly as I would one of my students. *OK, Kate. Feel your body relax. Notice the random fluctuations of your mind and—*

A vicious snarl ripped through the silence, startling me out of my catnap. I sat straight up, eye pillow falling to the floor with an undignified thump.

What the heck?

When had a dog fighting ring moved into the neighborhood?

A dog fight was the only plausible explanation for the commotion outside. Bursts of deep, frantic barking were followed by high-pitched yelping, all punctuated by the peace-shattering sounds of angry yelling. The phrases I could make out confirmed my suspicions. This had to be a dog fight, albeit one-sided.

"Control your dog!"

"Get that vicious beast out of here!"

And even a simple, "What the hell?"

I closed the door between the yoga room and the studio's lobby, hoping to block out the intrusive sounds. Snarls, shouts, and an occasional ear-piercing shriek continued to reverberate right through the wall.

Undaunted, I imagined that the sounds were merely clouds floating across my mental horizon. Most of those clouds were dark and ominous, like the deep thunderclouds preceding a hailstorm. But every so often I heard a soft voice, more like the fluffy clouds of childhood summers. I couldn't quite make out his words, but I could tell that the speaker was a man. From his tone, I assumed he was trying to calm beasts both human and animal.

It wasn't working.

Neither, for that matter, was my attempted meditation.

I'd obviously have to shift tactics.

I tried drowning out the clamor with low, soft chanting. Then I increased the volume. But even as I belted out *Om Santi*, my favorite mantra for peace, I felt my jaw start to tighten. My fingernails bit deeply into my palms. My shoulders crept up to my ears.

An entirely different mantra began pounding through my head: *Don't get me angry; you wouldn't like me when I'm angry.*

A series of yelps and the words "I'm calling the cops!" zapped me like a cattle prod. I leapt from my mat and stormed across the floor, determined to put a stop to that infernal racket. I hurled open the door and came face-to-face, or rather face-to-snout, with the source of the commotion. Not more than five feet away from the studio's entrance stood a paunchy, dark-haired man and the biggest, skinniest, meanest-looking German shepherd I had ever seen. Don't get me wrong. I like dogs. I love them, in fact. It's their human counterparts I could sometimes do without. But this frothing beast was no Rin Tin Tin. A long line of drool oozed from its mouth. Its sharp white teeth glinted in the sunlight, and its wiry black topcoat still stood on end from the prior scuffle. The dog was obviously rabid.

I didn't recognize the man standing next to the frightening creature, but I did recognize his activity. He worked as a vendor for *Dollars for Change*, a well-regarded local newspaper that published articles about homelessness and poverty while employing those same homeless individuals as salespeople. Ordinarily I would have welcomed one of their vendors outside my business. If nothing else, supporting the paper demonstrated yoga's principles of kindness and compassion.

But this was *not* an ordinary circumstance. I absolutely could not allow that disgusting dog to raise a ruckus outside my studio. The prenatal class would have a fit. Suffice it to say that pregnancy hormones didn't always leave expecting moms in the best of moods. My moms-to-be liked their yoga practice. They *needed* their yoga practice. And they needed to be serene while doing it. If a noisy dog fight disturbed their peaceful experience, I'd be the one getting barked at.

Thinking less than yogic thoughts, I marched up to the pair, determined to put a stop to the chaos.

"What in the world's going on out here?"

The human half of the dastardly duo held a leash in one hand, newspapers in the other. He smiled at me and said, "Sorry about all the noise. I'm George, and this here's Bella. What's your name?"

"Kate Davidson, but—"

"Well, nice to meet you, Kate. I'd shake your hand, but mine are full, so Bella will have to do it instead."

The vicious beast walked up and calmly sniffed my hand. I prayed she wasn't about to ingest my fingers.

"Bella, say hello!"

Upon hearing her owner's command, the giant hairy monster-dog immediately went into a perfect sit and sweetly offered me her paw. Maybe she wasn't rabid after all. Just huge and ill-mannered.

"Don't mind Bella," he continued. "She's very friendly to people. She just doesn't like other dogs much. She'd be fine if people kept their unruly mutts to themselves, but they think if their rude dog wants to play, Bella has to as well." He shook his head in disgust. "I don't understand some people!"

I tried to interrupt, to tell him that *his* dog was the problem, but he didn't give me the chance.

4

"Bella and I are new to this neighborhood, and we're supposed to sell papers near the market. I tried setting up by the north entrance, but there's a pet store at that end. Pete's Pets, I think it's called? The owner was a nice enough guy and all, but selling there was a disaster with all those dogs going in and out. Bella wasn't happy at all." He shrugged. "So I guess we're going to have to hang out here instead."

I bit the inside of my lip and considered my options. Up close, George wasn't exactly the paragon of health I wanted standing outside my business. His friendly smile exposed yellowed teeth in need of significant dental care, and if the sharp, ammonia-like smell was any indication, neither he nor Bella had taken a bath in quite some time. At three-thirty in the afternoon, I could smell whiskey on his breath, and I suspected this most recent drink hadn't been his first of the day. It would also likely be far from his last. I only knew one thing for certain: if George didn't frighten my students away, his loud, intimidating, fur-covered companion would.

I needed them to leave, but honestly, I didn't want to say it out loud. After all, I taught yoga for a living. People expected me to be calm and collected at all times. I wasn't allowed to be mean, or even irritated, for that matter. I hesitated as I tried to come up with the perfect words to make him want to move, if not out of the neighborhood, then at least across the street.

Fortunately (or perhaps unfortunately), one of my favorite students picked that very moment to walk up with her five-month-old Lab pup, Coalie. "Hey, Kate!" she said. "I hoped I'd run into you! Do you still have space in your Core Strength class tonight?"

Coalie was as rude and friendly as Labs everywhere. She couldn't stop herself if she tried. She ran up to Bella, wiggling her entire body with glee, and covered Bella's muzzle in sloppy wet puppy kisses.

Bella wasted no time. Faster than a 747 and stronger than a freight train, Bella pinned Coalie to the ground between her front legs, snarling and air-snapping on either side of Coalie's neck. I heard the sound of canine teeth chomping together and imagined soft puppy bones shattering between them.

My student screamed. Coalie yelped. George grabbed Bella's collar while I reached in between razor-sharp teeth to pull Coalie from the jaws of death. The three of us wrestled the two dogs apart, but not before my student almost died of heart failure.

"What's wrong with you?" she yelled. "Keep that vicious monster away from my baby!"

George quickly apologized, but said, "No damage done. Bella was just teaching that pup some manners." He pointed at Coalie. "See, it's all good!"

Coalie, oblivious with joy, seemed unscathed and ready to dive in again. Tail wagging and butt wiggling, she pulled with all her might, trying desperately to get back to Bella.

Bella had other plans. She sat next to George, glaring directly at that pup with a patented Clint Eastwood stare. *Go ahead,* she seemed to say. *Make my day.* My soon-to-be-former student ran off as quickly as her legs would move, dragging the still-happy puppy behind her.

"See you in class tonight!" I yelled to her rapidly retreating back. I doubted I'd be seeing her anytime soon.

Yoga reputation be damned. I had to get rid of this guy.

I put my hands on my hips and stood nice and tall, taking full advantage of my five-foot-three-inch frame. "Look. I can't let you stay here with the dog. She's obviously frightening people. You have to leave." I paused a moment for emphasis, then added, "Now."

George stood a little taller, too. "Look yourself, lady. The last time I checked, I'm standing on city property. I have every right to

6

be here. You don't own this sidewalk, and you can't stop me from making a living on it." He glared at me, sharp eyes unblinking. "We *Dollars for Change* vendors are licensed, and no matter how much you don't like us, the city says we can be here."

"There's no 'us' I don't like," I replied, frustrated. "It's your dog. And you may have every right to be here, but the dog is another story. What do you think Animal Control will do if I report a vicious dog attacking people outside my store?"

George stepped back, pulling Bella closer. Seattle had the toughest dangerous dog laws in the nation. We both knew what would happen if I made that call. "You wouldn't do that!" he said. "Bella's never hurt anyone."

I planted my feet stubbornly. "Try me."

George gave me a wounded look and gathered his papers, shoulders slumped in depressed resignation. "OK, we'll go. But I thought you yoga people were supposed to be kind." He shuffled away, shaking his head and mumbling under his breath. Bella followed close by his side.

"Crap," I muttered, watching their slow departure. "Crap, crap, crap, crap, crap."

He was right. Like all good yoga teachers, I had extensively studied yoga philosophy and tried to live by it. The teachings were clear: A yogi should respond to suffering with active compassion. And George was clearly suffering, whether he realized that fact or not.

Threatening to call the cops on George's dog may have been active, but it wasn't all that compassionate, to him or to Bella. I felt like a cad. My solution probably wasn't what the teachings had in mind, but it was the best I could come up with on short notice.

"Hang on there a minute!" I yelled as I ran to catch up with him. Out of breath, I said, "You're right. I overreacted, and I'm sorry. How many papers do you have left to sell today?"

George stopped walking. When he turned to look back at me, his eyes sparkled with an unexpected hint of wry humor. "About thirty."

The calculations weren't difficult. I wasn't completely broke—yet—but thirty dollars wasn't a drop in the bucket. On the other hand, my Monday evening classes were popular, and I had to get this guy away from the front door. Mentally crossing my fingers that the toilet wouldn't break again, I said, "Wait here. I'll be right back." I hurried back to the studio and grabbed thirty dollars from the cash box.

"If I buy all of your papers, will you be done for the day?"

"Yes ma'am, and that would be very kind of you." He gave me a broad, yellow-toothed smile. "Bella and I appreciate it very much."

He took the money, left the papers, and wandered off, whistling. Bella happily trotted behind him.

"Well, that wasn't so difficult," I said, patting myself on the back. "I should follow the teachings more often!" I went back inside and finished my considerably shortened practice. I chose to ignore the quiet voice in my head telling me I'd just made a huge mistake.

TWO

I DON'T KNOW WHAT possessed me to think that becoming George's best customer would keep him away from the studio. It must have been one of those mental delusions the *Yoga Sutras* warned me about.

Less than twenty-four hours later, I was elbow-deep in my least favorite activity—updating the studio's database—when the Power Yoga class entered Savasana, a pose of quiet rest. Vedic chanting flowed from the studio's speakers, filling the lobby with sounds of cherubic bliss.

Ahhhh…just the excuse I was looking for.

I cracked open the door to the yoga room, intending to eavesdrop as the instructor lulled her students into a state of samadhi—yoga-induced ecstasy. I returned to my chair, leaned back, and closed my eyes, mentally transporting myself out of the lobby and into the practice space.

In my mind's eye, I savored the room's peaceful atmosphere. Dimmed incandescent lights reflected off unadorned yellow-beige walls, illuminating the space in a soft golden hue; meditation candles cast dancing light beams along the maple floor; a fresh-cut bouquet of soft pink tulips decorated the altar, symbolizing the rebirth of spring. The room currently held twenty practicing yogis, but in my imagination, it was mine. All mine. I practically purred, feeling as contented as a recently fed kitten.

The teacher's voice soothed my nerves and dissolved salt-like grains of tension from behind my eyes. "Release your weight into the mat. Imagine that your muscles are made of softened wax, melting on a smooth, warm surface." My jaw muscles loosened. My shoulders eased down from my ears.

She continued her spoken lullaby. "With each inhale, imagine a white light entering the crown of your head and pouring through your body, illuminating every cell." A soft sigh escaped from my lips. "With each exhale—"

The now-familiar sound of barking drowned out the teacher's voice and jolted me awake.

Loud, angry barking.

My momentary tranquility vanished. As if in one motion, my jaw tightened, my shoulders lifted, and my hands clenched into tight fists. An embarrassing litany of swear words spewed from my lips.

I jumped up from the desk and frowned out the window. George and Bella were outside my door again, this time with a much larger stack of papers. Bella was no happier than the day before at the parade of dogs passing by. How *dare* they think they could walk on *her* sidewalk!

George couldn't have picked a worse place to hawk his wares if he tried. The walkway in front of the studio was practically a canine superhighway. It connected the building's parking lot to its street-level businesses. Serenity Yoga occupied the southern-most unit. The north end was home to the promised land of doggy delights known as Pete's Pets. The PhinneyWood Market and Zorba's Greek Deli separated the two.

As of this moment, the only thing keeping Seattle's treat-starved canines from an infinite supply of dog cookies was the sidewalk's newly acquired guard dog, Bella. If I wanted Serenity Yoga to live up to its name, I'd have to come up with a better strategy than buying the daily production of newspapers.

My customers didn't look at all peaceful as they grumped out of class. Neither did their teacher, for that matter. She stared out the window, scowling. "Who's the guy with that awful dog, Kate? Can't you make him leave?"

I smiled, pretending to be in charge. "Don't worry. I'll deal with it." *Though I have no idea how.*

I joined George and Bella on the sidewalk. "How's it going today?"

"Sales are OK, but I've got lots of papers here if you need some more," he replied, grinning.

I couldn't help but grin back. I may have been stubborn, but I knew when I'd been outsmarted. "Look. We need to come up with a compromise. You obviously want to set up shop here, and you're right; you have every legal right to do so. But I can't have the noise, much less the terrified customers. What do you propose we do?"

"It's not Bella's fault, you know. I've trained her some, and she's a good dog." He smiled at Bella, scratching the soft spot behind her ears. "You're a good girl, aren't you, sweetie?" Bella let out a heavy sigh and leaned into his touch. "She just never had a chance to get to know other dogs very well."

I suspected he was skillfully changing the subject, but I didn't press him. I asked another question instead.

"Why not?" I asked. "Is she a rescue?"

"Sort of. You see, before I got this paying gig, I used to live down south in a park near this ritzy neighborhood. Nice houses, great big yards, obviously plenty of money. People there throw away more food every week than most people eat in a month. I made out pretty good."

"They let you go through their trash?"

"Not exactly, but they didn't stop me, either. That's one nice thing about being homeless. People don't see you. They don't *want* to see you. It reminds them how good they've got it and makes them feel guilty, you know? Most of the time Miss Bella and I just blend into the background."

I had a hard time imagining this man-beast combo blending in anywhere, but I let it go. George continued his animated speech, barely even pausing for breath. He was obviously a practiced story-teller—and I had a feeling he'd shared this particular tale many times before.

"Honestly, people would be shocked if they knew how much I see and hear. And I'm no dummy," he said, emphatically shaking his head. "Most folks assume I'm too stupid or lazy to make it on my own, but I wasn't always homeless. I even used to have my own business. But people look right on through me as if I'm not even there.

"Anyway, this little puppy showed up at one of those houses one day. No more than three months old." He leaned down and ruffled Bella's ears. "Cutest little thing you ever saw, weren't you, Pumpkin? And would you believe it, they chained this lovely girl here up to a stake in the yard. I guess they thought she was a guard dog." His lips wrinkled in disgust.

"Those fools never played with her, never even took her out of that yard. Not once did I see them give her any affection. As if giving her a few kibbles and buying a stupid dog house were enough to make her want to protect them and their precious belongings. I watched for over two months as they let this little girl grow more and more frustrated. Of course she started barking and digging and whining. Who could blame her?"

"Didn't she bark at you?" I asked. "I mean, if you were prowling around her yard, I'd assume she'd have sounded the alarm."

"Nah, she liked me, poor little thing." George knelt on the ground and hugged Bella close. "I was the one person in her life that actually paid attention to her. I'd come by late at night when everyone was asleep. I'd talk to her, scratch her ears—I'd even share some of my loot from the trash. She and I became best buddies.

"Well, one night she started howling; lonely, I think. The noise must have royally pissed the creep who owned her, because he marched right out of that fancy house of his and kicked the crap out of her." His eyes hardened. "And her still a puppy! Well, that was it as far as I was concerned. I couldn't stand there and watch him abuse this sweet little thing. I waited a couple of hours, until I figured he'd gone back to sleep. And then I marched right into that yard, unhooked her chain, and took her. She's been with me ever since."

"Wait a minute" I interrupted. "You *stole* her?"

George stood up tall, holding his head high. "No, ma'am," he said, sounding slightly offended. "Absolutely not. I have my vices, that's for sure. But I am not a criminal, and I do not steal. No way. I *rescued* her."

Snatching a puppy from her own yard sounded a lot like stealing to me, but I decided not to argue the point.

"Of course, I couldn't stay down south anymore. That jerk might not recognize me, but he sure as heck would know his property. Bella and I went on the road that night and came up here to Seattle.

That's been almost a year now. Saving Bella was the best thing I ever did."

It was a beautiful story—but beside the point. "Regardless of how you got Bella," I interjected, "we still have a problem. She can't stay here. Why don't you leave her at home while you work?"

George's face remained deadpan. "Ma'am, not to state the obvious, but we're homeless. Where exactly would I leave her?"

I had to admit, he had a point.

I looked up and down the block, trying to come up with a solution. Seattle prided itself on having more dogs than children, so finding a dog-free zone to park Bella wouldn't be easy. The sidewalk on my side of Greenwood Avenue would never work. Hundreds of animals walked this path daily on their excursions to Pete's Pets.

The other side of the street didn't look much more promising. Tying Bella to the bike rack on the corner might work, but the nearby crosswalk would be problematic. I scanned farther south. Mocha Mia, the neighborhood's most loved coffee shop, had an outdoor sitting area that was shaded by large green and white umbrellas. Unfortunately, it was also pet-friendly. On warm days the crowded, chained-in space was practically a doggy day care. Tasmanian Devil-like whirlwinds of fur, coffee, china, and baked goods flashed through my mind.

No good.

My eyes finally landed on the block's most infamous dive bar, The Loaded Muzzle. The retail space next to it had been empty for months. Only the most desperate of drinkers ventured to that end of the block. If Bella barked at those poor souls, they'd be too anesthetized to notice. I pointed to a half-dead tree between the two businesses. "Why don't you tie her over there? That part of the sidewalk doesn't get much foot traffic, and there's plenty of shade."

George looked downright insulted. He forcefully shook his head. "No way. I'd never leave Bella over there by herself. That place is scary. Besides she goes crazy when she's tied up alone—sometimes she even hurts herself trying to get loose. She's still scarred from what that jerk of a prior owner did to her. She only feels safe when she's with me." He crossed his arms. "Bella and I stick together. We're family."

George and I were clearly at an impasse. I would never call Animal Control, and he knew it. Time ticked on as we stared at each other, each waiting for the other to give ground. Finally, inspiration struck. "Wait here," I said. "I have an idea."

———

The chime on the door to Pete's Pets sang out brightly as I walked into a veritable cornucopia of pet delights. Brightly colored squeaky toys, rhinestone-studded collars, and a thousand varieties of designer pet foods lined the shelves. These were obviously not Alpo dogs.

"Welcome to Pete's Pets. May I help you?"

Those words came from a man with the most gorgeous blue-green eyes I'd ever seen. That's all I noticed before I realized the rest of his face was hidden behind a scraggly, disgusting beard. Beards always gave me the shivers, and not in a good way. I knew it was superficial of me, but I couldn't stand beards, and I tried not to get too close to the people underneath them.

My best friend Rene teased me incessantly, claiming I exhibited all the classic signs of pogonophobia. Clearly she exaggerated. Just because some psychologist coined a fancy term for "fear of beards" didn't mean I was neurotic.

It was completely understandable, really. Whenever I saw a beard, I wondered what its wearer was hiding. I could never get past the defects that might be buried underneath all that unsightly hair, not to mention the food crumbs, saliva, and multilegged critters that might have taken up residence inside. In a word, gross. So in spite of his cool eyes, thin waist, and approximately six-foot frame, this man was not my type. Bummer.

I got right down to business. "Hi. I'm Kate, and I need to buy the biggest cage you have."

"Sorry, we don't sell bird supplies, but I can give you directions to an aviary supply store in Ballard. What kind of bird do you have?"

"No, I need a dog cage."

"Oh," he replied, looking surprised. "You must mean a crate! Follow me and I'll show you where they are."

We walked past bright yellow tennis balls, a zoo's worth of stuffed animals, and carefully balanced pyramids containing every kind of dog treat imaginable. We finally arrived at the back of the store and an area littered with so-called crates of all different shapes and sizes. Some were made of plastic, others of wood. Some contained metal rods that looked unmistakably like jail bars. Each boasted four walls, a ceiling, a floor, and a door with a lockable front. Frankly, they all seemed like fancy cages to me, but who was I to argue?

"Now, what kind of dog do you have?"

"It's not my dog. But I think it's a German shepherd. A big one. I mean huge." I spread my arms out as wide as they would go. "So a cage that fits something between a large horse and a small elephant will probably do."

He laughed. "A big shepherd used to hang out here with her owner, but they moved down by the yoga studio." He paused. "Hey, wait a minute, I recognize you! Don't you work there?"

"I own it, actually. And that shepherd's the dog I'm talking about. She's freaking out my customers. I hope if we put her in a cage, she won't bark and seem so threatening. Otherwise, I'll have to dig an access tunnel to my business underneath the sidewalk."

"I know what you mean," he said, grinning. "Bella's actually a pretty good dog, but she sure doesn't like other dogs getting into her business." He held out his hand. "It's great to meet you after all this time! I'm Michael, and I own this store."

I dropped my hand and stared at him, dumbfounded. "Seriously? Your name is Michael and you own a shop called Pete's Pets?"

His blue-green eyes sparkled. "Well, I wanted a memorable name, and all I could think of for Michael was Michael's Magpies. That name seemed to seriously limit my clientele. Besides, Pete's Pets was catchier." He winked and smiled wider. The crinkles around his eyes hinted that he smiled a lot.

I laughed in spite of myself and hoped *my* eyes were wrinkle free. Michael might not be my type, but that didn't mean *I* shouldn't look irresistible. He turned around to grab a crate, and I got a good look from behind. A sense of humor and a nice rear. Really too bad about the beard.

When he turned back toward me, those same eyes sparkled flirtatiously. "You know, we small business owners should help each other out. I'd like to learn more about yoga." He flashed a beguiling smile. "Want to go out for coffee some time?"

Crooked smile or not, I wasn't fooled. He clearly had no interest in perfecting his Downward Dog, or discussing the cat chow business, for that matter. The business he had in mind was of a more romantic nature.

The thought of spending time with him was appealing. He was obviously intelligent, except for the crazy idea he had of running his own business. And he might even be attractive underneath all that facial hair. For a blissful moment, I allowed myself the luxury of daydreaming. I imagined sharing a bottle of cool, crisp Chardonnay, curled up next to a roaring fire. I mentally snuggled in close to his broad chest, hugged his lean waist, and leaned in to kiss his ... *fur-covered lips.*

Nope. That ruined it. The mental image of all those tiny microbes swarming from his face to mine interrupted my daydream and brought me back to reality. I didn't know what lurked in that disorganized tangle of facial hair, and I wasn't about to find out the hard way. I just couldn't shake the subtle wave of nausea.

"Thanks, but I'm so busy with the studio I barely have time to brush my teeth, let alone go out."

"I hear you," he replied. "Been there myself. In fact, I'm planning to hire some help soon, if you know anyone interested. The pay will be crap, but I hear the boss is fabulous." I laughed in spite of myself. "As for that coffee, I figure it never hurts to ask." He winked. "You have to like a dog lover."

I winked right back. "Maybe you'll meet one someday."

Ultimately, he sold me an extra-large collapsible wire crate that would hold Bella during the day and fold flat for storage behind the studio at night. The extra-large crate came with an extra-large price tag, but I swallowed hard and gave him my credit card, silently praying that the early morning yoga class would fill the next month. Either that or I'd have to keep the thermostat set pretty low this winter.

I crossed my fingers and hoped that, like I'd been taught, everything happened for a reason. Maybe there'd be a silver lining in all this. After all, hot yoga was all the current rage, but it was bound to die out eventually. Maybe I'd make my fortune in shivering cold yoga.

Michael threw in a few dog cookies to soften the blow. Bella was impressed.

THREE

LESS THAN TWENTY-FOUR HOURS later, I ventured across the street to Mocha Mia for a sacred girl's coffee date with Rene. While I waited for her to finish ordering one of her thousand-calorie desserts, I sipped my nonfat soy latte and considered—not for the first time—how Mocha Mia's eclectic décor represented everything I both loved and hated about the Greenwood neighborhood.

Sparkling Tiffany-style lamps sat atop ancient, scarred wooden tables, which were surrounded by a mismatched assortment of formal dining room chairs. The café's exquisitely framed paintings competed for wall space with flyers for local businesses and crude crayon drawings taped up by neighborhood school children.

Even the drinks were a study in contrasts. Each artisanal beverage was served in a faded coffee mug that had either been scavenged from a local thrift store or donated by one of the cafés many loyal patrons. Today's barista had obviously chosen a cartoon theme; my nonfat latte was topped by a Curious George coffee swirl and served in my favorite Looney Tunes mug.

Likewise, the neighborhood around Serenity Yoga seemed trapped between the forces of decay and renewal. Frozen by a poor economy and various environmental factors, the Greenwood business district sandwiched ghetto-like empty buildings in between trendy new construction—like a sort of architectural split personality. Well-dressed professionals and trendy antique shops vied for dominance with addicts and skid-row-type bars. It wasn't yet clear who would win.

I chose to open Serenity Yoga in these unusual surroundings for two very simple reasons: the rent was cheap and the studio's mixed-use building was only a ten-minute drive from my home in Ballard. I ignored The Loaded Muzzle and the early morning drinkers that frequented it. I ignored the annoying sounds that reverberated through the ceiling from the apartments above. I even ignored the empty storefronts of several recently failed businesses. I should have known better.

I would have continued beating myself up over my poor business acumen, but Rene sat down with a flourish and waved her hand in my face. "Earth to Kate...Are you there?" She pointed at my mug. "No fair. You got Tweety Bird." She deposited her double chocolate mocha on the table with a disappointed thud. "That barista hates me. She always gives me one of the boring brown pottery mugs." Rene stopped talking long enough to swipe her tongue through a heaping mound of chocolate-drizzled whipped cream.

I considered pointing out the whipped cream mustache adorning her upper lip, but I launched into the story of my frustrating week instead. I told Rene all about the studio's new smelly salesman, his horse-dog companion, and my collection of unread newspapers. I'd finally gotten to the part about buying a giant dog cage, when she shoved her palm in front of my face, interrupting.

"Wait a minute. Let me get this straight. You met a perfectly good guy, and you turned down a date because he had a *beard*? Are you *crazy*?" Rene's voice belted across the cafe. She clearly wanted everyone inside Mocha Mia to hear about my transgression. Perhaps even the pedestrians walking by on the sidewalk.

Don't get me wrong, I loved Rene; she'd been my best friend since grade school. But most of the time I still wanted to kill her. She had this annoying habit of homing in on my nonexistent love life like a heat-seeking missile. I wanted to complain about the annoying drunk outside my studio, not get all goofy-silly about a cute guy in a pet store. I sipped my coffee and jealously eyed the pastry on her plate, tempted by the sweet smell of vanilla icing. Maybe if I stole her cinnamon roll, I could distract her and get back on topic.

"I knew I never should have told you," I replied. "And it wasn't a date. He invited me to a business meeting. Besides, I'm very happy on my own. The last thing I need is some stupid man distracting me from the business. I barely have time to think as it is!"

"Come on! You haven't been out on a date in more than eight months!"

"It hasn't been that long, has it?" (It had been nine months, three days and seven hours, to be exact.)

She shook her head in disgust. "You would have sabotaged a relationship anyway. You know how you are. You fall head over heels for the first couple of weeks, and then suddenly Mr. Perfect turns into Mr. Perfectly Awful."

"It's not my fault you keep setting me up with jerks."

She looked at me incredulously. "Jerks? Are you kidding me? You've gone through every one of Sam's single friends. And I can assure you, my husband does not hang out with jerks. What was wrong with Troy?"

"Too dumb. Couldn't hold his own in a conversation with a doorstop."

"How about Chris?"

"Too boring. Going out with that guy was like taking a triple dose of Ambien with a Valium chaser."

"Sean?"

"Too rich. What do I have in common with a guy who owns a yacht named *Pocket Change* and flies to Vail every other weekend?"

"OK, what about Carl? Surely, you can't find fault with him."

"That guy was a football fanatic. I have no intention of spending my Sunday afternoons hanging out with a bunch of beer-drinking, junk-food-belching sports nuts in their man cave. Spare me."

Rene glared at me in frustration. "You dated him for two weeks in April. There *was* no football. You look for any excuse to dump and run. Ever since your father died, I swear you've become commitment phobic."

I shifted uncomfortably in my chair. Rene didn't realize it, but she was getting a little too close to the truth. Make no mistake, I enjoyed a fun night out with a guy as much as the next girl. But ever since that dreadful night with my father, I couldn't stand the thought of relying on someone else—or having him rely on me.

"I am not commitment phobic, I assure you. I simply have relationship ADD." Rene rolled her eyes. "Seriously," I continued. "Give me a break. I just haven't met the right guy yet. But when I do, I can assure you his face will be clean-shaven and baby smooth." I leaned back and took a deep swig of coffee. "You know, ever since you married Sam, you've become obsessed with setting up all of your friends. Just because you're Mrs. Marital Bliss doesn't mean the rest of us have to join you."

"I know, but I do worry about you," she said, sighing. "You're not getting any younger, you know."

"When did thirty-two become an old maid?"

Rene pretended not to hear me. "And you spend *waaay* too much time in that yoga studio. You're not the only teacher there, you know."

"Maybe not, but the other instructors only teach a few classes a week, and they certainly don't help manage the studio. I can barely get them to take out the garbage."

"Come on, Kate. You don't have to personally oversee everything, and you know it. Frankly, I'm beginning to think that you bury yourself in work to avoid dealing with your own issues."

She was right, of course. But that didn't mean I had to admit it.

"How can I possibly avoid my own 'issues' when I have you to remind me of them? Besides, it's hard to meet people unless you hang out in bars or join some online dating service. Neither of those is really my thing. How am I supposed to meet someone?"

"That's exactly my point!" she said, scowling. "You claim you can't date anyone from the studio, yet you spend all of your time there. This pet store guy may have been your last chance. I don't want to visit you ten years from now only to be surrounded by a hundred cats. You may not mind being the crazy cat lady, but I'm allergic!"

"I don't even own one cat, Rene. But I do own a business. And in spite of what you seem to think, the studio needs my attention more than I need any man." If I had any hope of getting out of this coffee shop with my ego intact, I needed to change the subject. "Speaking of which, are you coming to flow yoga tonight?"

"Yes, I guess I'd better," Rene replied, eating the last bite of pastry and licking the frosting-coated whipped cream off her lips. "I love these sticky buns, but they *stick* right on my ass. I've got to work off the calories somehow. You know, I love your studio, but you really do need to turn up the heat. Nothing like an hour or two of hot yoga to sweat all those nasty carbs out of your thighs."

Another reason to hate Rene. As long as I'd known her, I'd never noticed an ounce of body fat mar those perfect legs. She ate cinnamon rolls, I crunched celery. She had the kind of body found in the swimsuit edition of *Sports Illustrated*, I had thunder thighs.

Hmm … Maybe she had a point about that hot yoga thing …

"Now finish up that disgusting soy latte and let's get going. I've got a pet store owner to check out. If you're not going out with him, maybe one of my other friends will."

———

Time zipped by, and before I knew it, three weeks had passed. The great crate experiment with Bella went reasonably well. Caging Bella like a zoo animal wasn't the most elegant solution, but the setup cut down on the daily noise and drama, which were my main concerns. After all, how could students find their internal Zen if they were forced to inhale flying fur before breath practice and listen to dog fights during meditation? Bella still barked occasionally, but significantly less than before. She seemed basically happy as long as she could be close to George.

For his part, George kept to his selling schedule like a full-time corporate job. He'd arrive at eleven each morning and sell until seven at night. Over time, I stopped noticing his pungent aroma and started looking forward to seeing his friendly face outside my window.

I felt oddly comforted by his presence—as if I had a private security guard on duty from eleven to seven every day. George assured me that he and Bella watched out for me; that they kept would-be prowlers from sneaking in the finicky front door when I wasn't looking.

He wasn't perfect, by any means, but he stayed relatively sober each day until his selling shift ended. Then he ambled off with Bella and a bottle for his evening reprieve from the struggles of daily life. If I hadn't known he was destroying his health and shortening his life span, I would have found a sort of symmetry and beauty to the simplicity of his existence.

Every now and then, I'd pick up sandwiches for us at the Phinney Wood Market. On sunny days George, Bella, and I packed up our lunches and headed to Greenwood Park, a small oasis of green a few blocks north of the studio. This hidden, two-acre play space restored my faith in the untapped potential of the Greenwood community.

Adopted by a group of dedicated neighborhood activists, Greenwood Park had recently been transformed from the run-down site of a defunct nursery to a beautifully maintained community gathering place. The park's many amenities included something for everyone: Pea-Patch vegetable gardens, multi-use sport courts, futuristic-looking children's play areas, and a large open lawn suitable for Frisbee, volleyball, and spirited games of fetch.

But for the three of us, Greenwood Park was simply a tranquil place to relax and spend precious minutes chatting in the shade. I liked listening to George's stories, and he obviously loved telling them.

Much to my surprise, he *had* owned a business.

"It was one of those dot com startups that were all the rage in the late nineties. I started the company out of my house, which wasn't all that unusual back then." He fed Bella the last bite of his ham and cheese sandwich. "What *was* unusual was that we almost made it. We were *this* close." He held up a thumb and forefinger about a quarter inch apart.

"We worked night and day, and I never had so much fun in my life. I wasn't as young as most of the kids forming the startups in those days, but I could work twice as hard. My partner and I built the company to over fifty employees in three short years. We were growing so fast we could barely keep up." He smiled and looked wistfully off into the distance. Although he gazed toward the playground, his eyes seemed blank—as if he had traveled to some better, faraway place.

I hated to make him return, but I wanted to hear the end of the story. "What happened?"

He turned back and shrugged. "Bad luck combined with bad decisions, I guess. First the tech market bit the dirt; then our investors got nervous. So I took a couple of creative financing risks and, well, let's just say they didn't pay off. We went bankrupt almost overnight." His voice grew sad. "Broke my heart the day I had to tell everyone we were closing the doors."

As I listened to George's story, my heart broke too, for him and for others like him. The failure he described could happen to anyone, even me. Being forced out of business was my worst nightmare—one that might soon come true, if business at the studio didn't pick up. I didn't know how to help, so I kept listening, hoping that would be enough.

"My partner was furious. He never understood the financial side of the business, and to be honest, I didn't tell him about our money issues until it was too late." George paused, shaking his head. "Helluva way to lose a friend.

"But the worst part was telling those fifty-three people that they were out of a job. Several of them had families to support. Every single one of them had put 110 percent into building the company, assuming their hard work would pay off in the end." He rubbed his eyes, as if even remembering that day left him exhausted. "All for nothing."

He stared at the ground for a full minute, the laughter of children paradoxically filling the silence. When he continued, his voice sounded heavy, defeated. "That night I went out and got plastered for the first time. Just couldn't take how I had let all those people down. One drink became two, became three. The next night, three drinks became four, and well, the rest is history." He absently stroked Bella's fur.

"My biggest regret is what my drinking did to my family. My wife finally gave up and divorced me, not that I blame her. I wasn't exactly a good husband. I got drunk every night and disappeared for days at a time. She gave me plenty of chances to go into rehab, and I said no to every one of them. Last I heard, she had remarried and moved to Denver. I haven't spoken to my daughter in years."

As his voice trailed off, I sensed an opportunity. Maybe alcoholism and homelessness didn't have to be the end of his story.

"What about now? Have you considered getting help? Your wife may have moved on, but I'm sure your daughter would love to see you again. It's not too late, you know."

He sighed. "I keep thinking that one day I'll get my act together. But honestly, for now this life suits me. I sort of like disappearing into the woodwork. Nobody's counting on me, except Miss Bella here." He patted her affectionately. "No rent to pay, no employees' lives to ruin. Heck, I even get to meet nice people like you occasionally." I smiled. People didn't call me nice every day.

"Besides, I can't possibly go into rehab now. What would happen to Bella? I may not be much, but I'm all she's got." Bella stared steadily at him, drooling and hoping for one last morsel. He ran his hand down her side. "I'm getting worried about her, though. Does she look skinnier to you?"

I looked more closely; she *did* look thinner. Bella had been skinny the first day I saw her, but not like this. Her ribs clearly showed, and her formerly shiny black fur appeared dull and brown. Even her eyes seemed sadder, more desperate somehow.

"Now that you mention it, yes," I replied. "If you're having trouble affording food, I can always help out a little." I had my own financial worries, but an extra ten or twenty dollars a month wouldn't break me.

"Well, you know I never look a gift anything in the mouth, so if you want to buy us some dog food, I sure as heck won't stop you. But she's not underfed, believe you me. She eats better than I do." He touched his nose to Bella's and cooed. "I feed you lots, don't I, Missy Girl?"

He turned back to me. "But she's always ravenous and she's getting grumpier, too. She never liked other dogs much, but she only used to bark when they got in her face. Now she goes after them even when they're clear across the street. And she keeps getting skinnier and skinnier. At first I thought she was having another growing spurt, but this seems different. I even caught her eating dirt yesterday."

"Wait a minute. You mean she's not done growing yet?" That wasn't the most relevant comment I could make, but I couldn't help but be dumbfounded. The Bella-beast was already ridiculously large.

George smiled with obvious pride. "She's a big one, isn't she? A vet told me once that she'd be 100 pounds by the time she stopped growing. I think she could top that. She's got at least six months' growth left in her. I'll bet she hits 110. She's a purebred shepherd, but some days, I swear she's part malamute."

More like part horse.

"And she's a smart one, too," he continued. "It only took me twenty minutes to teach her to 'say hello.'" Bella looked up expectantly at the familiar command. "But I *am* worried about her, and people have started to harass me about her weight. They assume I'm intentionally starving her or that I can't afford to feed her. A couple have even threatened to turn me in to the Humane Society." He scowled, clearly offended. "As if I'd ever hurt Bella!"

"Anything I can do to help?"

"Thanks, but I don't think so. I'm taking her to the free vet clinic by Southcenter next weekend. Hopefully they'll figure out what's going on."

"Next weekend?" From what George described, I was afraid Bella might not make it that long.

"I'd like to take her in sooner, but they're only open one weekend a month."

I hesitated, vacillating between idealism and realism. A true friend would offer to pay for an earlier appointment. But I had my own money issues. "I wish I could help but—"

George responded with an insincere smile. "Don't you worry, ma'am. Bella likes the folks at the free clinic, and they're good with her. I wouldn't take her anywhere else."

"How are you going to get Bella all the way to Southcenter?" I could at least offer him a ride.

"It's pretty easy, actually. Bella loves riding the bus. The drivers even keep a stash of cookies for her. We'll get there, no problem."

I guiltily counted the days until that fateful appointment. Bella got alarmingly thinner, and George's face grew more concerned. The angry words outside my door changed from "Control that beast!" to "If you can't afford a dog, you shouldn't have one!"

I wanted to throw open the door and tell those obnoxious strangers what they could do with their rude opinions. I stopped myself only by imagining the headline: "Yoga Teacher Starts Fist Fight Outside Studio." I even tried practicing loving-kindness meditation. But instead of feeling waves of love flow from my heart, I felt white-hot daggers of indignation shoot from my eye sockets. Buddha needn't fear for his job any time soon.

Saturday finally arrived. I waved goodbye, sent George positive energy, and waited, hoping for good news. I looked for George Saturday evening, to no avail. Saturday turned into Sunday, turned into Monday, turned into Tuesday. Although I searched for him every day at eleven, he failed to show up for his route.

Unaccountably depressed and fearing the worst, I went on with my life. What else could I do?

FOUR

"You have got to be kidding me," I muttered. I punched the numbers in again, but the studio's calculator stubbornly refused to change its mind. "This can't be right. How can we possibly be down to $300 in the studio account?

"No new candles this month, I guess. Maybe I'll ask students to reuse paper cups and bring their own toilet paper." I tossed the traitorous device to the side. Grumbling felt good, but it didn't change the bottom line. My bank account gave the phrase *going for broke* a whole new meaning.

For the 937th time, I wondered what malfunctioning brain synapse compelled me, of all people, to open a yoga studio. The day I got my foot behind my head would be the day I chopped it off at the ankle, and my short, stubby legs hardly merited the cover of *Yoga Journal*. As for achieving yoga's supposed blissful state of samadhi? Well, let's just say that I had yet to discover the path to enlightenment.

But in life's toughest times, yoga kept me going.

So when my father passed away and left me his house and a small inheritance, the choice seemed obvious. I quit my stable, good-paying, full-benefits job and opened Serenity Yoga.

I started by designing the studio's layout and décor, naïvely agonizing over every detail. I shopped for hours at New Age stores all across Seattle, looking for the perfect selection of door chimes, water fountains, meditation cushions, and Tibetan singing bowls. I replaced the carpeting in the studio's single practice room with solid maple flooring and strategically placed colorful pots filled with tropical plants all around the reception area. I even hung motivational artwork that implored my students to "live well, laugh often, and love much." At the time, I thought every detail was crucial. At the time, I thought I was creating a sanctuary of physical and emotional healing.

I can only plead temporary insanity.

As my accountant had told me several times since, anyone with half a brain would have realized that I was constructing a 1,500-square-foot money pit. Forget dining on caviar and sipping Dom Perignon. At the rate I was going, Top Ramen and tap water would soon become unaffordable luxuries.

Now that I was lucid again, one thing was brutally clear: teaching yoga was the most rewarding way to go broke on the planet. Yoga was a six-billion-dollar-a-year industry, so someone out there was obviously making money. Maybe the millionaires all operated those mega "hot box" yoga studios popping up everywhere. Or perhaps the riches were found in producing DVDs and selling designer yoga duds. Yoga's megarich certainly weren't getting that way running small neighborhood studios.

Fortunately, I had a full schedule of private clients the rest of the week. If none of them canceled and I timed things perfectly, I might not have to raid my personal savings account again. Alicia arrived right on time, as usual.

"Hey, Alicia. It's great to see you."

My words were true, for multiple reasons. Alicia was one of my favorite students, and I always enjoyed spending time with her. But more relevant to my current predicament, Alicia was also the studio's landlord.

Landlord or not, broke tenant or not, I hesitated. Today wasn't one of Alicia's good days. She looked pale, tired, and significantly older than her true age of thirty-three, and her normally perfectly tailored clothes hung on her frame like hand-me-downs from a heavier sister. I gritted my teeth and plunged ahead anyway. "I hate to ask this, but money's a little tight this month. Can I give you the rent check a few days late?"

I expected at least token resistance, especially since this was the second time I'd asked in four months. But Alicia smiled and said, "Sure. Don't worry about it. I'll talk to my bookkeeper and let him know. And I'll make sure he waives the late fee again."

I sighed in relief. "Thank you. I'll get the check to you as soon as I can. I hope I'm not causing you any problems."

"Don't be silly," she said as she rolled out her mat. "Waiting a week or two for your rent money is the least of my concerns. I'm happy to help."

She was right. About money being the least of her concerns, that is. Calling Alicia rich would have been an understatement. But as Dad used to say, money can't buy everything. In her case, money couldn't buy time—at least not enough of it.

Alicia was diagnosed with stage IV malignant melanoma last February. She celebrated her thirty-third birthday hooked up to an intravenous cocktail of immunosuppressing, hair-destroying experimental drugs at Seattle's Fred Hutchinson Cancer Research Center. Chemo or not, the survival rate for her condition was so low that her doctors didn't even talk about it, except in hushed tones when they thought she couldn't overhear.

I looked at those statistics myself. In most cases, Alicia's doctors were probably right. In her case, however, those highly schooled, super-experienced medical professionals might just be mistaken. Alicia was determined to fight. And I'd seen too many miracles to completely discount her.

She used to love strong yoga practices, and I envied her ability to do complex balance poses with seeming grace and ease. Now she practiced yoga in an attempt to find that same grace and ease in the balance of her daily living. From what I'd seen, her inner strength put her former physical capabilities to shame.

I led her through a gentle restorative sequence designed to support her struggling immune system. We began with a few cycles of Nadi Sodhana—a breath practice also known as Alternate Nostril Breathing—to balance Alicia's energy system and focus her mind. After a few minutes, we added some simple, gentle movements. Our first pose was Chakravakasana, loosely translated as Sunbird Pose.

Alicia had done this posture dozens of times in the past, but I verbally coached each repetition anyway, hoping my voice would drown out any worries that might be echoing through her mind. "Please come to hands and knees." She folded a blanket and placed it under her kneecaps, then positioned her palms on the floor underneath her shoulders. "As you inhale, extend your spine, lengthening it from the crown of your head to the tip of your tailbone." Alicia's spine grew subtly longer. "As you exhale, pull in your belly and move your hips back toward your heels." She moved her hips toward her feet, bent her elbows, and rested her forehead on the floor in a position called Child's Pose.

I continued coaching her. "On your next inhale, come back to hands and knees. Keep your elbows soft and your belly lightly engaged. Continue this motion, linking every movement with your breath. Each inhale, return to hands and knees; each exhale, fold back to Child's Pose."

As Alicia moved, her breath became slower and subtly deeper; the chemo-induced stiffness eased from her joints; the tired-looking wrinkles diminished around her eyes. I would even have sworn that her prana—yoga's invisible life-force energy—grew stronger.

Alicia didn't have much stamina, so I kept our practice short. But that didn't make it any less powerful. By the time I rang the chimes at the end of our session, she seemed utterly transformed. She looked lighter—softer somehow. The circles under her eyes were less pronounced; a slight smile graced her lips. Our time together fed her in ways more powerful than food, rest, or a cabinet full of prescription medication ever could. Working with Alicia reminded me why, in spite of its challenges, I loved my profession.

We said our goodbyes as Alicia reached for the door. She paused after opening it, looking confused.

"Didn't you lock up before we started?"

"I thought so, but the door must have stuck. It's been giving us some trouble lately."

Alicia pushed, pulled, and rattled the handle in a futile effort to lock it. "Kate, I wish you had told me. This isn't safe. I'll have Jake come by tomorrow to take a look."

Oh no, not Jake. I resisted an urge to hide behind the display of yoga blocks. Even the thought of spending time alone with Alicia's husband, Jake the Jerk, made the hair on my arms stand up.

OK, so his last name wasn't actually "the Jerk." I added that part. To be honest, I'd never liked Jake, or his dark brown goatee, either. But until recently, I hadn't seen him very often. All that changed the day Alicia received her diagnosis. She quit her full-time job as property manager to become a full-time cancer fighter. Jake hired himself as her replacement.

I had no idea what Alicia saw in Jake, but she wasn't alone. My female students used adjectives like gorgeous, funny, interesting, and intelligent to describe him. I used words like sleazy and used-car salesman. He stood a little too close, touched a little too much, and volunteered to come by after hours a little too often for my comfort.

So when the toilet overflowed, the heat stopped working, or anything else in the studio broke down, I did whatever I could to avoid calling him. I would have rather waded through waist-high raw sewage than spend an hour alone with that man. Dealing with a finicky front door was nothing.

"Don't worry about it, Alicia. All you have to do is jiggle it to the right, push quickly to the left, then pull it out and snap! There it goes, right into place!" For once the gods were with me. Right on cue, the door finally latched shut.

Alicia looked skeptical.

"Honestly, it's no trouble at all." I fibbed. Fixing that door had been on my to-do list for weeks. "Please don't bother Jake. I know he's busy, and I don't want him wasting his free time over here."

Alicia furrowed her brow. "Well, I don't know ... I'd feel responsible if something happened."

"Seriously, it hardly ever causes problems. Maybe it's extra humid today." I kept talking before she could reply. "I promise, if it causes any more trouble at all, I'll give Jake a call. Besides, I've already spoken to the other instructors. Everyone knows to double-check the door before they leave. And if they forget, well, we don't have anything here worth stealing, anyway."

I gave her my most confident smile. Lying didn't count if you crossed your fingers, right?

Alicia wasn't convinced, but she didn't have enough energy to argue, either. So I successfully avoided spending time alone with Jake, while the door continued to squeak, stick, pop open, and otherwise annoy the heck out of me.

It seemed like a good trade-off at the time.

FIVE

"KATE, ARE YOU IN there?" Jake rattled the studio's door handle the next morning as I hid, crouched among the dust bunnies under the front desk. For once, the infernal lock held. "Kate?" Alicia must have told him to stop by the studio.

I glanced at the clock. Eleven-fifteen. Bummer. The instructor for the lunchtime meditation class wouldn't arrive for another thirty minutes. I'd locked myself safely inside the studio, hoping to work on the monthly newsletter. Instead, I was trapped, knees screaming, hunched under the desk in the world's sloppiest Half Squat.

I pinched back a sneeze and nestled up to the filing cabinet, determined to wait Jake out until the end of time—or at least until an unsuspecting yoga teacher discovered my mummified corpse. Jake knocked a few more times, then dropped an envelope through the mail slot.

I held my breath, waiting.

Silence. Was it safe to come out?

"Well, hey there, gorgeous. What are you doing here?"

Jake's voice startled me and I jumped, bumping my head against the drawer. Who was he harassing now? I rubbed the bump on my head and considered my next course of action. I wanted to know who Jake was stalking, but if I stood up, he'd see me for sure. I decided to play hide and go peek instead. I scooted to the window, parted the leaves of the schefflera tree, and cautiously looked outside. Jake sidled up to Jenny, a student from my nine o'clock prenatal class.

"I don't think they're open," he said.

"Oh, no, they *can't* be closed!" Jenny wailed. "I forgot my purse inside! I was so blissed out after class that I walked all the way home before I realized I'd *driven* to the studio. So then I walked back to get my car, only to realize I didn't have my purse. I left it by the yoga mats. And my car keys are inside it!"

Several non-yogic phrases entered my mind, but I managed not to say them out loud. Still using the plants as cover, I crawled out from behind the desk, snaked along the wall, and craned my neck to peep through the door to the yoga room. Damn. There sat Jenny's purse, plain as day, on top of the yoga mats. I skulked back to my hiding place by the window and continued eavesdropping.

Jenny wept. "How can I possibly take care of a *child* if I can't even remember a *purse*! I swear all of these pregnancy hormones have given me that forgetfulness disease. You know, the one old people get? Oh lord, what's it called again?"

Alzheimer's, I silently answered.

"Don't worry, honey," Jake replied, wrapping his arm around Jenny's shoulders. He hugged her close and whispered in her ear. Jenny covered her mouth and blushed, tears suddenly abated. I glowered at Jake through my leafy green canopy. I knew it was customary to put your hand on a pregnant woman's belly, but I could

39

have sworn I saw Jake's hand wander to an entirely different part of Jenny's anatomy.

This conversation had to stop. I couldn't just sit here and allow Jake to harass Jenny. Not even if she appeared to enjoy it. Not when I had the keys to her getaway vehicle.

I reluctantly abandoned my sanctuary and sneaked back across the floor. Once inside the yoga room, I stood up, dusted off my pants, and pounded the achiness out of my thighs. Then I grabbed Jenny's purse, pasted on a fake smile, and confidently strode back across the lobby.

"I thought I heard someone talking out here," I said, as I unlocked the door. "Sorry to keep you waiting, but I was using the restroom." I held up the purse. "Is this yours?"

"Thanks, Kate," Jenny replied, gratefully taking it from my hands. "I swear this pregnancy brain is going to be the death of me." She glanced at her watch. "Oh no! And now I'm late for work!"

"See you later, sweetheart!" Jake yelled as Jenny hurriedly waddled to her car.

Irritation crawled up the back of my neck to the top of my scalp. "What do you want, Jake?"

Jake's flirtatious smile vanished. He picked up the envelope he'd dropped through the mail slot. "I stopped by to give you a copy of your rental agreement."

I must have looked confused, because he kept talking. "Alicia told me your rent check's going to be late again. This is the last time, Kate. Alicia may be a pushover, but I'm in charge now. From now on, you'll pay the fifty-dollar-a-day late fee, like everyone else." He edged closer, his dark, bristly whiskers advancing dangerously close to my cheek. "Unless, that is, you want to start giving me some private lessons?" His expression feigned innocence, but the implication was clear. Even thinking about it made me want to toss my morning muffin, so to speak.

One look at my face, and Jake wisely stepped back, holding up his hands. "Mellow out, Kate. I was kidding."

I resisted the urge to stomp on his foot.

He grinned. "But think about it, just in case." He handed me the envelope and walked away, whistling.

———

I still felt slimy after the meditation teacher left two hours later, so I cleansed myself with a short yoga practice. I was literally hip deep in the luscious stretch of Pigeon Pose when I heard the magnificent sound of Bella's unmistakable bark. George was back! I grabbed a dollar for a paper and ran to greet him.

I threw open the door and froze. George wasn't alone. The stranger standing next to him wore a bulky camouflage jacket and pushed a bicycle piled high with a mountain of army green duffle bags. No smile graced his dirt-smudged face; I had a feeling it never did. I couldn't quite hear them, but based on their low, almost growling tones, I suspected they were arguing.

I rubbed my hands up and down my arms, shivering. I felt uneasy about this stranger, though I couldn't quite articulate why. It wasn't his disheveled clothes or even his thick, dark beard. In some odd, intuitive way, I sensed his energy. It felt jagged, unpredictable somehow—like an irritable mountain lion, newly escaped from its cage.

"Is everything OK over there?" I asked. The stranger muttered something to George, handed him a black nylon gym bag, and walked away, grumbling and pushing the bicycle beside him.

I walked up to George. "Are you all right?"

"I'm fine," George said. "Just a little disagreement over property rights."

George and I watched the departing stranger, now half a block away. Bella growled softly at his retreating shape.

"Bella, you hush now," George said. He ruffled Bella's ears before smiling at me. "Don't you worry about Charlie there, ma'am. He's a friend of mine. He likes to act all gruff, but he's harmless enough. He even hides my stuff when I can't watch it. Sometimes I just have to remind him it's mine, not his." He patted the gym bag. "But it's all good now."

I would have probed further, but I got distracted. "Hey, Bella looks better!"

Bella seemed happy and energetic; I could even have sworn that she smiled. Her ribs were still visible, but her eyes sparkled, and she looked like she'd put on a pound or two.

George, on the other hand, looked awful. His dull, depressed eyes were underscored by purple-gray smudges, and his shoulders rounded forward in an uncharacteristic slump.

I kneeled down to scratch Bella's neck. "I've missed you two the last ten days. I was starting to get worried."

"Sorry about that," George replied. "We've been out of town. Bella's tests took three days to come back, so I stayed down south. It's not like I have a phone they can call with the results."

I was almost afraid to ask. "What did you find out?"

"It's not good. Bella has EPI, which is an autoimmune disease. Evidently, she can't digest food anymore. That's why she's always hungry and keeps losing weight no matter how much I feed her."

"I've never heard of that."

"Neither had I. It's pretty rare, but over half the dogs that get it are German shepherds. That's what made the vet think of it. He gave me some medicine to mix with her food, and so far it seems to help."

George's dismal demeanor confused me. "Well, that's good, right? At least now you know what's wrong with her, and she's starting to get better."

George sighed and absently rubbed Bella's fur. "I suppose. But the medicine's expensive. The vet gave me a bottle that had been donated to the clinic, but it normally costs over $200."

No wonder he seemed so sad. George could never afford $200 medicine. "That *is* expensive," I replied. "But we'll figure out a way to get you a refill if she needs it. Maybe I can host a fundraising event."

The grim line of his mouth turned into a sad smile. "That's very kind of you, ma'am, but a bottle only lasts two weeks, and Bella will need this medicine for the rest of her life."

My heart sank. "The rest of her life?" I could never raise that much money.

"Yes, otherwise she'll starve. The vet even hinted that I should put Bella down, but I couldn't do that. She's my life, and she's so young, you know?" He looked away to hide the tears in his eyes. "She's not even two yet!"

"Oh, George, I'm so sorry."

I moved to hug him, but he turned away and shook off my touch. I didn't know what else to do, so I stood silently with him for several awkward moments. Finally, he wiped his eyes and vigorously shook his head, as if forcing himself back to reality. When he turned back to face me, his heartsick expression had been replaced by one of stubborn determination.

"Don't you worry about us, ma'am. I have a plan. Bella needs me and I *will not* let her down. No way."

"What are you going to do? Do you think your family will help?"

He hesitated, as if choosing his words carefully. "My family isn't an option. But I've been thinking, and someone owes me. They don't know it yet, but they're going to help."

That didn't sound good. "George, what are you up to?"

He set his jaw stubbornly. "Don't worry about it. All I can say is, I have a plan."

Worry nibbled at the lining of my stomach. "How in the world can you get an extra $400 a month, George? You can barely buy dog food for Bella, much less expensive medicine. You'd have to rob liquor stores or sell drugs to get that kind of money."

George crossed his arms, frowning. "I told you before," he said through clenched teeth. "I don't steal, and I don't do or sell drugs. So get off that. Besides, what I do with my life is none of your business."

He was up to something, and it couldn't be good. Nibbling worry escalated to biting agitation. I knew George wouldn't like what I was about to say, but I said it anyway. "Maybe you could find Bella a new home."

He didn't have to reply. His stiffening shoulders told me exactly what he thought of that idea. For a brief moment of sanity, I hesitated, wondering if I should go on. But fear for George drowned out all reasonable thought. I knew I might regret it, but I kept talking.

"I hate to say it, but maybe the vet was right. Maybe you should even consider—"

George's expression turned from cold anger to retching disgust, like he'd discovered a smear of dog waste covering his shoe. "What is wrong with you?" he hissed. "Would you give up on a family member because she got sick? Would you get rid of a child because she was expensive?"

"No, of course not," I snapped back, insulted. "But Bella's not a child, George. *She's just a dog.*"

As soon as the words left my mouth, I wished I could take them back. George's look was clear. I was no longer a pile of dog dung. Now I was his best friend—and he'd just learned that I'd slept with his wife, strangled his puppy, or committed some other sin of unforgivable betrayal. He shook his head in disbelief. "I honestly thought you were different. I thought you'd understand."

I'd already gone too far, but I kept on going. After all, George was clearly blinded by emotion. I had to make him see reason. "Look, George, I get it. You don't want to put Bella down, and I can understand that. But you can't keep her. I'll help you find another home for her. I'll even help you find another do—"

He hurled his papers to the ground. "Now she's *replaceable*? I don't know why I thought you were so special. You're as bad as everyone else—worse even. You *pretend* to care." He glowered at me with disgust. "I'm done talking with you. If you don't want a paper, then get out of here so I can sell it to someone who does."

I wanted to continue our conversation. I wanted to help. A part of me even wanted to apologize. But I was stubborn, and we were both angry. I turned on my heels and stomped away, dollar bill still in hand. I slammed the studio's door, then jiggled and pulled and kicked and swore until it finally clicked into place.

"Stupid door. Just as cantankerous as that old man." I pulled off my shoes and threw them in the corner. "Don't know why I'd want to help him anyway. Ungrateful jerk disappears without a word for over a week, then shows up here expecting me to—"

I paused. *Hey, wait a minute…*

George's timeline was incomplete. Bella's test results took three days to come back. Why then, had George been gone for ten? I couldn't imagine that he'd blithely sacrifice a week's income, given his financial problems. What had he been up to?

————

The rest of the day went by in a blur of private clients, teachers' meetings, and group classes. Before I knew it, the students from my Core Strength class had departed, and I was ready to head home. I'd steadfastly avoided George the rest of the day, and now he and Bella were gone to wherever they went each evening.

Time had cooled my fiery temper, and I felt bad about our argument. I should have known better than to suggest George get rid of Bella. She was the closest thing to family he had. I vowed to apologize as soon as I saw him the next day.

My only goals in that moment, however, were to close up shop and go home. At almost ten o'clock, the dueling temptations of a hot bubble bath and a cool glass of Chardonnay beckoned me. But first I had to prepare for the next day's classes. I blew out the candles, swept the yoga room's floor, and emptied the garbage cans. I quickly wiped down the sink in the studio's single unisex bathroom, grateful for once that the space didn't have showers. From there, I headed to the small alcove of yoga props just off the back entrance. I untied the chaotic tangle of cotton straps, folded the pile of carelessly tossed blankets, and created three organized stacks from the Jenga-like structure of black foam yoga blocks. I finished by neatly stacking the mats.

Practice space done, I moved to the lobby, where I vacuumed the floor and watered my thirsty jungle of plants. I was about to restock the flyers outside the studio's front entrance, when I heard the sounds of a heated argument.

To be honest, nighttime arguments weren't all that unusual in this section of Greenwood. After nine at night The Loaded Muzzle and its sister bars were the only businesses open, and the neighborhood drunks weren't exactly known for their quiet discussions on local politics and art.

I normally ignored them, but for some reason this felt serious. I cracked open the door and pressed my ear to the void, trying to eavesdrop. The yelling stopped as suddenly as it began.

Nothing but silence. Not the easeful silence that enveloped your mind after the most blissful of meditation practices. Not the friendly silence that followed a fight between buddies, after they had shaken hands and made up. Not even the sad, desperate silence of loneliness. This was a more ominous silence. The silence between the jarring final notes of a horror movie's theme song. The silence before the knife shot through the shower curtain in *Psycho*. The silence that punctuated the seconds until the evil monster attacked the heroine from behind.

Great. And now I had to walk out into the parking lot. Alone.

Should I call the cops? If I called the police and it turned out to be nothing, I'd feel pretty stupid. I wasn't a little girl anymore. By the age of thirty-two, I should be able to take care of myself. Besides, the police had better things to do than walk paranoid yoga teachers through empty parking lots.

Dad schooled me well in self-defense, but I owned little in the way of protection. The yoga teachings were clear: violence was not an option; therefore, I did not own a gun. I looked around the studio. A yoga strap would help only if I wanted to whip my would-be killer into submission. My newly organized yoga blocks? I could throw one at him, I supposed, but the lightweight foam brick wouldn't do much damage. If only I'd purchased the heavy wooden ones instead. I supposed I could try to smother him with one of the blankets…

"I wonder if it's too late to open a martial arts studio?" I said to the empty room.

The deadliest options I found were a stapler and a pair of round-nosed scissors. Vowing to buy pepper spray first thing the next morning, I grabbed my flashlight, turned on my cell phone, and prepared to press the autodial button for 911, just in case.

I opened the door and cautiously looked left and right. Nothing. No sounds except the traffic along 85th Street; no smells but the yeasty aroma of stale beer. Nothing unusual at all. I inserted the key into the lock, and started at the sound of someone throwing out the trash. *Good lord, you're jumpy. No more Friday night horror fests for you.*

I played the flashlight along the pavement in front of me, wishing there were more people out on the street. I had nothing but my internal dialogue to keep me company.

See, nothing to be afraid of here, just the normal cats, cars, and an occasional empty beer can. I heard a metallic bang, yelped, and practically leaped out of my skin. *Just the garbage can lid. You really need to drink less caffeine, jumpy girl.*

As I tiptoed to the end of the parking lot, the flashlight illuminated a mound of old clothes. *How odd. Someone threw out a jacket and pants.* I moved closer. *Actually, it looks like a whole pile of clothes.*

I froze. *Wait, are those shoes?*

My stomach churned. *Oh, no,* I silently prayed. *Please, God, please don't let that be what I think it is.*

Acid bile rose in my throat as I moved the flashlight's beam across the shape. It wasn't a pile of clothes at all. It was a person—a man—surrounded by a pool of thick, dark fluid.

I recognized the sickening, coppery smell. It was blood. A *lot* of blood.

I resisted the urge to scream and run. Instead I turned him over to see if he was still breathing. The minute I saw the deep indented gash in his forehead, I knew saving him was hopeless. I pressed the button to make the 911 call I now dreaded, took two steps away from the body, and vomited.

It was George. And Bella was nowhere to be found.

SIX

"MA'AM, I NEED YOU to wait in the patrol car. The detectives will be here soon to take your statement."

"I can't stay here," I begged. "I have to find Bella! She's a large black German shepherd. She never left George's side, and she must be terrified." I frantically looked left and right. "I'm sure she's around here somewhere. Please let me go look for her. She hates being alone."

I'm sure I sounded insane. All things considered, a stray dog should have been the least of my concerns. But focusing on Bella allowed me, if only for a moment, to avoid thinking about George's death. And I couldn't think about that. Not then. It was too awful.

"Ma'am, there's obviously no dog here, and I need you to come with me before you destroy any more evidence." The officer took me by the arm and led me away from George's body. As we walked past the small crowd of pointing and whispering onlookers, I felt strangely guilty, as if I were the murderer, not merely a witness.

Everything seemed surreal, like the flashing, disparate images of a childhood nightmare. Circling police lights pulsated in an oddly patriotic collage of red, white, and blue. The zigzag aura of an impending migraine tugged at the edges of my vision, and I knew throbbing pain was sure to follow. The officer opened the car door and nudged me inside. I didn't *want* to sit in the car. I wanted to go home. I wanted to crawl into bed and pull the covers over my head. Barring that, I would have preferred rotting in a nice, dark prison cell, far away from all this insanity. I considered telling the officer exactly that.

I sat in the car.

"The detectives in charge will be able to answer your questions. Now wait here and let us do our jobs." He firmly shut the door.

It seemed like a hundred years, but actually only twenty minutes passed before detectives Martinez and Henderson had time to question me. Petite and pretty, with dark hair, brown eyes, and a serious look, Detective Martinez obviously played the good cop to Henderson's bad one. Bearded, slightly paunchy, and well on the far side of forty, Detective Henderson wasn't the slightest bit interested in my worries about Bella.

"I already told you," I said wearily. "I don't know anything. Now please let me go! I have to find Bella. George wouldn't have wanted her to be alone."

"Ma'am, answer the question," he replied. "What were you doing out here when you found the body?"

I would have screamed in frustration, but the sound might have exploded my pounding head. "For the hundredth time, I heard fighting and I got worried. I decided to make sure everything was OK on my way home."

"If you heard a fight, why didn't you call the police?" Henderson asked, leaning forward. I assumed he was trying to intimidate, not sicken me. But the warmth of his garlic-infused breath sent another wave of nausea roiling through my stomach. And his scruffy mat of saliva-encrusted facial hair didn't help. I swallowed hard to avoid vomiting a second time. Lord, didn't anyone shave anymore?

"If what you say is true, you're lucky *you* didn't get your face bashed in." He stepped his feet wide and glanced at Martinez. "This kind of thing happens all the time. Couple of drunks fighting over money or booze. One puts up a little too much resistance and gets beat up or worse. Could even have been a drug deal gone bad. A young woman like you should have more sense than to get in the middle of it."

"I'm telling you, that's not what happened," I replied emphatically. "George had a drinking problem, but he didn't do drugs, and he wasn't violent."

Henderson leaned back and crossed his arms. "All right, then, what's your theory?"

My eyes burned with looming, frustrated tears. "I don't know, maybe he got mugged."

"Why on earth would anyone mug him? He obviously didn't have much money." Henderson leaned in close again, going for the jugular. "Unless there's something you're not telling us…"

Dad taught me to be tough—to stand up to bullies and never give them the satisfaction of seeing me cry. But my head pounded, my body ached with exhaustion, and I couldn't hold back anymore. Tears streamed down my face. "I don't know anything! Please, please, *please* let me go, so I can look for Bella."

Martinez gave Henderson a "back off now" look. "Just a few more minutes, ma'am," she said. "How did you know the deceased?"

"I told you that already. He sells—" I bit back a sob. "I mean, he *sold* the *Dollars for Change* newspaper outside my store. We became friends."

"See, that's what I don't get," Henderson sneered. "Why would a pretty young thing like you be friends with a deadbeat like him?"

At that moment, Detective Henderson joined Jake the Jerk on my short list of truly odious people. My tears stopped. The hair on the back of my neck rose. An image of my fist smashing into Henderson's face entered my head and refused to leave. Cold-cocking him would land me in jail, so I looked at him steadily and enunciated clearly.

"George wasn't a deadbeat. He had an addiction. There's a difference."

Martinez stepped between us. "Did the victim have any enemies?"

"No, George was a sweet man. People aren't always courteous to the homeless, but I can't imagine why anyone would hurt him." I remembered the incident with Charlie. "He did have an argument with someone earlier today, but he said it was nothing—that they had it all worked out." I described the dispute over the black duffel bag. "The guy seemed kind of odd, but George said they were friends."

"We didn't find a bag with the body, but we'll look into it," Martinez assured me. "But if this 'Charlie' isn't a regular in the area, he might be hard to track down. And the bag is probably long gone by now."

"Did anything else seem different than normal?" Henderson asked.

"Not really. George had some money worries, but I think he had a plan to fix that."

The two detectives exchanged a knowing look. Henderson spoke. "Perhaps he decided to consort with the wrong people to get that money and got himself killed for his efforts?"

I felt my face flush with anger.

"George was the *victim* here. You keep forgetting that. George was an alcoholic, not a criminal. And if he planned to meet with someone dangerous, why didn't he take his dog? Bella would never have let anyone hurt him."

They were about to press me further when a uniformed officer interrupted. "Excuse me, detectives. You might want to take a look at this. We found a dog in the alley behind the pet store. It might be the one the witness has been talking about."

I jumped out of the police car, pushed past the two detectives, and ran as fast as my legs would take me. Bella's low bark filled the air as I rounded the corner.

She huddled, cowering in the back of her crate. "That's her! That's Bella!"

Martinez grabbed my arm before I could open the cage. "Don't touch anything! That crate is evidence. Wait until we call Animal Control." Bella snarled and lunged against the door. "Besides, that dog looks dangerous. The Animal Control officers will know how to handle it."

Animal Control? Wasn't that a fancy name for the dog catcher? Were they going to take Bella to the pound?

"There's no need to call anyone," I quickly replied. "Bella's not dangerous, she's just upset. I'm sure I can calm her down."

"Maybe so," Martinez replied. "But we still need to call Animal Control. They'll take her to the shelter and contact her owners."

I imagined Bella trapped in a cage, surrounded by strangers and barking dogs. "But there's no one to contact. Her owner is dead."

"They'll call his next of kin, in that case. If no one claims her in seven days, they'll assess her. If she's deemed adoptable—" She paused and glanced at Bella, still ferociously barking in the crate. "If she's *safe* to adopt, they'll try to find a home for her."

I knew the chances of that were somewhere between slim and none. In this horrible economy of home foreclosures and double-digit unemployment, more and more people were forced to give up their pets. Normally easy-to-place animals were euthanized every day. And Bella wouldn't be easy. Not only did she have behavior problems, she had an expensive health condition.

Bella clearly needed an advocate. I hesitated, but just for a second.

"Let me take her. I promised George that if anything ever happened to him, I'd find Bella a new home." I lied. George and I never talked about anything of the sort. Like most people, George simply assumed he'd outlive his dog.

Martinez looked at Bella, who was still snarling and showing her teeth. "Sorry, I can't take the risk."

Out of desperation, I named the one person I thought she'd trust. "Call Detective O'Connell at the West precinct. He was my father's partner, and he'll vouch for me." I pulled out my phone. "He's probably off duty now, but I have his home number in my cell." Martinez looked doubtful, but she gave the number to a uniformed officer, who walked away to make the call. Sensing that the drama was over, the other officers left to continue processing the crime scene. Bella finally stopped barking and sat in her cage, watching me intently.

"Your father's a cop?" Martinez asked.

"Was. He died two years ago."

"I'm sorry. Was he young?"

The answer was yes. He was only fifty-three the day he died. But I couldn't talk about my father's death. Not with a stranger. Especially not so soon after finding my friend's body. I changed the subject instead.

"Hey, look. That's Bella's leash over there. If you open her cage, I swear I won't mess anything up. I'll carefully put on her leash and take her home. I'll come right to the station if you have more questions, but please let me leave. I need to go home, shower off this horrible night, and collapse into bed."

The officer came back wearing a lopsided grin. "O'Connell vouches for her. Says she's a pain in the ass but otherwise harmless."

Bella continued to sit still, now quiet and apparently calm.

"You'll come right to the station if we call?" Martinez asked.

"Yes, immediately. I promise."

Martinez looked to the side for a moment, thinking. "I'm probably going to get my ass chewed for this, but OK. You've had a tough night. No need for me to make it any tougher. Go ahead home and take the dog with you; she's your responsibility now." She gave me a stern look. "Don't make me regret this."

Martinez opened the crate. I hooked on Bella's leash and coaxed her out. Bella seemed stressed and unsure, but she came out quietly, gently swishing her tail back and forth.

So far, so good.

At least until Detective Henderson walked around the corner. One look at him and Bella rose up like a hound from Hell. Her hair stood on end and foam sprayed in all directions, as she lunged, barked, and viciously snapped her teeth. I could barely hold onto the leash as she pulled me to the ground. One more second and I'd have flown through the air like a kite behind her.

Martinez grabbed the leash. Henderson took three quick steps back and drew his weapon.

Adrenaline surged through my body. "Don't shoot her!" I begged. I couldn't bear the thought of another death. "I don't know why she's doing this. She must be terrified!"

"Get that dog under control or I *will* shoot it!" he yelled.

Martinez and I dragged Bella around the corner. Once Henderson was out of sight, Bella stopped lunging. Although she appeared to calm down, her facial expression belied her true feelings. She stared at the building with laser-like focus, as if daring him to make another appearance.

Martinez frowned. "Are you sure you want to take that animal home with you?"

"Not exactly," I admitted. I slowed my breath, trying to calm my fractured nerves. "But honestly, I've never seen her do anything like that before. And George wouldn't want Bella to go to the pound. She won't last a day there. I'd rather keep her with me for now."

I looked at Martinez with what I hoped was an expression of steady confidence. "Who knows? Maybe George's family will take her. I'm sure we'll be fine."

"It's your funeral," Martinez said shaking her head. "But fair warning. Don't let her go after an officer again. A cop won't hesitate to shoot a dog that attacks him or another person. We protect human life over animal. Every time."

SEVEN

"HEY, BACK THERE, KEEP it down," I muttered to the snoring monster in my back seat. Bella wasted no time in claiming my ancient Honda Civic as her own. As soon as I opened the door, she crawled behind the driver's seat, curled up, and immediately fell asleep for the three-mile drive southwest to my home in Ballard. She seemed surprisingly comfortable. Perhaps riding the bus taught her what to expect from a moving vehicle. Perhaps the small, dark space reminded her of her crate. Or perhaps she simply passed out, exhausted from the trauma of her evening.

I should be so lucky.

As we neared our destination, I worried about how the neighbors would react to my new roommate. They had a hard enough time adjusting when *I* moved back in. They liked me well enough, but a yoga teacher was a poor substitute for a twenty-five-year veteran of the police force. Maybe if I told them Bella was a police dog and signed her up as block watch captain, they'd be more welcoming.

Dad and I moved into the 1920s bungalow back when Ballard was best known as a sleepy Scandinavian fishing village. In the last decade, it had been radically transformed. Most of the small, single-family homes had been torn down, and the Nordic-themed businesses had relocated, along with most of the area's Scandinavian residents. Today, the Ballard neighborhood was an ethnically diverse Mecca of multi-story apartment buildings, trendy new restaurants, live music venues, and enough microbreweries that it was now known as a music and beer destination.

When Dad first died and left me his house, I wasn't sure I could stand to live there—too many memories, you know? I considered selling it for about a minute, but the thought of my childhood home being torn down and replaced by some fancy new McMansion quickly squelched that idea. So I made it my own by painting the exterior a soft shade of violet and filling the flowerbeds with pink roses, multi-colored tulips, and bright yellow sunflowers.

The two-story, 1,400-square-foot house wasn't much by most people's standards, but I'd grown to adore it. Probably because it safeguarded the very memories I'd been afraid to confront. The top level contained the master bedroom and a spa-like bathroom, complete with a jetted bathtub—the one luxury Dad had permitted himself. The main floor was made up of the requisite kitchen, living room area, and a half-bathroom suitable for guests. Just off the kitchen sat my childhood bedroom, now a combination office and storage space.

I didn't have much of a yard, but my tiny piece of grass was enough for what Bella needed right then. Standing next to her and holding the leash, I deeply regretted not getting the yard fenced. Some things should be done in private. One look at her output and I realized I'd need to buy some dog waste bags. Big ones.

That duty completed, I took her into the house and unhooked her leash. She ran from room to room, frantically sniffing, as if expecting an evil intruder around every corner. Her only pit stop was a brief visit to the guest bathroom, where she drank her weight in water—from the commode.

Satisfied we were alone, she sat in the middle of the kitchen floor and stared at me with big brown wolf-like eyes.

"Bark!"

"What do you want now?"

She barked again.

This wasn't one of Bella's typical vocalizations. It didn't sound particularly angry, or even excited. This single, distinctive, sharp bark said, "I demand something. *Now!*"

I had no idea what she wanted. I ignored her and tiredly sorted through the day's assortment of bills and junk mail.

Bella's bark grew louder and more insistent.

"Quiet! You'll wake up the neighbors!"

She walked closer and barked directly in my ear. I could only assume she thought I was deaf.

"I don't know what you want!"

She continued her loud conversation.

"Oh, for God's sake, shut up and let me think!" I slumped in a chair and rubbed my aching temples, unsure which was worse—my pounding head or my growling stomach. It was well after midnight, and I hadn't eaten since lunch.

I sat up straight. "Hey, wait a minute. Are you hungry?"

Bella answered with another series of staccato barks.

We had a problem. I had no idea when George had fed Bella last, or even what she ate, other than leftover ham sandwiches. I vaguely remembered something about her illness that made food problematic, but I was too brain-dead to recall the specifics. And it was far too late to visit a pet store.

I went to the fridge instead, Bella tagging close behind. "Let's see what I've got: lettuce, tofu, a couple of apples, milk..."

I took a whiff and almost gagged again. Straight into the trash.

"Forget the milk. Hummus, carrot cake..."

Bella leaned in closer and started drooling. I snatched the tasty morsel away before she had a chance to grab it. "Absolutely not. The carrot cake's mine. Salad mix, bagels..."

Bella groaned. A vegetarian household obviously wasn't conducive to late-night doggie dining.

I looked at her and shrugged. "Sorry, girl. I don't have anything for you."

Bella showed her frustration with three more ear-splitting barks.

"I get it! Shut up. I'm thinking."

I finally remembered Ballard's twenty-four-hour Super Mart. I knew grocery store kibble was frowned upon in most doggy circles, but these were desperate times.

———

Twenty minutes and a grocery store run later, Bella had mercifully stopped barking. She was too busy wolfing down dog food from my favorite crystal serving bowl. I added food and water bowls to my shopping list.

I looked at the clock and almost cried. It was one-thirty, and my early morning class started at six. I'd never felt so bone-weary in my life. My head still throbbed, and my stomach ached from hunger. But all I could think about was sleep—deep, dreamless sleep. "Come on, Bella. It's bedtime." I showed her the bedroom. She hopped on the bed and flopped down, lying squarely on my pillow.

"Sorry, pooch. This is where I draw the line. I sleep on the bed. You sleep on the floor."

I grabbed a blanket from the closet, laid it on the floor and pointed to it. "For you." It took some convincing, but Bella finally relented. I collapsed on the bed and closed my eyes.

Huge mistake.

Images of George's body, sounds of sirens, the smell of blood, and the full knowledge of the evening's horror invaded every crevice of my being.

Bella paced the room, panting and whining. I tried to coax myself to sleep with "Kate's Sleeping Pill," my favorite breath practice for insomnia. No good. The horrible memories refused to leave. But at least now the room was quiet. At least that infernal whining had stopped.

My mind froze. My eyes flew open. Why *had* the whining stopped?

I rolled over and locked eyes with Bella. Her accusing glare scolded me. We stared each other down for what seemed like an eternity. Finally, I realized what was bothering her. Bella was used to sleeping on the ground, but not alone. She and George had lain next to each other every night for as long as she could remember. Changing that now seemed cruel.

"OK, you win. Come on up, but only for tonight." I slapped the bed beside me.

Bella hopped up, turned a quick circle, and sank down next to me with a heavy sigh. Her brow furrowed, her ears drooped, and her head hung low. I could tell she knew something had changed. She didn't know what or why, but she knew it was bad. Frighteningly bad. Life-changingly bad.

I suspected Bella couldn't understand me, but she deserved an explanation nonetheless. So I told her that George was gone, but that he had loved her more than anything. I also promised her that, although I couldn't keep her, I would make sure she was safe until I found someone who could.

I owed that to George.

You see, I firmly believed that George's death was at least partially my fault. That if I had listened more and judged less, I might have prevented this awful night. I deeply regretted my stubbornness in not apologizing. I regretted suggesting he euthanize Bella. I even regretted not buying that damned paper. No one else would have blamed me for what happened, but I definitely blamed myself.

As I finished the story, Bella rested her chin on my belly, closed her eyes, and fell asleep. The warmth of her body on mine felt oddly comforting, and I finally relaxed enough to do what I'd needed to do for hours. I broke down sobbing as I held Bella and allowed her rhythmic breathing to rock us both to sleep.

———

When I arrived at the studio the next morning, the area seemed unfathomably normal—as if the prior evening's nightmare had never occurred. I'm not sure what I expected. News helicopters buzzing overhead, vying for the opportunity to video an empty lot? Armed policemen standing guard over parking space 137? At least some black and yellow crime scene tape warning people to stay away from the now desecrated area.

I yearned for a physical marker—an acknowledgment of what had been lost. But no telltale chalk drawing outlined the place where George's body had lain. The only echo of the prior night's evil was a subtle red tinge, left by the blood from his shattered brow.

Thankfully, my students didn't yet know about the murder; I could never have faced retelling the story so soon. But I knew my reprieve of silence would be short. The death of a homeless man might not make the early morning headlines, but it would be all over the local news blogs by noon.

I needed a better story than the one I had now, both for my business's sake and my own. "Drunk Dies in Drug Deal Gone Bad at Yoga Studio" wasn't exactly the free publicity I'd been hoping for. And no matter what the police thought, I didn't buy their theory. George had not died in some drunken altercation. I had to find out what really happened last night, not just for George, but also for myself. Otherwise, I'd never feel safe closing up the studio again.

Detective Martinez had been kind, but Henderson was obviously in charge, and I'd freeze to death in Hell before I got more information out of him. Luckily, I had another source—if he was still speaking to me. I hadn't been a very good friend to John O'Connell since my father's death. In fact, I'd been more like a stranger. But if I thought about that, I'd chicken out for sure. So I pushed all non-yoga thoughts to the side and tried, unsuccessfully, to focus on teaching my class.

I barely remember the seventy-five minutes of mindless blather that tumbled out of my mouth, but suffice it to say that the session wasn't my best effort. I fidgeted through the beginning breath work; I said left when I meant right and fingers when I meant toes; I impatiently drummed my fingers against the hardwood floor during Savasana. And although I don't know for certain, I'm pretty sure that I made the class do Warrior I three times on the same side. My students didn't comment on my lack of verbal acuity, but they popped up like Pop-Tarts at the end of class and tried not to make eye contact as they said their goodbyes. Part of me felt bad about their awful experience, but most of me was simply relieved the ordeal was over.

As soon as the last student grabbed her yoga mat and scurried out the door, I joined the monster-dog snoozing in my car and drove south on I-5. Destination: the Seattle Police Department's West Precinct. I pulled up to a shady spot in front of the familiar cement building, placed my hand on the car door handle—and froze, seemingly super-glued in place.

"I don't know, Bella. Maybe this wasn't such a great idea."

I hadn't seen John in months, and I hadn't visited the West Precinct in even longer. Being at the station reminded me too much of Dad. I wasn't proud of my actions, but I had to move on with my life, and avoiding painful reminders seemed like the best strategy. But that strategy wouldn't work today. Today I needed information.

I sat in the car for what felt like a century, trying to gather enough courage to enter the building. I'm still not sure how I convinced myself to actually walk through the front door, but seeing John's beaming face was worth every step.

"Katydid! I haven't seen you in forever!" He crushed me in one of his famous bear hugs. "Where have you been?"

"John, I go by Kate now. You know I always hated that nickname."

"Nonsense. You'll always be little Katydid to me." He made a circling motion with his index finger. "Now, let me take a look at you."

I reached my arms out to the side and spun around for him, just like I did as a little girl.

"Beautiful as always," he said, smiling. He pointed to the elevator. "Now let's go talk."

I looked at the floor as the elevator doors closed behind us. "I'm sorry I didn't return your calls, it's just—"

John held up his palm. "You don't have to say anything, Katydid." I heard a catch in his voice. "Believe me, I know. I miss him, too." We rode the rest of the way to the tenth floor in silence.

When we arrived at his desk, John got right to business. "That was some phone call I got last night. How'd you go and get mixed up in a murder?"

"I'm not mixed up in it; I just found the body. But thanks for vouching for me. I would have gone crazy if they hadn't let me go home. They kept asking the same questions over and over again, but I didn't have any answers. I was simply in the wrong place at the wrong time."

"That can happen, Katydid, that can happen." He playfully nudged me on the shoulder. "Hey, I hear you adopted the vic's vicious dog. Funny, you always struck me as one of those crazy cat ladies."

"Why does everyone say that? It's not funny." I gave him a dirty look, and he was smart enough to look chagrined. "Besides, I'm not keeping the dog. I just didn't want her to end up in the pound. That's why I'm here, though. I didn't get off to a great start with the detective in charge, and I need your help."

John pulled out a chair and motioned for me to sit. "How's that?"

"George, the victim, mentioned once that he had family. I got the impression that at least his daughter is local. Can you get me her phone number? I'd like to offer my condolences and see if she's willing to take Bella."

I didn't fool him, at least not completely. He remained standing and peered at me through narrowed eyes. "Katy, what are you up to?"

"What do you mean?" I asked, trying to look innocent.

"You know exactly what I mean. You have a bad habit of sticking your nose in where it doesn't belong. It used to drive your father nuts. He always said you took after your mother that way: nosy, argumentative, and stubborn."

"Very funny, John." I held back a smirk. My temperament may have driven my Dad nuts, but I *clearly* inherited it from him. But I didn't share that insight with John. Instead I gave him the Scout's Honor sign. "I swear. I'm not up to anything. I just want to get this dog off my hands."

John crossed his arms and gave me *the look*—the same look Dad used to give right before he caught me in a lie. Seasoned psychopaths couldn't hold up to *the look*. How could I be expected to fare any better?

"But you're right. I wouldn't be averse to learning more about what happened to George. He was a friend of sorts, and I don't buy the detectives' theory of what happened."

John leaned against the edge of his desk. "I'm not working the case, but from what the officer told me last night, your friend was killed in some drunken brawl. Sorry, Katydid. I know that's not what you want to hear, but it's probably what happened, all the same."

I was afraid he'd say that. John and Dad might have solved George's murder in the old days, but I wouldn't put money on Henderson today. Seattle's priorities had changed. In this time of deep, city-wide budget cuts, Seattle barely had enough money to keep convicted criminals in prison. The city had zero resources to waste on low-profile cases that would likely go unsolved. I envisioned George's cold-case file covered in dust, buried in a warehouse full of forgotten boxes.

My voice grew a tad louder than I intended. "But John, that doesn't make any sense! I told Henderson last night. George didn't have a violent bone in his body. And he always had Bella with him. His being alone has to mean something!"

John actually had the nerve to pat me on the shoulder. "Katydid, leave crime fighting to the professionals. I know you mean well, but stick to stretching hamstrings or whatever it is you do in those yoga classes of yours. Keep your nose clean and safe. I promised your dad that if anything happened to him, I'd keep you out of trouble. And that's a promise I intend to keep."

"I'm thirty-two, John, not thirteen. You don't need to keep promises you made to my dad when I was a teenager."

"It doesn't matter. A promise is a promise is a promise. And you'll always be the same cute little brown-eyed girl to me." He stood up and looked at me squarely, without even a trace of a smile. "Stay out of this. That's an order."

I knew that look, too. I didn't respond well to edicts, but arguing was pointless, at least for now. "OK, John, you win. I won't talk to George's daughter about his death." *At least not until I meet her in person.* "But I still need to find out if she'll take this dog off my hands. Will you please get me her phone number?"

I didn't exactly lie, but I don't think John believed me, either.

He sighed. "Go home, Kate. I'll see what I can do, and I'll call you if I find anything. But if you want my advice, take the dog to the pound and go on with your life. Nothing good can come from your snooping around in this. Nothing good at all."

EIGHT

I DROVE AWAY FROM the precinct with more questions than answers, but for now, I was forced to wait and hope that John uncovered some useful information. In the meantime, I needed to clear my head. My mind felt sluggish from lack of sleep and the residue of last night's trauma. Bella's digestive system, on the other hand, wasn't sluggish in the slightest. She needed to do some clearing of an entirely different nature.

Discovery Park would meet both of our needs perfectly. Full of wooded trails, open beaches, and scenic picnic areas, the park seemed like the perfect place to gather my thoughts and let Bella do her business. The sun peeked through the clouds and provided a welcome contrast to the chilly morning breeze. A damp, earthy smell permeated the air, left over from the prior week's rain. The universe seemed to be offering me hope—reminding me that after every dismal storm, the sun eventually reappeared. I turned toward the warmth, closed my eyes, took a deep breath—and gagged.

In the name of all that was holy, *what* was that smell?

Bella had relieved herself of her digestive burden. Without going into too many details, suffice it to say that Bella's late night dog chow dinner had not agreed with her.

"Sorry, pup. Looks like we need to find a new brand of dog food. I'll add that to our list." Bella looked at me gratefully. A trip to Pete's Pets was definitely in order.

But not now. Now, I needed to think. I wandered through the park, oblivious to my surroundings. Instead of living in the present or even planning for the future, I obsessed about the past. Where had George gone for those missing days? He hadn't volunteered much information about his time away, and I'd been much too busy harassing him to ask. I mentally kicked myself for not listening—for not being a better friend. George might still be alive, if only I'd acted differently.

A sudden tightening of the leash interrupted my guilt trip. Bella froze in her tracks. She stood stock-still, muscles tense, leaning forward. I turned to follow her gaze. What was she glaring at?

I saw them too late.

A jogger exercising a golden retriever ran right at us. Bella and I had no time to escape; they were only a few feet away. I wrapped the leash around my hand, pulled Bella in close, and braced myself for the inevitable explosion. Bella lunged, pulling forcefully on the leash. She snarled, snapped her teeth, foamed, and growled. Cujo would have been friendly in comparison. I planted my feet and did my best impression of a 130-pound anchor.

All things considered, I thought I did pretty well. The leash held, my wrist remained intact, and Bella's teeth touched nothing but air. The jogger, however, was not impressed. "What's wrong with you, lady? Control your dog!"

"She's not my dog, sorry!" I replied, as he ran off into the blessed distance. If I were him, I'd have kept on running. No good could come from tempting Bella again. But that crazy jogger did a one-eighty and charged right back to us, yelling.

"Yeah, right! Sure she's not your dog. People like you drive me crazy. You know, if you didn't starve that dog, she might not be so vicious. You should be ashamed of yourself!"

People like me?

What was his problem? Bella certainly wasn't going to win Miss Congeniality, but she hadn't gotten anywhere near him, or his dog for that matter. And how could he think I was purposefully starving her? Who would be cruel enough to intentionally starve a dog, but responsible enough to take it for a morning walk?

If Jogging Man wasn't going to keep running, Bella and I would. One quick left turn and off we ran down a different path, the jogger's ranting echoing behind us.

"That's right. Run away and keep on running! I ought to call the Humane Society. Some people shouldn't be allowed to own animals!"

I used to smile, nod, and pretend to agree when George said, "You know how people are." I didn't know what he meant then, but I certainly understood now. Fostering Bella was going to be a lot harder than I had originally anticipated.

After that, we avoided other dogs. When we saw one, we'd jump off the trail or run full-speed in the opposite direction. I even found a sort of rhythm to it. Not a soothing rhythm, certainly not a relaxing rhythm, but a rhythm nonetheless. See a dog, run for your life. See another dog, run for its life.

But dogs were easy. Bella's reaction to other dogs was consistent and predictable. Her reaction to people—not so much. Most, she treated like long-lost friends or at least potential dog food providers.

But occasionally she'd see someone and go crazy, snarling and lunging like she'd done with Detective Henderson.

I was both confused and intrigued. On the surface, Bella's behavior toward people seemed random, but I suspected she reacted to something specific. I simply needed to figure out what. John might not want me looking into George's murder, but even *he* couldn't object to my solving "The Case of the Cantankerous Canine." And as a yoga teacher, I had the right skill set. Each time I worked with a student, I watched, reflected, and looked for patterns: patterns in movement, patterns in breath, even patterns in thought. How much harder could it be with a dog? As we continued walking, I closely observed, trying to solve the riddle of Bella's aggression.

First we ran into a woman with a toddler. "What a beautiful dog!" she exclaimed. "Is she a purebred?" Bella sat down and offered to shake hands. "How cute! She gave me her paw!" The red-haired munchkin-child giggled uncontrollably while Bella covered her face with wet German shepherd kisses. I opted to keep Bella's toilet water drinking habit to myself.

Later, we encountered a groundskeeper on lunch break. He relaxed in the shade, preparing to take the first bite of his tuna sandwich. "Isn't it a gorgeous day?" he said, smiling. He stood up, leaned forward, and held out his hand. "I used to have a shepherd like that when I was a kid. They're great dogs. Can I pet him?" Bella pulled toward him, suddenly drooling profusely. "Hey there, big guy ... Whoa!"

Bella ignored the empty hand he offered and snatched his sandwich from the other, swallowing it in two large gulps. Then she nudged, licked, sniffed, and flirted, clearly hoping for seconds. I sheepishly apologized before dragging Bella away.

I continued making observations, and Bella continued introducing herself to new friends. All went well until I spotted an overweight man with a long white beard. "Look, Bella," I whispered, pointing in his direction. "That guy looks like Santa! All he needs is a red hat and a black belt and—"

That's all I got out before Bella went berserk. She barked, danced on her toes, and waved her tail straight in the air, attempting to look as large and menacing as possible.

There was no jolly "ho ho ho" from this Santa. Instead, he yelled unrepeatable phrases, waved his cane in the air, and threatened to bludgeon Bella if she took even one more step toward him.

"Seriously, Bella," I whispered as we hurried away. "Who doesn't like Santa?"

Bella had no comment.

And so it went. Women and kids were never a problem. Men, however, were a conundrum. Although Bella generally liked men, occasionally she'd see one and go berserk. I looked for commonalities, to no avail. It didn't matter how close or far they were, how short or tall, how fat or thin. It didn't matter if they limped, jogged, or sat in the shade. It didn't matter if they wore a backpack or carried a bag. It didn't even matter if they were eating a tuna fish sandwich.

I wondered if there was some sort of "bad man" stench only Bella could smell, but that seemed unlikely. The answer, when it appeared, practically slapped me in the face. How could I, of all people, have been so blind? Bella calmly explored the trail about twenty yards behind a tall blond backpacker. He turned around, and Bella went crazy. I could barely hold on to her. The difference? When he turned, Bella saw his face. *He had a beard.*

If I'd ever needed proof, I had it now. This was one smart dog.

"Bella, it's not that I don't agree with you," I whispered. "But sometimes you have to keep your opinions to yourself. If you want a new home, you'll have to change your attitude." She looked at me stubbornly as if to say, *you first.*

I needed help.

———

I strode purposefully past the brand-new "Help Wanted" sign in the window of Pete's Pets, grabbed a basket by the door, and started filling it with the bare essentials. *Water and food bowls, check. Extra large pick-up bags, check. On second thought, grab two boxes of those. Chew toys. Do I really need those?* I turned away until I envisioned Bella dismantling my dining room table. *Better get several kinds of chew toys.*

Next up was food. What to do about food?

Obviously, last night's dining disaster couldn't be repeated. I scanned the mind-boggling array of choices cramming the shelves. Bags of kibble vied for space with foods that were canned, dehydrated, freeze-dried, and frozen. Some contained the meats of my childhood, such as beef, chicken, lamb, and fish. Others were made of more exotic ingredients, including rabbit, venison, buffalo, and brushtail—whatever that was. I even saw one made of kangaroo. Gross!

As if that weren't bad enough, the next aisle contained yet a different choice. Evidently, once you figured out what you wanted *in* your food, you had to decide what you wanted *out* of it. That aisle boasted foods that were soy-free, corn-free, gluten-free, and grain-free. I was beyond confused.

I searched the store looking for someone who could make sense out of the chaos. I found Michael stocking designer cat litter.

One look at the glorified bags of soon-to-be-garbage, and I could see where all those missing dog food ingredients had gone. This display featured cat litters made of corn, wheat, peanut shells, and pine. Non-politically correct cat owners could also go inorganic. Then they could choose between clumping, non-clumping, or something called "crystal."

Whatever happened to using a good old sandbox? Obviously the pet industry had gone as crazy as the yoga industry. I was pretty sure cat owners needed fifty-five kinds of kitty litter as much as yoga students (who practiced barefoot) needed yoga shoes.

Michael looked surprised to see me, but he left his stack of cat box accouterments to talk.

"Hey, I'm sorry about what happened last night. I heard you found the body of the *Dollars for Change* vendor that was killed."

I shuddered. "Yes, it was pretty awful. I still can't believe it."

"The building manager came by and told me. Somehow violence seems worse when it happens to someone you know."

"Jake the Jerk was by? Glad I missed him." Oops. Did I actually say that out loud?

Michael smiled. "He's a piece of work, isn't he? I don't know what Alicia sees in him. Most people seem to like him, though. I guess you and I have better taste."

I changed the subject before I said something else I'd regret. "I need some help. I'm taking care of George's dog until I can find his daughter, and I don't think the food I bought at the Super Mart is working for her."

Michael flinched as if slapped in the face. "You fed her grocery store food? That stuff is nothing but fillers and trash. I wouldn't feed it to a cockroach."

"Yes, I get that. But it was an emergency. Besides, I think Bella may need special food. You know, the kind you feed sick dogs." I looked at Michael expectantly.

"Sorry, Kate, I'll need more information than that. Does she have food allergies?"

"No, I would remember that. Bella has a disease, but I can't think of what it's called." I looked away, trying to recall what George had told me about Bella's illness. "All I can remember is that it has lots of letters, German shepherds get it, and she needs special food or she'll starve."

"Bella has EPI?" Michael asked.

"That's it! I can't remember what it stands for, though."

"Exocrine pancreatic insufficiency. That's too bad. EPI is serious. One of my customers has a shepherd with it. I think you'll need more than special food for Bella, poor thing. No wonder she's so skinny."

"So, what do I do?"

"I'm not sure, but my customer will be. Let me call her." He went to the desk and started typing. A minute later, he grabbed his cell phone and went into a room marked "Private."

While Michael made the call, I killed time looking at the "Pet Services" bulletin board. A few dog training flyers caught my eye. One who guaranteed results with issues ranging from separation anxiety to aggression sounded promising. I pulled down the flyer and put it in my pocket. I wouldn't need this information, but Bella's next owner might.

Michael returned with a sheet of paper and a determined look. "OK. Here's the scoop. Bella needs enzymes to digest her food. They're prescription, so you'll have to buy them from a vet."

I sighed and rolled my eyes toward the ceiling. Michael pretended not to notice. "My customer agreed to help you out in the meantime. She recommended a food, and she'll donate enough medicine to last a couple of weeks. But she said you can't just give Bella the medicine. You'll have to prepare her food a special way for it to work."

"That sounds complicated," I complained. "I'm not going to have Bella long. Can't her next owner deal with all of this?"

"Absolutely not," he said, without hesitation. "Until Bella gets the enzymes she needs, you may as well not feed her at all. You wouldn't starve her until she got a new home, would you?"

Of course I wouldn't. But I also remembered what George told me about the price of that medicine. A couple of weeks wasn't much time to find Bella a new owner.

"Tell you what," Michael said. "Let's ring up your supplies, and I'll throw in a five-pound bag of food to get you started. I'll call you when I have the enzymes. In the meantime, is Bella here? I'd like to say hi to her."

I looked at Michael's bearded face. The mental movie of Bella saying hi to him was a cross between *The Three Stooges* and *Friday the 13th*. "Sorry. Not a good idea. She doesn't like men with beards."

"Really? I hadn't noticed that. I thought she just didn't like other dogs." He scanned the shelves and grabbed a small bag of food. "Don't worry, she'll like me. I'm great with dogs."

"I don't know..."

"Seriously, it'll be fine." Michael leaned against the counter, folded his arms, and cocked his head. "Tell you what. Let's make a bet. Bring Bella out to the parking lot. I'll meet her there, where there's lots of space." He pointed to my overflowing shopping basket. "If she doesn't like me, I'll give you all of this stuff for free. I'll consider it my donation to a dog in need."

"And if she *does* like you?"

"Well, then," he said, lifting his lips in a hairy grin, "in that case, you owe me a date this Saturday night."

"A date?" He had to be kidding.

"Yes, a date. I have a feeling we'd really get along. You like to act all tough, but you're actually pretty sweet underneath all that bravado. As for me, well, I'm an amazing catch." I stared at him, speechless. "Let Bella be the judge," he continued. "If she likes me, you have to give me a chance. If she doesn't, well, who am I to argue with a dog as smart as a German shepherd?"

It seemed like a safe bet. That beard looked exactly like a Brillo pad—dark, scratchy, and teeming with bacteria. Bella would eat him for lunch. I, on the other hand, would get free dog supplies and a chance to knock some of the cockiness out of this overly confident male.

"You're on."

NINE

BELLA WHINED WITH ANTICIPATION as I unlocked the door and released her from her mobile prison cell. She scrambled out of the car and voraciously sniffed her new surroundings while Michael moved toward her slowly and nonchalantly, as if out for an afternoon stroll. Bella spied him and froze; she stood completely still, ears pricked forward, intently staring. Her eyes practically burned holes in his chest. I smiled and chuckled to myself. This was going to be fun.

Michael edged nearer, until he was about five feet away. Bella moved tentatively toward him three steps, then backed up again. I wrapped the leash around my wrist, took up the slack, and held on tight. No doubt about it. Bella was about to explode.

"Woo, woo, woo." Bella's vocalization was soft, almost mumbled. She was obviously concerned about Michael, but this was a far cry from the vicious attack I expected.

Michael crouched down and looked at the ground. "Hey, Bella girl," he said in a low, soothing tone. He held out his hand, fingers in a fist—to avoid their amputation, I assumed. "Loosen the leash," he said. "Let her come up and sniff."

Against my better judgment, I gave Bella an additional foot of lead. Still woo-wooing, she tentatively reached toward Michael and sniffed his outstretched fist. I held my breath, silently praying. I wanted to win the bet, but not at the expense of Michael's right hand. I mentally cursed myself for agreeing to this insanity.

I couldn't believe the transformation that came over that dog. One whiff, and her tail started wagging slowly back and forth; her facial expression softened; her ears relaxed. She let out a soft "woof!" and nestled right up to Michael, excitedly nudging his hand with her nose.

"Remember me, Bella girl? I'm the cookie man." He turned toward Bella and opened his fist. In it was a heart-shaped dog cookie. Bella snatched it up with the joy of a child taking a chocolate-covered Drumstick from the ice cream truck man. She snarfed down the yummy morsel, then proceeded to crawl all over Michael, licking and nibbling at his hairy face.

"I know! It's great to see you again, too!" He laughed, vigorously scratching her sides.

I'd been conned.

"No fair! You already knew her!"

"You didn't think I'd let Bella hang out near the store without giving her cookies, did you?" He rubbed his hand back and forth across the top of Bella's head. She wiggled her entire body with glee, clearly reveling in doggy heaven. "Bella's always loved me."

"The bet is off," I whined. "You cheated."

"Absolutely not. At no time did I say Bella and I were strangers. You assumed." Michael winked and edged closer. I marveled at his courage. I was, after all, about to kick him in the shin.

"You have no one to blame but yourself," he said, grinning. "But don't worry. You can get even by ordering champagne with dinner on Saturday. Maybe that will make up for the small fortune you're about to spend on dog supplies."

I shook my head and watched in amazement as Bella continued to play and flirt. "I still can't believe she likes you. She hates men with beards."

"To tell you the truth, until Bella got a good whiff of me, I thought you might be right. She must be stressed, but that's not surprising. After all, her whole world's been turned upside down. She probably doesn't know who to trust.

"So," he continued, "Saturday night? I've got great taste in restaurants, so dress nice. You like Italian?"

Great. Just what I needed. A date with a beard covered in pasta sauce.

———

Six hours later, Bella and I returned home. The day's yoga students were safely tucked in their beds, and Bella was more than tired of hanging out in the car. I dragged in the jumbo bag of dog supplies and prepared Bella's new organic, hypoallergenic, grain-free kibble according to the instructions provided by Michael's Good Samaritan customer. Her note indicated that getting the enzyme dosage right was a "trial and error" process. I laughed. It figured. Nothing about Bella was easy. But since I was already going through the "trial," I might as well add the "error."

I ground up the kibble, added water and medicine, and mixed up the moist, disgusting-looking concoction in Bella's brand-new food bowl. Bella watched with anxious anticipation. The instructions said her food should be the consistency of oatmeal, but to me it looked like something significantly less appetizing. Bella didn't seem to notice. She danced and drooled, clearly ready to devour her dinner. I set the timer. "Sorry, girl, it needs to sit for twenty minutes."

"Bark!"

I ignored her.

She responded with two more ear-splitting barks.

"There's nothing I can do," I said in my most authoritative voice. "We have to wait at least twenty minutes." I handed her a bone-shaped piece of plastic. "Take this chew toy."

Bella retired to the living room and half-heartedly gnawed on the bacon-flavored dog pacifier. She looked less than pleased, but for the moment, I had won. Score one for the human.

When the timer went off, Bella snarfed down her meal in two minutes flat. It must have tasted better than it looked.

Bella's dining requirements satisfied, I could finally attend to my own needs. Nothing sounded better than a good book and a long, hot bath. I was about to dip my toes in lavender-scented bliss when I noticed the light blinking on my answering machine.

"Hey, Katydid, it's John. I have some information on that woman you're looking for. Give me a call."

I threw on a robe and grabbed a pen. "Bella, our luck may be changing."

O'Connell answered on the first ring. "Great. I was hoping you'd call. I spent some time on the phone with Detective Henderson today. You were right, by the way. You didn't exactly make a good impression. Is it true you barfed all over his crime scene?"

Lack of sleep left me irritated. "Well, pardon me if I'm not used to stumbling over dead bodies."

"Settle down, Katydid, settle down. No need to get your drawers in a bunch. I'm doing you the favor, remember?"

I bit back my snarky reply and stared longingly at the bathtub. "Sorry, John, but I'm in a hurry. Do you have something for me?"

"Henderson's convinced your friend's murder was a drunken brawl gone bad," he continued. "They haven't found the murder weapon yet, but nothing about this looks premeditated—more like a fight that got out of control."

"I don't buy it, John," I argued. "George wasn't the fighting type. And Greenwood may not be Mercer Island, but we're not exactly Belltown, either. We don't have a lot of street crime in this neighborhood." I tapped my pen on the notepad, thinking. "Maybe I should talk to Henderson again."

John's irritation surged through the phone line. "Katy, we made a deal. I'd get you some information to satisfy your curiosity, and you'd stay out of this. A murder investigation is no place for an amateur, especially one who's also a witness."

"But—"

"I mean it, Kate," he barked. "Keep messing in this investigation, and you're liable to really screw it up. Now are you going to fight me, or are you going to be a good girl and let me tell you how to contact the vic's daughter?"

I scowled and made a gesture—the kind not readily accepted in polite company. Nobody called me a "girl." Especially not a "good girl." Not even my father's oldest friend. I didn't feel the slightest bit guilty lying to him, under the circumstances.

"You're right, John. I'm out of my league. I'll stay out of the investigation and leave it to the professionals. You found George's daughter?"

He exhaled with relief. "Good job, Katydid. As it turns out, you were right. She's local, sort of. Her name's Sarah Crawford and she lives in Issaquah. I've got her number here." I wrote it down.

"Detective Henderson didn't think she'd be too happy to speak with you, but that's your concern. I did my part."

I disingenuously thanked him for his help, hung up the phone, then immediately picked it up again. The bath would have to wait. I had no idea what to say, but under the circumstances, I figured the fewer details, the better.

"Hello, Ms. Crawford? My name is Kate Davidson. I have something valuable of your father's that you might want."

TEN

"Don't worry, girl, they'll love you. After all, you're family."

I hoped I was right. As Bella and I drove across I-90 the next morning, I worried about our reception. My phone conversation with Sarah had been brief, and I didn't volunteer much information. I certainly didn't tell her that the "item" I planned to deliver was of the canine variety. Sarah sounded tired—too tired to think clearly—so I talked fast and used vague terms like "father's most precious possession" and "family heirloom." I may have even fibbed a little about my connection to the Seattle Police Department.

I felt bad about deceiving her. The yoga teachings clearly promoted honesty. But my story was an exaggeration, not really a lie. I may not *officially* work for the police, but they *did* give me Sarah's phone number. Besides, there were extenuating circumstances. My work with Bella was a mission of mercy. I pulled into the driveway and hoped for the best.

The property was exactly what I had envisioned for a Bella-sized dog. The pale yellow house nestled in the corner of a gorgeous green lawn. Large fir trees blocked neighboring houses from view and would provide cool, dappled-gray shade puddles, perfect for napping on hot summer afternoons. I smiled as I imagined Bella happily protecting her yard from intruding cats, wandering deer, and hapless mailmen.

"Bella, this is perfect. Look at that huge fenced-in yard! You'll be able to run and play all day." Bella did, indeed, look impressed as she smashed her nose against the car window. "I don't see any other dogs, so unless there's one in the house, you'll have this place all to yourself. And look! There's a tricycle in the front yard. I'll bet a kid lives here. You love kids!"

I smiled to myself. *I guess sometimes stories do end "happily ever after."*

"Wait here. I'll go butter them up for you."

As I walked up the sidewalk, I examined Bella's new home. Bright white shutters and the smell of freshly mown grass hinted that the property was well cared for. Children's toys littered the lawn, and bright orange poppies bloomed along its edges in well-tended beds. Saying a silent prayer to God, the universe, or whatever else was in charge, I rang the bell.

The woman who answered the door had the weary look of young mothers everywhere. She wore a clean-but-wrinkled blouse and frayed jeans that weren't quite stylish enough to have been purchased that way. Her red-rimmed eyes showed evidence of recent crying. A blue-eyed toddler clung tightly to her leg with one hand and held a plastic dump truck in the other. The remnants of a peanut butter and jelly sandwich colorfully decorated both his face and his blue-striped T-shirt. I smiled as I imagined ruffling my fingers through his adorable, soft-looking brown curls.

"You must be Kate. I'm Sarah, and this here's Davie. Davie, say hello."

I half expected Davie to walk up and offer me his paw. Instead, he smiled and leaned into his mother's leg, shyly hiding behind it. "I'm Davie," he said, rocking back and forth. "I'm gonna be three." He held up the correct number of fingers. Sarah gave him a gentle hug and opened the door wider.

"Come on in. My husband, Rick, is out back, but we can talk inside."

I followed Sarah to a neat and functional living room. Well-worn rugs covered its wooden floors, and the dirt-colored furniture looked sturdy and easily cleanable—well suited for the inevitable mishaps of life with a toddler. I could easily imagine Bella curled up by the fireplace or hiding under the kitchen table, begging for unwanted table scraps from her new young best friend.

Sarah gestured toward the corner. "Davie, why don't you go play with your trucks?" To me, she said, "Please have a seat. I'm sorry, I don't have much to offer you. Would you like a cup of coffee?"

I declined her offer as we both sat down.

"My father's death took us by surprise, and I haven't had time to go to the store. Even in a death like this, there's so much planning."

"A death like this?" I asked.

Her facial expression was blank, almost numb. "It's not like we're going to have a funeral or anything. My father didn't have insurance, and we don't have much money." She shrugged. "Besides, who knows if he even had friends anymore? I wouldn't have a clue who to invite to a memorial. I thought it would be simple enough to have him cremated, but I still have to make all these decisions. Like, what am I supposed to do with the ashes? I don't want to keep them, but I have no idea where to scatter them. As far as I know, the place Dad loved best was some liquor store."

I winced before I could stop myself. Her acrid tone surprised me.

"I'm sorry if that sounded cold, but my father and I weren't close. Not for years."

"I would imagine that makes it even harder," I replied. "So much unfinished business."

"I suppose. But telling Mom was the hardest part." She rubbed her eyes, whether from exhaustion or grief, I couldn't tell. "Mom claims to have gone on with her life, but even after all this time, I think she still loved him."

"When was the last time you saw your father?"

"Last weekend, but before that it had been a very long time ..."

My yogi sense tingled on high alert. George told me he hadn't spoken to his daughter in years. What made him reconnect with her last weekend? And more importantly, did visiting Sarah somehow lead to his murder?

I waited, hoping Sarah would volunteer more information. But she stared off into space, her echoing silence broken only by a ticking clock and the wooden clunking of Davie's dump truck as it deposited blocks into an imaginary landfill.

I gently prodded her. "At least your father was able to spend some time with his grandson before he passed."

Sarah stiffened. When she looked back at me, all traces of wistfulness were gone. Her lips thinned to a tense line. "I never said that I let him see Davie." She stood up. "I don't mean to be rude, but I don't want to talk about my father anymore. You said you have something for me?"

I had no choice but to drop the subject—for now.

"Yes, but it's hard to explain. If you come outside, I'll show you."

Sarah followed me to the yard, Davie clinging tightly to her hand once again. I opened the car door and clipped on Bella's leash.

"Bella, say hello."

As trained, Bella walked up to the pair, sat down and raised her paw. Davie giggled, clearly delighted, while Bella nudged his hands looking for treats. Finding none there, she moved on. Dog saliva dripped from Davie's chin as Bella licked peanut butter from his face. No doubt about it; Davie and Bella were in love.

Sarah was not.

She looked at me, trembling with ill-disguised fury. "You have got to be kidding me," she snapped. "This is what you brought? This stupid *dog*?"

I took two steps back, pulling Bella in close. I'd expected Sarah to be surprised, even annoyed by my deception. Frankly, I deserved a harsh word or two. But this reaction was much, much stronger than that. Her facial expression connoted an intense, hidden rage. The type of rage best left buried deep inside or explored from the safety of a psychiatrist's couch.

The Sarah I faced now was not the same woman who'd offered me sustenance only moments before. I tried to reconnect with that calmer, more rational Sarah. "I'm sorry I deceived you. I know you're having a tough time right now, really I do. I lost my own father a couple of years ago. I know my timing is terrible—"

"You have no idea." Sarah interrupted, practically vibrating with anger. I pressed on, hoping to penetrate the fortress she'd built between us.

"I know how hard it is to lose someone you love unexpectedly. How hard it is to leave things unsaid. But Bella can be such a gift for your family. She can form a connection—a bridge—between you and your father. When my father died, I longed to be close to him again. I would have given anything to still have a part of him with me." A sob caught in my throat. "Anything." I paused to take a breath. Sarah remained silent. I hoped that meant I was getting through.

"Your father adored Bella," I continued. "And part of him still lives within her. He'd want nothing more than for the two of you to be together."

Sarah said nothing. Her body was rigid, her face stone cold.

Desperation overwhelmed me. I had to make her understand—I had to do right by George. "I know you and your father had a difficult relationship. I get that. I know he put you through things I can't possibly comprehend. But perhaps Bella is his way of reaching out to you. Perhaps through her, you and he can re-create a relationship of sorts. She's a great dog and she obviously likes your son. Your dad loved her so much—"

"Believe me," Sarah exploded, "I know he loved that frigging dog. More than he loved anything else, including me." She shook her head, outraged, as tears streamed down her face. "Do you know how many years Mom and I begged him to go into rehab? How many times I asked him to be part of my life? He never once considered it.

"Then, after all these years of nothing—no contact whatsoever—he showed up on my doorstep last Saturday, expecting some kind of redemption. He even had the nerve to tell me that he wanted to be a grandfather to Davie." She pointed a shaking finger at Bella. "That this *stupid dog* taught him the importance of family. He promised to go into rehab if I took his *precious pooch* and helped pay for its medical bills."

I wanted to interrupt. To say something—anything—that would calm her, but Sarah didn't give me a chance.

"I practically slammed the door in his face. I told him I wouldn't give him one penny. I swore I'd kill him before I'd let him anywhere near my son—that he'd never hurt Davie the way he hurt me." Her bitter tears turned into frustrated, aching sobs. "I can't believe how naïve I was. I thought now that he was dead, he couldn't hurt me anymore. But he's still the same selfish SOB he always was, even after death. Even now, all he wants is another favor." She took one final, seething look at Bella. "Well as far as I'm concerned, he and that mangy mutt can both go *straight to Hell.*"

Before I could tell Sarah that her father really did love her, before I could share any of his regrets, before I could explain that caring for Bella was George's damaged way of making amends, Sarah was gone. She stormed back to the house, dragging the bewildered toddler behind her. I stood frozen, still stunned, as the screen door's slam echoed around me.

I laid a calming hand on Bella's shoulder. "Well, sweetie, that didn't go exactly as I had hoped. I guess we'd better head back."

I had every intention of leaving, and leaving quickly. Sarah was less than rational; lord knew what she'd do if she came back and found Bella and me still on her property. But before I could get Bella loaded in the car, the screen door opened again, and a tall, somber-looking man rushed out. He had Davie's blue eyes and those same tempting curls.

"Bella, wait," I said, tightening her leash. "I think we're about to meet the man of the house." I closed the car door and returned to the yard.

"I'm sorry about my wife," Rick said. "She's usually quite level-headed. She rarely loses her temper. But all of this has really caught her off guard." He looked back at the house and lowered his voice. "First her father shows up here, asking for money. I've never seen Sarah so furious. Not that I blame her, not one bit.

"Then, a few days later, she finds out he's dead. I don't think she's gotten over the shock yet, much less the guilt of how they ended things. I'm honestly not sure who she's angrier with—her father or herself." His eyes hardened. "But soon enough she'll realize she has nothing to feel guilty about. I never knew her father before last week, but if you ask me, that deadbeat had a lot of nerve showing up here after all that time." He clenched his fists. "My only regret is that I didn't throw him off the property myself."

Sarah and Rick weren't exactly vying for president of George's fan club. Either one of them might have wanted George gone—permanently. I tried to empathize, but all I felt was righteous indignation. George had been flawed, that much was certain. But he was a good man. A good man who had been brutally murdered. And nobody, including his family, seemed to care. Nobody, that is, except me.

"Just how angry was your wife?"

Rick flinched, startled. "What do you mean?"

"Her father was murdered, you know."

His mouth dropped open. "You can't possibly think Sarah had something to do with that."

I remained silent, hoping he would continue.

"You've got to be kidding! My wife wouldn't hurt a fly! Besides, what would she have to gain by murdering her father?"

"Rage can be a powerful motive." I looked pointedly at Davie's tricycle. "For that matter, so can protecting someone you love. Exactly where were the two of you on Tuesday night?"

Rick's face turned bright red from his neck to his scalp. "Are you serious? Where we are every night. We have a toddler, for God's sake. By eight o'clock, it's bath time. If we're lucky enough to get two minutes together, we collapse on the couch and watch TV." He took a step back and narrowed his eyes. "Why are you so interested, anyway? The cops said this was an open-and-shut case. A violent death isn't all that surprising, given my father-in-law's life." His upper lip lifted cruelly. "Live on the street, die on the street. It was merely a matter of time."

I glared at him, appalled. "I don't believe that for a minute."

"So what?" Rick countered. "That still doesn't mean Sarah or I had anything to do with his death. Sarah's father didn't exactly have a shortage of enemies. A lot of people suffered when that business of his went under. Any one of them might have felt completely justified putting a brick to the old man's head."

He pointed to my car. "Now please, for my family's sake, take that dog, get off my property, and don't ever come back here again." Like his wife, he stormed off, slamming the screen door behind him.

Two questions plagued my mind as Bella and I drove way. First, no one had mentioned a brick. If George was killed with a brick, how did this guy know it?

Second, what on earth was I going to do with Bella now?

ELEVEN

As I drove across the I-90 bridge back to Seattle, I came up with the perfect plan—so perfect I wondered why I hadn't thought of it before. All I needed was a little preparation. This time I wouldn't rush in and improvise, like I'd done with Sarah. This time I would strategize carefully and execute flawlessly. I left Bella parked in the shade, went inside the studio, and did a quick meditation practice to visualize my success. In my mental motion picture I was cute. I was convincing. I was irresistible. No one could possibly have said no to me.

Mental preparation complete, I turned to the physical. I smiled in the bathroom mirror, removed an errant piece of spinach from between my teeth, and pulled my makeup tote out of my purse. I added a little extra blush, some smoky black mascara, even the tiniest amount of shiny pink lip gloss. The clothes I wore would have to do, but I smoothed out the wrinkles and brushed off the dog hair. I hadn't practiced flirting in quite some time, but I figured it was like riding a bike—once you learned, you never forgot.

I locked the studio's front door behind me and pep-talked myself down the sidewalk. When I arrived at my destination thirty seconds later, I popped in a breath mint, flashed my biggest, brightest smile, and added the teensiest sway to my hips. The bell on the door announced my arrival as I purposefully strode through the entrance.

"Welcome to Pete's Pets, can I help you?"

My smile vanished.

Sitting behind the desk was a woman—a child, really. She was no older than twenty. Her thirty-six D chest contrasted nicely with her size six hips, and her too-tight top and hip-hugging jeans left nothing to the imagination. I glanced back at the window. The "Help Wanted" sign was conspicuously missing.

"Um … I'm um … looking for the owner. I mean … I'm looking for … you know … Michael."

Brilliant, just brilliant. You have such a way with words.

"He's busy right now, but maybe I can help. I'm Tiffany."

Seriously? Tiffany? Who in the world named their kid Tiffany? Parents who raised brain-dead sex kittens, that's who. My esteem for Michael, not all that high to begin with, dropped several notches. My self-confidence rose by twice that amount, and with it, my ability to speak.

"I need to speak with Michael. It's personal. When will he be back?"

Perhaps I shouldn't have used the word "personal." Perhaps I should have continued stammering. Regardless, her attitude toward me changed. Her smile thinned to a smirk, and her eyes shrewdly narrowed. She looked me up and down, mentally sizing up the competition. "I didn't say he was *gone*. I said he was *busy*."

Game on.

If this licentious Lolita wanted a catfight, I'd show her my claws. I considered spraying her with my newly acquired vial of pepper

95

spray, but decided that would probably be overdoing it. I impaled her with my oh-so-sharp-witted tongue instead. "Well, in that case, do you have any idea when he will get *un*-busy?"

No reply. I was as inconsequential as a housefly—annoying, but not worth the effort of swatting. She stared at me, clearly asserting her authority. I had two choices: I could either leave, or I could provide more information.

I chose option three.

I planted my feet and did my best impersonation of a statue, staring right back at her. Time ticked on, both of us childishly refusing to give ground. I imagined decades passing while we continued our passive-aggressive struggle for dominance. In my mind's eye, dust and cobwebs covered us both, as our hair turned white and numerous body parts sagged with the inevitable effects of gravity.

Tiffany finally stood up, sighing. "If you wait here, ma'am, I'll try to find him."

Ma'am? Who was she calling *ma'am*?

She walked, or more accurately sashayed, back to the storage room. In a voice more than loud enough for me to hear, she said, "Michael, there's some older lady out here who insists on talking to you."

Michael emerged from the storage room, looking confused. His gaze bounced from Tiffany, to me, then back to Tiffany again. He tried, unsuccessfully, to suppress a grin.

"Hey, Kate. How's that food working out for Bella?"

"Much better, especially now that I've figured out the enzyme routine. But that's not why I'm here. I need to talk to you for a minute." I looked pointedly at Tiffany. "Alone."

Michael nodded for her to return to the cash register. She reluctantly left, but flashed me a look on her way. *Don't celebrate,* it said. *This battle is far from over.*

"What's up?" Michael asked.

"I took Bella to meet George's daughter today, and our visit didn't go well. I don't think she's going to take her."

"That's too bad."

"Yeah, but my dad always said things happen for a reason, and I came up with a great idea!" I flashed my biggest, brightest smile.

"I don't like the sound of this at all," Michael replied, frowning in return.

It was time to use all those skills I rehearsed in my visualization. I leaned in closer, played with my hair, and batted my mascara-covered eyes. Michael responded by taking a step back, crossing his arms, and looking at me suspiciously. Undaunted, I tried my next move. I coquettishly looked away for a moment, only to accidentally lock eyes with Tiffany.

Tiffany's evil stare sapped my superflirt sex appeal faster than kryptonite. Instead of embodying the irresistible temptress of my imagination, I suddenly felt inadequate—like my pants were unzipped, I wore lipstick on my teeth, or I had toilet paper stuck to the bottom of my shoe.

I continued anyway, talking considerably faster. "Well, you like Bella, and she adores you. You said yourself that you're good with dogs, and what better person to take her than someone who owns a pet store! You have all the food right here and lots of toys. You're obviously the right home for her!"

Michael shook his head slowly. "Sorry, Kate. As much as I'd like to, there's no way I can take Bella."

This was *not* the response he gave in my visualization.

"Why ever not? You two are perfect together!" I paused and realized the obvious. "Wait a minute. Do you already have a dog?"

"No, and I can't. My apartment doesn't allow pets."

I stepped back and looked at him incredulously. "Doesn't allow pets? What kind of idiotic animal lover lives in a place that doesn't allow pets?" Insulting Michael while throwing a temper tantrum wasn't in my plan, either, but I was frustrated.

"I thought the apartment would be temporary. I've been saving to buy a house, but the economy is terrible and business is slower than I'd hoped. Even in this abysmal housing market, I'll be lucky to have enough money for a down payment by the time I'm seventy-three.

"Besides, I don't have time for a pet," he continued. "I hope hiring Tiffany will help, but until now I've been working twelve-hour days, every day. That's not fair to an animal, especially a dog."

I stepped back and frowned, reassessing my strategy. Michael was the solution to my problem; he simply didn't know it yet. I hadn't counted on the no-pet housing fiasco, but I had another idea. I added a tiny pout to my lips. "Gosh, that's really too bad. I guess I'll have to take her to the pound." I sighed and looked at the floor in pretend despair. "They'll probably put her down ..."

I walked away, counting the seconds. At five, I turned back around and looked at Michael with what I hoped was an expression of guileless innocence. "Unless, that is, you could keep Bella in the store. She'd love it here. You'd be with her all day and then she could guard the place for you at night!"

Michael wasn't fooled. "Come on, Kate," he chided. "You know that would never work. Bella would go after every dog that came in here. I'd be out of business in a week!" His expression turned wry. "Besides, you can't con me. You'll never put down George's dog. Sorry, but I'm out. You'll have to find another sucker."

"What in the world am I going to do?" Flirting didn't work; throwing a temper tantrum didn't work. I don't know what possessed me to think whining would fare any better.

Michael didn't seem moved by my plight. "The first thing I'd do is buy a bigger bag of dog food. That five-pound bag I gave you will only last a few days. I can connect you with some no-kill shelters, but honestly, Bella's going to be hard to place. People generally want to adopt healthy dogs. She's got an expensive disease. That's strike one."

"But that's not her fault—"

"And her behavior issues are strike two. You know I like Bella, but she's not an easy dog. Whoever adopts her is going to have a lot of training in their future."

I had gone through my entire repertoire of persuasive tactics: flirting, cajoling, guilt-tripping, and begging. Michael wasn't coming to Bella's rescue. "I guess you'd better give me that list of shelters," I said, resigned. I grabbed a second five-pound bag of kibble, hoping it would last the week. Surely I'd find a place for Bella by then. Michael followed me to the cash register.

"Kate, this is Tiffany," he said. "She moved into the apartments upstairs a few weeks ago and noticed my 'Help Wanted' sign. She started work here today."

Tiffany flashed Michael a sparkling white smile—the kind you see in toothpaste commercials. "Michael, would you please help me ring this up? The computer is so confusing…"

Great teeth or not, she was obviously dumb as a post.

Michael joined her behind the desk. She leaned into him, using a bit more body contact than strictly necessary. Michael leaned away and glanced up at me, wearing a sheepish grin. "We still on for Saturday night?"

"Sure!" My voice sounded overly excited, even to my own ears. Why should I care if Michael associated with tramps? Going out with him was simply my penalty for losing a bet. I turned my vocal volume and my enthusiasm both down a notch.

"I mean, yes, we're still on, but I'll have to make it an early night. I have to teach early the next morning."

"Oh, really?" he replied. "I looked at the schedule. Your first class is at noon. According to my calculations, that means I don't have to get you home until eleven on Sunday."

"Don't get your hopes up, Romeo," I said, starting to smile again.

"Yeah," Tiffany replied. "I'm sure she needs her beauty sleep."

I signed the receipt, grabbed the bag of dog food, and quickly left the store before I did bodily damage to the little tart.

"Pick you up at seven o'clock sharp!" Michael yelled as I slammed the door behind me.

If Tiffany was the kind of woman he liked, this was going to be the shortest date in history.

———

I stomped back to the studio and stormed past the surprised looking teacher checking in students at the front desk. The yoga room was occupied, so I barricaded myself in the storage room and pulled out my cell phone. I was in a foul mood anyway. I might as well pick a fight with John O'Connell.

"Was George bludgeoned with a brick?"

"Well, hello to you, too, Miss Katy. How nice of you to call."

"Sarcasm doesn't suit you, John," I said testily. "Now tell me. Was he killed with a brick or not?"

"Simmer down, Katy. As far as I know, they still haven't found the murder weapon. But no, it wasn't a brick. From the shape and size of the wound, the coroner thinks it was something smooth and heavy, like a baseball bat or a bottle of some kind." He paused. "Hey, wait a minute, why do you ask?"

"I went to the daughter's house today, and something's not right there. I think she or her husband might be involved in George's death."

John's suspicion turned to irritation. "Now wait one cotton-pickin' minute, little one. You promised me you would stay out of this."

I hesitated, wondering how much to tell him. "I took Bella to George's daughter, exactly like I told you I would. It's not my fault Sarah and her husband started volunteering information. But I'm telling you, someone needs to talk to them. They're hiding something."

"Katy, Katy, Katy," John replied, sounding disappointed. "I knew you'd stick your nose in this. You always do. But as it happens, I've been keeping my eye on the case. You're wrong. The daughter and her husband have solid alibis."

"They were with each other, right?"

"Well, yes."

"Did anyone else see them? How do you know they're not lying to protect each other?"

John exhaled the long-suffering sigh of a parent dealing with an obstinate teen. "Katydid, I already told you. You're making too much of this. There is absolutely no evidence that this wasn't exactly what it appears to be: two drunks fighting over a bottle or a buck."

"But, John—"

"But nothing, Kate," he interrupted, clearly annoyed. "Be quiet now and listen. I'm sorry your friend got killed, but there's no great conspiracy here. You're in way over your head, and frankly, you're starting to make a fool out of yourself. Now I'll say this one final time. Let the professionals do their job and stay out of it!"

I slammed down the phone in a gesture of frustrated determination. John's reaction was exactly what I'd feared. If the police were going to stick to their asinine theory, I didn't have a choice. I would have to solve George's murder myself.

TWELVE

I spent the next several hours grumbling to myself about sleazy pet store clerks and incompetent police detectives. Before I knew it, Alicia had arrived for her Thursday afternoon appointment.

"I'm so glad to be here," she said as she walked into the studio. Each step was achingly tentative, as if moving took almost more effort than she could bear. Dark smudges beneath her eyes contrasted starkly with pale, translucent skin. Her hands trembled slightly as she unrolled her mat.

"How do you feel today?" I asked.

"Well, I have good days and bad days, you know. This is one of the tough ones." She smiled wanly. "But your life is more interesting than mine, anyway. How are you?"

We chatted for a few minutes, though I studiously avoided all but the most superficial of topics. I generally liked to keep my personal life private, but Alicia seemed to appreciate our small talk, as if hearing about the minutiae of my life gave respite from the Hell that was her own.

When we were ready to begin, I invited her to lie on the mat and completely relax, releasing her body into the embrace of the earth. I started by leading her in a centering, breath-focused meditation.

"Allow your mind to be anchored in this present moment. Not concerned with the past, not worried about the future. All that matters is now. Every time your mind wanders, simply bring it back to the sensation of your breath." Alicia closed her eyes and began lengthening her breath. "Each time you inhale, imagine a white light entering your lungs, filling your body with life-giving energy." Her rib cage visibly widened. "Each time you exhale, imagine a dark fog exiting your nostrils, carrying with it all tension, exhaustion, and fear." Alicia wiggled her shoulders and settled deeper into her mat. I would have sworn that the room itself sighed.

After several more minutes of meditation, I guided her through a sequence of yoga poses designed to be gentle, yet purposeful, subtle, yet powerful. Light traces of color returned to her cheeks; worry lines eased from her brow. As I witnessed Alicia's transformation, I felt myself relax. Even after years of experience, I was amazed at how teaching yoga to others could so deeply and personally impact me.

We wrapped up her movement practice with a treasured period of rest. I asked Alicia to lie on the floor with her body draped over a bolster. She extended her legs straight out on her mat and arched her spine over the oval-shaped cushion. Once her head, neck, and back were safely in place, she reached her arms out to the side and faced her palms toward the ceiling. This restorative, heart-opening position subtly built energy, something Alicia so desperately needed.

She rested in silence for ten minutes, until I rang the chimes and asked her to finish her practice. "Begin with small movements, such as wiggling your fingers and toes or even simply taking a deep breath or two. When you're ready, roll to your side for a moment, then gradually press yourself up to sitting."

Alicia slowly sat up, looking not exactly healthy, but at least refreshed. A slight smile graced her lips, and a light pink color enhanced her cheeks. We brought our hands together in prayer position, planning to end the practice by saying Namaste: "The light in me honors the light in you."

"Nama—"

What the heck?

The studio lights shattered our Zen-like practice, flickering on and off like strobe lights in a seventies disco—from Hell. The newest of the many annoying idiosyncrasies of the space.

"I'm so sorry about that," I said. "I'll go turn them off."

Alicia smiled. "Seems like I should be the one apologizing. We must be having problems with the electrical system again. I swear whoever built this building should have his license revoked. I'll tell Jake to come and take a look at it."

As if my week wasn't going badly enough. "Don't worry about it," I said quickly. "I'll call an electrician."

"You have got to be kidding," Alicia chided. "Do you have any idea how much they charge?"

Unfortunately, I did. The last time I had an electrical issue, the bill was well over $1,000. Jake was terminally annoying, but if he could fix the problem, he was also free.

"Perhaps you're right," I admitted. "Maybe it's a problem with the dimmer switch. I'd be foolish to call an electrician for that. Have Jake give me a call and we'll set up a time for him to come over."

"It might be a few days," Alicia replied as she rolled up her mat. "This whole murder business has everybody in an uproar. The police have been questioning all the tenants, and poor Jake has been on the phone nonstop. Nobody feels safe with violent drunks and drug dealers setting up shop in the neighborhood. There's even talk of starting a neighborhood watch."

"Honestly, I don't think anyone has to worry."

Alicia stopped, surprised. "What makes you say that?"

I hesitated, feeling suddenly vulnerable. "This would seem crazy to a lot of people, but I think you'll understand. I've dedicated my life to teaching and practicing yoga. Most people think yoga is simply a form of exercise, but as you know, it's much deeper than that. It's about mindfulness, about focus. It helps us see things as they truly are." Alicia hadn't burst out laughing yet, so I continued.

"As a yoga teacher, I notice subtleties that most people overlook. It's not intuition, exactly, but it sure feels that way. I sense things in my gut, and when I do, I'm almost always right. And my gut tells me the murder was personal.

"Besides, I knew the man who was killed. I overheard a fight right before I found his body and—"

Alicia's eyes widened. "Oh my gosh, I totally forgot. You found the body! How callous of me! I sometimes get so caught up in my own world that I completely forget about other people. I'm so very sorry."

I smiled. "You're not exactly self-centered, Alicia. And even if you were, you have a pretty good excuse."

"Maybe, but still…" She paused. "Hey, wait a minute. You knew the guy who was killed? I thought he was a transient."

We continued talking as we moved to the lobby. "Not exactly. He was part of the homeless community, but he lived in the neighborhood. He sold *Dollars for Change* in front of the studio. He and his German shepherd were out there almost every day. Didn't you see them?"

"Now that you mention it, I do remember a man with a big dog out there. But honestly, I didn't pay much attention to him. Seems like those guys are everywhere." She looked at me quizzically. "But I still don't get it. The police told Jake that the man was killed in some kind of drunken brawl."

"I know, that's what they keep telling me, too," I replied. "But they're wrong. And I won't let it go. I won't stop looking until I learn the truth."

Alicia handed me a check for the day's session. "I know this sounds terrible, but I hope you're right—that the murder was personal, that is. I hate the thought of Greenwood being taken over by criminals. Several of our renters have threatened to move, and the stress is driving poor Jake crazy." She stopped at the door. "You know, I'm not around very much, but Jake's here all the time. Maybe the two of you should put your heads together. Who knows? You might remember something important. I'll have him give you a call."

Great. I was already an untrained, self-appointed Sherlock Holmes. Now I was stuck with Jake as my Watson.

THIRTEEN

THE NEXT TWO DAYS went by in a blur. I didn't exactly forget about George's murder; I just got caught up in the mundane tasks of everyday life.

When I wasn't being dragged around a local park by Bella, I taught classes, paid bills, called customers, and performed the myriad of other duties that consumed my life as a small business owner.

Part of me felt like a failure. Four days had passed since George's murder, and I still had no idea who might have wanted to kill him. The more rational part disagreed. If I truly wanted to honor George's memory, finding a good home for Bella had to come first.

I took Michael's advice and started contacting rescue groups. I called every group I could find in the greater Seattle area—even some in eastern Washington. He was right. Finding a no-kill rescue willing to take Bella wouldn't be easy. Most of the rescues I contacted were full and would be for the foreseeable future. The shelters that had space often weren't equipped to deal with Bella's disease. Those who were willing to jump that hurdle said a firm and final no as soon as they learned about her behavior issues.

I finally found Fido's Last Chance—a rescue specializing in hard-to-place dogs that were literally one step away from euthanasia. I hated putting Bella in that category, but I was getting desperate. After thirty-seven firm answers of "no," a "maybe" sounded downright promising. I crossed my fingers and set an evaluation appointment.

On to the next project: paying off my ill-conceived bet with Michael. Our date was to begin in two short hours, and Rene reveled in date-preparation heaven. She invaded my home with half her wardrobe, determined to make me look, if not sexy and glamorous, then at least presentable. She balked, however, at Bella's participation in *Extreme Makeover: Kate Edition*.

"A dog? Seriously? If you wanted a dog, why couldn't you have at least gotten something cute and hypoallergenic, like a toy poodle or even one of those labradoodles? You know how bad my allergies are!" She sneezed, a bit more dramatically than strictly necessary. "You've gone from being the crazy cat lady to the creepy dog lady!"

"I'm sure you'll live, Rene," I replied drolly. "Besides, I already told you. I'm not keeping her. She's only staying here until I find her a permanent home."

Rene looked around the room, exasperated. "How am I supposed to help you land this guy when everything you own is covered in dog hair? As if your clothing tastes weren't bad enough." She sighed and rolled her eyes toward the ceiling.

"Give it a break, Rene. Tonight's my way of paying off a bet. It's not *Love Connection*."

"Don't be silly. This is the first date you've had in months. I'm not about to let you blow it." She held up an outfit. "How about this dress and those red stilettos?"

"Those shoes are great," I replied, "as long as he's planning to carry me everywhere." I tried them on to make her happy. "Criminy! How small are your feet, anyway?"

"Fine. Forget the shoes. At least you own a decent pair of black pumps. Wear those. And try on this little black dress." She handed me a dark cloth the size of a handkerchief.

It was easier to acquiesce than to argue. I tried them on. I had to admit, the pumps *did* make my calves look good. The dress, however, made me look six months pregnant—with twins.

Rene shook her head. "Ditch the dress. That's no good. How about my charcoal miniskirt and your bright blue blouse?"

I put them on.

"Hey, not bad!" she exclaimed.

I had to agree with her. I usually wear skirts specifically designed to camouflage my flabby upper thighs. But to my surprise, this short skirt made my legs look, if not quite model-thin, at least less Miss Piggy-like.

"Unbutton the top two buttons of the blouse," Rene ordered.

I obeyed. I could always button them back up later.

Rene stood back to assess her work. "Much better. Now, take everything off so I can iron it." She furrowed her brow. "But what *will* we do with that hair?"

I knew better than to argue with Rene when she was on a tear, but all this effort was silly. I had no intention of ever going out with Michael again. I could understand getting all dressed up for a *first* date, but who in their right mind spent this much energy getting ready for a *last* date?

Sixty minutes later, the chosen outfit hung wrinkle-free on the bathroom door, my hair was pinned in an up-do with so much hairspray a tornado couldn't tear it loose, and my fingers and toes shimmered with Rene's sparkly, deep red nail polish—a shade auspiciously called "Walk of Shame." *Subtle, Rene. Real subtle.*

Rene finally allowed me to rest—but only while my nails dried. I sipped herbal tea, savoring the spicy aroma of ginger, while Rene nibbled almond orange biscotti. Bella stood sentry, quietly begging and drooling.

"I'll trust you to do your own makeup," Rene said, waving her index finger back and forth. "But don't make me regret it." Tired of harassing me about my appearance, she turned to a new topic.

"So what *is* the story with the dog? I thought you'd be rid of it by now."

"I thought so too. But I can't find anyone who'll take her. I don't suppose you and Sam are up for a new roommate?"

"Absolutely not," Rene replied, shaking her head vigorously. "The only dog to enter *my* house will be small and hairless. This drooling, furry monster doesn't even come close." She pointed to her saliva-covered jeans. "Look at my pants—she slimed me!" Rene pretended to be annoyed, but her affectionate smile revealed her true feelings. She leaned forward, touched her nose to Bella's, and cooed, "You're a stupid, disgusting monster-dog, aren't you?" Bella leaned into Rene's touch, groaned deeply, and gazed at her with unmistakable adoration.

Rene reached under the table to give Bella the last bite of cookie. "I have to admit though, she does grow on you. It almost seems like she can stare right into your soul. Too bad she's so darned big. Are you sure she isn't part horse?"

I laughed. "I used to say that myself, but now that I've gotten used to her, I don't really notice her size. I can see why George loved her so much."

Rene stopped teasing. Her face turned uncharacteristically serious. "I can't believe I'm about to say this, but why don't *you* keep her? You obviously like her, and she seems right at home here. Other than being a German shedder, she's not so bad. I can always load up on Benadryl before I come over. At least then I won't have to worry so much about you being alone."

I carried our dishes to the sink. "Honestly, Rene, part of me wishes I *could* keep her. But that wouldn't be fair to either of us. Bella needs a family that can devote more time to her. With me, she spends most of the day alone."

"Can't she hang out with you at the studio?"

"Are you kidding? I tried that. It was a disaster. Bella barked at everyone who came to the door. The postman even threatened to stop delivering our mail. Seemed like every ten minutes, I had to take her out to the car or lock her in the bathroom."

Rene shrugged. "I still don't see the big issue. Leave her here. Most dogs stay at home while their owners work. Bella will be fine."

I laughed. "Tried that too. She barked, howled, and drove my neighbors nuts." I poured myself a glass of water. "She's quiet when she's alone in her crate, but I can't leave her caged for ten hours a day. I've resorted to taking her to work with me and leaving her in the car."

"In the car? Is that safe?" Rene asked.

"It's certainly not optimal, but it's safe. I reserved one of the covered spots by the studio's back entrance. On warm days, my car's cooler than the house."

I took a long drink. "It's not fair to her, though. I bring her into the studio while I close up at night, but she's still cooped up most of the day. Besides, I'd go bankrupt feeding her, let alone paying for her $400-a-month medicine. As it is, I can barely afford to feed myself."

"How much money do you have left from your dad?"

"About $4,000, but I need some of that for taxes. The Department of Revenue isn't nearly as forgiving as Alicia."

"I thought business was picking up."

"It is. I'm not *paying* to work at the studio anymore—at least not most months—but I'm still not drawing a regular salary." My gaze didn't quite meet Rene's. "So as much as I'd like to keep Bella, I can't."

Rene could read me like a human lie detector—even when I didn't realize I was lying. She leaned back, crossed her arms, and looked at me skeptically. "Nice try, Kate. I know you better than that. Everything you said is an excuse. You'd find a way to make it work; you always do. And Sam and I can always help out in a pinch." She forced me to make eye contact, insisting I tell her the truth. "What's really going on here?"

I opened my mouth to argue but stopped, suddenly dizzy. Irregular-feeling heartbeats fluttered in the soft pit of my throat. Rene was right. Those *weren't* the real issues. Even thinking about a future with Bella pushed me right to the edge of a panic attack.

I pretended to be calm as I returned to the table. "Honestly, Rene, even if I could work out everything else, I don't think I can stand the loss."

"What loss? What are you talking about?"

"Bella's going to live, what, another eight years, maybe ten, max? And who knows what effect her disease will have on her life span. Then she'll die and I'll be all alone again."

Rene looked confused. "What do you mean?"

"Do you remember what I was like when Dad died? I could barely get out of bed. The grief was so intense, I thought it would kill me."

"But honey, that's normal! Everybody grieves when they lose someone they love. And in spite of your squabbles, you and your dad were practically inseparable. Of course you were depressed for a while!"

"Grieving may be normal, but not like this. It lasted for over a year." Even talking about that time brought back an unwelcome feeling of nausea. "I didn't want you and Sam to worry, so I put on a good front and pretended to be OK. But I felt empty inside for a very long time. In some ways, I still do." I looked down at the table. "It's like Dad took a piece of me with him when he died, and I never got it back. I simply learned how to function without it." I bit my lip to keep it from trembling.

"I know I'd fall in love with Bella. How could I help it? I'd get used to having her in my life, used to her company—then she'd be gone." My eyes burned with held-back tears. "I can't do it again, Rene. I simply don't have any pieces left to give."

Rene leaned forward and touched my arm. "Oh, sweetie, you can't be serious. You can't possibly go through life without loving. I'd rather die myself than lose Sam, but that doesn't stop me from loving him all the same."

"I know, Rene, but that's different. At least you and Sam have a fighting chance of living out your lives together. With Bella, I already know the ultimate outcome."

If Rene's confused look was any indication, she still didn't understand. Frankly, neither did I. Not really. That last fight with my father had changed me in ways I still didn't fully comprehend. I flashed back to that awful scene: the yelling, the accusations. The sound as the door slammed behind me. The words I couldn't take back no matter how hard I tried.

No. I couldn't, I *wouldn't*, talk about that night, not even with Rene. Prickly defensiveness edged out all other emotions. "I've made my decision, Rene. I'm not keeping Bella. I'm not willing to get attached to an animal that way. Now drop it."

Rene grabbed my hand earnestly. "Kate, this isn't healthy."

I ignored her.

"Have you considered counseling?"

Even my skin felt sharp, barbed like a porcupine's quills.

"I have a friend who's a psychologist. Maybe she could—"

"*Enough!*" I erupted, snatching my hand back. "A lot of people don't have pets. It's not a crime, or a sign of mental illness. I owe it to George to help Bella, and I will. But I'm not keeping her. *That's final.*"

Rene stared at me in shocked silence. I felt awful for snapping at her, but at least she got the message. I suspected I'd hear more from her later, but for the time being, she quit pushing. Instead she played the "Rene is a goofball" card, and for once I was glad for the charade. In fact, I had never loved her more. Instead of forcing the subject, instead of insisting that I confront my issues, she looked at her watch and pasted on a fake smile.

"Well, look at that, miss grumpy-pants. It's six-thirty! Your date will arrive in thirty minutes! I need to get out of here, and you, Miss Kate, need to get working on that face of yours. Do yourself a favor and don't go light on the makeup. You look exhausted."

Rene grinned slyly, "By the way, I went undercover and made an espionage visit to a certain pet store. I checked out your guy. He's gorgeous!"

"Oh, Rene, please tell me you didn't—"

"Don't worry, silly. I was subtle. I made up a story about a new pet kitten and everything. Which reminds me, you owe me twelve dollars and seventy-nine cents for kitten chow." She stood up, preparing to leave. "Be sure to call me first thing in the morning. I want details. Lots and lots of disgusting details." She grabbed her jacket and dashed to the door.

"Got to run, literally. I can feel that biscotti adhering itself to my thighs." She hesitated at the door, then ran back and gave me a deep, long hug. "You know I love you, right?"

Tears filled my eyes as the door clicked softly behind her. The room felt eerily, depressingly quiet in her wake. But in spite of my current melancholia, my decision about Bella was final. Rene might think my choice was unhealthy, but the *Yoga Sutras* disagreed. Attachment, they said, led to suffering.

What Rene called neurosis, I called self-preservation.

And so I reburied my fears, relocked the hole in my heart, and drowned out my dreary thoughts by playing my favorite Lady Gaga CD. Evidently, denial was a skill well-honed by practice. By the time I finished belting out the final lyrics of "Poker Face," I felt close to normal again.

Bella scoured the floor, looking for crumbs, as I continued to get ready. I put on my new favorite outfit and looked in the mirror, suddenly self-conscious. "What do you think, Puppy Girl? Does this skirt make me look good or just desperate?"

Bella refused comment.

I turned to the mirror, buttoned up the top two buttons of my blouse, then changed my mind and unbuttoned them again.

"What do we care? I don't even like this guy, and you only like his dog treats." I widened my eyes and liberally applied deep black mascara. "We girls can get along fine on our own. He's probably dating that twenty-year-old bimbo by now, anyway. Besides, I don't need any man. I'm a completely self-sufficient woman."

Bella lay down, sighed, and rested her head on her paws. *Go ahead, delude yourself,* she seemed to say.

I turned away from the mirror to glare at her. "What are you looking at, you hairy monster? You're the one who got me into this mess in the first place."

If that's how Bella was going to act, I'd keep my thoughts to myself. I gave her the silent treatment and continued my mental monologue. *I don't care what any man thinks of me, but I'd hate to be seen in public looking like a homely house frau. I'll just add some eye shadow, maybe a little concealer to hide those dark circles.* I looked in the mirror. An exhausted zombie-woman stared back. *Make that a lot of concealer.*

I glanced sideways in the mirror. I didn't look too bad for a woman in her thirties. As long as I remembered to pull my belly in, I'd be fine. I smiled to check out my teeth in the mirror. The minute I stopped thinking about it, the inevitable pooch below my navel showed itself again. *Lord, aging is a bitch.*

Bella sat up, tilted her head to the side, and watched me curiously.

"Oh, so now you're interested, Missy Dog? Well in that case, make yourself useful. Tell me how great I look."

Silence. Not even an appreciative sigh.

"Fine. Be that way. Do you think I have time for some breathing exercises?"

As if on cue, the doorbell rang. Bella charged the door, barking furiously.

Six-fifty. I should have known he'd be early. Bella alternated between hurling herself at the door and scratching it aggressively, as if she alone were our last defense against an ax-wielding psychopath. I could rest assured knowing I'd always be safe with Bella in the house—as long as the burglar rang the doorbell.

"Bella, shut up!" I yelled. I took a final glance in the mirror and sighed at the futility of it all. Where *did* all that dog hair come from?

I grabbed Bella's collar and dragged the barking, frothing beast away from the door to lock her in the bathroom.

I paused at the door and took a deep breath. *Here goes nothing.* After a count of three, I opened the door and came face-to-face with— a perfect stranger. A *gorgeous* stranger. Clean-shaven, dressed to the nines, lean build. He wore a great big smile and carried a bouquet of—

Flower-shaped dog cookies?

"I hope you don't mind," said the voice I immediately recognized as Michael's. "German shepherds are often territorial, and I didn't want to take any chances. I know this is supposed to be our first date and all, so I really should be trying to impress you. But I figured I should start by winning over Bella. After all, we already know your bark is worse than your bite. Bella's, on the other hand..."

I was stunned. Shocked really. Unable to move. But only for a moment. I slowly smiled, reached out, and took Michael's hand. In a voice so throaty and low I almost didn't recognize it as my own, I said, "Get in here."

I pulled him into the living room, wrapped my arms around his broad shoulders, and planted a long, hard kiss on those luscious, completely hair-free lips. I'm pleased to say he returned the favor.

We never did make it to dinner. But I have to confess, dessert was simply fabulous.

———

I rolled over a little after eight the next morning and opened my eyes. Bella glared back at me. Michael occupied her rightful spot on the bed, and she wasn't happy about it. "Sorry, sweetie," I whispered. "But sometimes a girl's gotta do what a girl's gotta do."

I flipped my back to her, ignored her silent recriminations, and snuggled up to Michael's softly snoring body. I ran my fingers across the ripples of his chest. Yes, there *was* a God.

The telephone's shrill ring interrupted my reverie. This early on a Sunday, the caller could only be Rene. I cursed myself for being too cheap to order voice mail. Michael would never sleep through her teasing, prying, and likely X-rated message.

"Hello?" I whispered, crawling out of bed and tiptoeing toward the bathroom.

"So, how'd it go?"

"Fine, but now's not a good time to talk. Can I call you back later?"

"What do you mean now's not a good time? Wake up, sleepy head! I've been waiting for hours! You can't get off that easily." There was a moment of blissful silence, in which I thought I'd fooled her. I actually thought I might get away with it.

I should have known better.

"Oh, my God!" she yelled, practically deafening me. "He's still there, isn't he? He spent the night! You little tramp!" In spite of her words, she sounded ecstatic. "OK, spill. I need details. Lots of delicious details."

"Shh! I'm hanging up now. I'll talk to you later." I gently, quietly, tentatively placed the handset back on the receiver and looked toward the bed, praying Michael was still asleep. He hadn't moved. For once, luck was on my side. I tiptoed back to bed and stealthily crawled under the sheets.

"Was that Rene?" asked an obviously amused Michael, his back facing me. "Tell her hello for me."

"Yes, she's such a snoop. I'm surprised she waited this long—"

My slow-witted mind clicked into gear. I sat straight up in bed, gathering the sheets around me. "Wait a minute! How do you know Rene?" Michael rolled over and put his arm around me, flashing an engaging and sexy grin. He said nothing.

I pushed him away. "That liar! She talked to you at the store, didn't she? She gave you Kate-specific dating advice! You two traitors conspired against me!" I didn't know which feeling was stronger: anger that they had plotted to thwart my resistance, or embarrassment that it was so easily overcome.

"Now don't be upset, Kate-girl. Our intentions were honorable." He pulled me back next to him and nuzzled my neck. "And we both like you an awful lot." I punched him on the arm. I tried to resist, but it was no use. I melted like cheddar on a grilled cheese sandwich. Who was I to argue? They obviously had me outnumbered.

FOURTEEN

MICHAEL AND I KISSED goodbye at eleven-thirty. I took the world's quickest shower, threw on my yoga clothes, and rushed to class, remarkably unstressed about my tardiness. When I opened the studio a scant two minutes before noon, the line of disgruntled students didn't faze me a bit.

I hadn't gotten much sleep the night before, but that didn't matter at all. I led my students through the entire range of yoga practices—sun salutations, inversions, reflective breath practices, and meditations—with a huge grin on my face and schoolgirl giggle in my voice. Instead of floating around the studio with the ease and grace of an evolved being, I skipped around the floor like a six-year-old with a bag of bright pink cotton candy.

I was in such a good mood that instead of hiding out at the front desk like usual, I joined in with the afternoon Yoga for Kids class. Six grade-schoolers, their yoga teacher, and I faced each other, mats in a circle, as we embarked on our journey—an African safari acted out in yoga poses.

We started standing in Mountain Pose, imagining ourselves at the base of Kilimanjaro. We barked like wild dogs, hissed like cobras, and roared like lions as we traveled through the Sahara desert and deep into the Congo rainforest. We pretended to soar through the Nigerian sky in Flying Warrior—a pose known in adult yoga circles as Warrior III.

I laughed so hard that I fell out of Boat Pose three times. At one point a young boy yelled, "Your boat is sinking!" I almost corrected him. I was clearly capsized, not sunk. But the word "capsized" was probably beyond his vocabulary. So I grabbed a stuffed giraffe and playfully threw it at him instead.

The teacher must have thought I was crazy, high, or both, but she had the good sense not to say anything.

My feet barely touched the floor from noon until five. I was obviously on a lucky streak. I'd found an exciting new love, but that was only part of it; I'd also located a new home for Bella. Today was her evaluation at Fido's Last Chance. I closed up early, grabbed a quick bite to eat, and started the long drive to the rescue's headquarters in Maple Valley.

I pulled in at six thirty, but hesitated before turning off the ignition. "Bella, are we at the right place?" I pulled out my glasses and double-checked the building number. Still the same. I could only hope that I needed new glasses.

To me, the word "headquarters" connoted a tall, light-filled skyscraper in the heart of a buzzing metropolis—or at the very least a small, run-down office in the middle of a deserted strip mall. The entire industrial complex of Fido's Last Chance, however, appeared to be a dilapidated house with a converted garage. A garage filled with dogs. Lots of dogs. Lots of loud, barking dogs. I walked to the door and tentatively rang the bell, hoping I was at the wrong address.

A matronly, smiling, and completely fur-encrusted woman answered the door.

"Hi. You must be Kate. I'm Betty." She peered around me, looking confused. "Where's Bella?"

"I heard all the barking and thought I'd better leave her in the car."

Betty laughed. "Good thinking, but I've locked everyone up for your visit. Now bring Bella on up here so I can take a look."

I returned a moment later with a panting, nervous, but at least reasonably self-controlled Bella.

"My, she *is* a big one, isn't she?"

"Bella, say hello," I said.

Bella, always the crowd pleaser, went into a perfect sit and offered Betty her paw. Betty smiled, grabbed it, and gave it a definitive shake. The uproar of the garage-incarcerated dogs grew louder, as if they could sense that their mistress was cheating.

"How many dogs do you have here?" I shouted above the din.

Betty counted on her fingers. "Well, I've got three of my own, and I'm currently fostering seven more, so I guess that makes ten." She stood taller, as if to deepen her resolve. "But I'm no hoarder, ten is my limit."

Ten? My God, *ten*? This woman must have been sent from the sixth level of heaven. Either that, or she'd recently escaped from a mental institution. I surreptitiously glanced around, looking for a discarded straightjacket.

"I don't know how you do it. I don't even have time for one, let alone one for each finger."

"Rescue is definitely a work of love," she replied, grinning. She opened the door wider. "Let's go to my office where it's quieter."

Betty led me to a dark, windowless room the size of a closet, covered in paw prints, dust, and fur. Loose papers covered every available surface. There was barely enough room for a small desk and two chairs, let alone two women and a jumbo-sized dog. Betty lifted a stack of papers off a visitor's chair and motioned for me to sit. Bella squeezed in beside me.

I wrinkled my nose. The distinctive, ammonia-like odor of cat box wafted from somewhere in the near vicinity. Bella's super-sharp senses picked up the scent as well. Her ears perked up; her eyes sparkled with interest; she pranced on the tips of her toes. She was entranced by something *very* exciting on top of the desk. Something she wanted to get to know more intimately. Something she needed to taste with her very own tongue. Betty looked at Bella and grinned.

"So you like Diablo there, do you?" She lifted a huge yellow tabby off the keyboard and placed him out of Bella's reach on top of the filing cabinet. "Diablo here is my resident dog trainer. He's not scared of dogs, though they probably should be afraid of him. He doesn't mind using his claws, and several of my foster dogs have the scars to prove it." She scratched behind the ears of the oversized jungle cat. "By the time my foster dogs leave here, they have certainly learned their manners."

She closely watched Bella dance and sniff the air around the filing cabinet. "Looks like your dog is basically good with cats. That's a positive thing."

"She's not my dog," I automatically replied. We both watched the canine-feline drama unfold. Bella stared intently at the filing cabinet, softly whining. I wasn't so sure about Betty's "good with cats" comment. A far as I could tell, Bella would have liked nothing better than to sink her teeth into the feline hors d'oeuvre of the day. Diablo, on the other hand, flattened himself rigidly on top of the filing cabinet and glared at Bella, claws fully exposed and ears plastered against his head. I envisioned flying fur, slicing claws, and spraying blood in my future.

"Maybe I should put Bella back in the car," I suggested, pointedly looking at Diablo. Diablo was, after all, the Spanish word for "devil." I was pretty sure I knew how that cat got his name. I didn't know whether Bella or Diablo would win the upcoming battle, but I didn't want to find out the hard way.

Betty didn't appear to share my concern. "Just leave them be," she replied. "They'll get used to each other soon enough." Betty sat down behind her desk and ignored the two feuding animals. Bella reluctantly left the filing cabinet to lie down on the floor beside me. Diablo half-closed his eyes and pretended to sleep.

Betty reviewed her notes. "So, this girl has EPI, eh? That's too bad. A serious illness narrows down the adopter pool considerably." She turned the page. "And you say she's not good with other dogs?"

"Hates them," I replied. "And she's not too fond of some men, either. She can be a real handful around a man she doesn't like."

Betty set down the papers and leaned back in her chair. "Well then, we have ourselves a problem, don't we? I didn't realize she wasn't good with men. That complicates things."

I didn't like the sound of that. "What do you mean?"

"Aggression toward humans raises my risk substantially." She put the cap back on her pen and laid it on the desktop. "There's a certain amount of liability in running a rescue, but aggressiveness, especially toward people, makes it worse by a factor of ten. Most places would euthanize her."

Seriously? I'd driven all the way out here only to be told to put Bella down? To my horror, I started to beg. "Please don't give up on her. It's not all men, just men with beards. She's a great dog and—"

"Enough," Betty said firmly, interrupting my plea. "If you want my help, you need to stop talking and let me finish."

I stopped talking.

"As I was saying, *most* places would euthanize Bella. But I'm willing to work with you."

"Really?" I smiled hopefully.

Betty didn't smile back.

"On two conditions." She held up her index and middle fingers. "First, you need to foster Bella in your home until she finds a permanent owner, and that could be awhile."

My begging amped up to pleading. "But your web site says that you have foster homes all over the state! Can't one of them take her in? They're probably much better equipped to deal with Bella's issues than I am. I'm not even a dog person—everyone knows I'm the crazy cat lady!"

"Give yourself a little credit. Looks like you're doing fine so far. Better than most, actually." She reached over to scratch Bella's ears. "In an ideal world, we probably *would* put Bella in a home with an experienced German shepherd owner. But our foster homes are all overfull, and they likely will be for a while. Do you honestly think I *want* ten dogs?"

I sensed that was a rhetorical question, so I didn't reply. She continued. "When I started this work, I thought I'd easily find homes for my special needs dogs. The reality's quite different. Very few people will adopt dogs with significant health issues. Dogs with behavior problems, well, I might die of old age before I find one of them a good home.

"Most of us here at Fido's Last Chance end up being what are called 'foster failures.' We try for years to find homes for these dogs, then end up adopting them ourselves because no one else will. Eventually, even we reach our limits."

Betty put her elbows on the desk and laced her fingers together. "So, Kate, like it or not, it's you or nothing. You're all Bella's got."

I knew I could change her mind; I simply needed to be strong. I stared her down, doing my best impression of an alpha dog asserting its authority.

Betty stared right back, not even blinking. I can't explain it, but I suddenly wanted to back up, look away, yawn, and lick my lips. If I'd been a golden retriever, I would have rolled on my back and shown her my belly in defeat.

"OK. I'll keep Bella for now, but only until something else opens up." I desperately hoped she was exaggerating about how long that would be.

"That's not all," Betty added.

"Second, you'll have to invest in some training. We can put Bella in the system tonight, but placing a special needs dog with aggression issues is next to impossible. So if I were you, I'd start calling positive trainers first thing in the morning."

"Positive trainers?"

"Yes. Trainers that use reward-based methods in their work. That kind of training may take longer, but it's more humane and, I believe, more effective in the long run than punishment-based methods."

"Maybe I should keep looking for a shelter with space," I said, discouraged.

Betty's years in rescue must have left her pragmatic. "I'm sorry, Kate, but I'm going to be brutally honest here. Even if you find a shelter that's willing to take Bella, an environment like that is too stressful. You'd be torturing her. Sensitive dogs like Bella never make it." Although she patted Bella with affection, her implication was clear.

"You have a decision to make. If you can't work with Bella, then you need to do what's right and let her go." In case I was completely oblivious, she added, "Go to doggy heaven, that is."

Betty and I stared at each other in silence. I thought about George and how much Bella had meant to him—how much she had enhanced his otherwise tragic life. Killing her wasn't an option. I signed on the dotted line.

"Beautiful," Betty said, standing and slapping her thighs. "Now we have one final item of business. Bring Bella over here and let me scan her for a microchip."

"She doesn't have one," I quickly asserted, hoping against hope that would close the issue. I'd neglected to share a couple of minor details about Bella's origins. I was afraid Betty wouldn't take a stolen dog.

Betty's eyes narrowed shrewdly. "How could you possibly know whether or not she's microchipped? According to your story, you got her from a dead homeless guy, and he found her abandoned."

Busted.

"Well," I said stammering, "maybe abandoned was too strong a word. She was more like lost. But she was much too young to have a chip, I'm sure, and—"

"Stop right there, child," Betty said, holding up her palm. "I can tell when I'm being hoodwinked. Now the truth, please. Spit it out."

I don't know why I expected her to be so gullible; Betty obviously knew people even better than she knew dogs. I reluctantly shared what I knew of Bella's early life, her mistreatment, and how George "rescued" her from her own front yard.

"So, you see, even if she has a microchip, Bella can't possibly go back to those people."

"I can sympathize, but it doesn't matter," Betty replied. "Before I place a dog, especially a purebred dog, I have to look for a possible owner. If I got caught placing stolen dogs, I'd be out of business like that." She snapped her fingers.

"Besides, how do you know your friend told you the truth? Maybe Bella wasn't abused at all. People steal puppies all the time. Sometimes they have the best intentions. They see a puppy tied up outside a grocery store and assume it's abandoned. Other times they steal a pup right out of its yard, like your friend did. Not because the dog is abused, but because it's cute.

"My point is, Bella may have a legal owner who wants her back. Her real family might have given up looking after all this time, but that doesn't mean she isn't wanted."

I listened to Betty's lecture in silence. I didn't like it. I didn't like it one bit. But how well did I know George, really? I agreed to the scan.

As Betty ran the scanner over Bella's shoulders, I closed my eyes and prayed. *Please, God, please don't let her be chipped. If you let this one thing turn out OK—*"

"Well, look at that!" Betty exclaimed. "I got a hit! We may be in luck." She pulled up a web site and entered a number. "The office is closed right now, but I'll give them a call first thing tomorrow."

My horrified expression betrayed my fears.

"Look, honey, don't worry so much," Betty said, patting my hand. "If Bella's original owners are the deadbeats your friend described, they either won't be registered anymore, or they won't want Bella back. If they *do* want her back, then they're probably a lot better people than you think." She stood up and grabbed a camera.

"In any case, we won't know anything until tomorrow. For now, get Bella to sit pretty. I'll take her photo and post her profile in the online adoption center. Then you should head on home and start calling trainers. If this microchip ends up being a dead end, you're going to have your work cut out for you."

FIFTEEN

AFTER A SLEEPLESS NIGHT of obsessive worry, I returned to the place I knew best: the wonderful land of denial. A kind, benevolent world in which Bella's microchip would be a dead end. A land in which I, and I alone, would control Bella's fate. In my fantasy, all Bella needed was a *tiny* bit of training. And if Bella needed training, by God, Bella would get training.

A small-time trainer who posted on pet store bulletin boards would never do. So as soon as I finished teaching the lunchtime yoga class, I opened the studio's desk drawer and pulled out the time-tested marketing tool of successful businesses everywhere: *The Yellow Pages*. I ultimately settled on the trainer with the biggest listing. I knew how much those ads cost; I practically cried every month when I wrote the check for Serenity Yoga's tiny, three-line listing. If a business could afford an ad that size—in color no less—it must have lots of satisfied customers, right? And the quarter-page advertisement contained musical phrases like "Quick results guaranteed" and "We do the hard work for you!"

The man who answered the phone was all too willing to work with me, in spite of Bella's issues. When I asked him about the cost, he quickly assured me. "We're not the cheapest, but you get what you pay for. And we take all major credit cards."

"Are you a positive trainer?" I asked.

"Absolutely," he replied. "I'm positive my methods work."

I hesitated a moment, underimpressed by his overdeveloped ego. But then I decided, what the heck? After so much negativity, Bella and I could use a little can-do attitude for a change. I set up an appointment for later in the week.

That settled and Bella's adoption profile online, I could finally focus on solving George's murder. But where to start? Almost a week had passed since that awful night, so the killer's trail was probably close to stone cold. I considered harassing Martinez and Henderson, but that seemed worthless; even if they were actively working the case, they'd be more likely to arrest me for obstruction than give out any useful information.

Thinking about George made my heart ache. I missed him, and I wished he and Bella were outside causing trouble. For a moment, I allowed myself the luxury of daydreaming. In my imagination George waved at me, smiling, as Bella happily drooled by his side. I handed him a one-hundred-dollar bill and said, "Keep the change." The paper's prominent headline declared: "Yoga Teacher Wins Lottery and Donates Half to Local Homeless Charities."

I knew the day's actual headlines said nothing of the sort, but it was *my* daydream, after all. Besides, I hadn't bought a paper since George's demise, so—

Of course! *I hadn't bought a paper*. But there was nothing stopping me from buying one, or from grilling its seller for information. A new *Dollars for Change* vendor had set up shop in front of the

PhinneyWood Market. Who knew what interesting information he might be willing to share, especially if I made it worth his while? The snitches on all my favorite cop shows opened right up when the savvy detective handed them a bank note.

I grabbed two ten-dollar bills from the cash box, vowing to cancel cable to make up for the expenditure. Watching television was a bad habit anyway, and I could always hone my detective skills at the library. If *Advanced Investigation Techniques for Dummies* and *The Complete Idiot's Guide to Solving Your Friend's Murder* hadn't been published yet, they should have been.

The new vendor didn't remind me of George in the slightest. Young, blond, wearing frayed jeans and Birkenstocks, he looked like a down-on-his-luck surfer dude, dreadlocks and all. I could easily imagine him on Maui's Baldwin Beach, living for the opportunity to catch the next big wave. A sweet, smoky smell emanated from his jacket—much sweeter than the average tobacco, if you know what I mean.

Hoping to get in his good graces, I handed him one of the tens and took a paper. "Keep the change."

"Thanks, lady," he said, pocketing the money.

"I'm Kate. I work over at the yoga studio. You're new here, aren't you?"

"Yeah, I used to sell over by the Mini Mart, but this is a much better spot—more foot traffic and better tips." He smiled, revealing a chipped front tooth. "Pretty sweet."

"I'd like to ask you a few questions, if you don't mind,"

"Time is money." He looked at my purse. "Got another of those tens?"

So much for my good graces strategy. Vowing never to pay up-front again, I pulled out the second ten-dollar bill.

"I'll give you this, but first we talk. I'm trying to find a new home for Bella, and I'm hoping you can help."

"Who's Bella?"

"She's a German shepherd I'm fostering. She belonged to George Levin, the man who sold *Dollars for Change* here before you." I lowered my voice. "Did you know he was murdered?"

"Yeah, I heard." He shuddered. "Gruesome. How'd you end up with his dog?"

"It's a long story, but I can't keep her much longer. I thought one of his friends would take her, but so far I'm not having much luck."

"I've been thinking about getting a dog myself. Everyone knows a dog increases the take, especially near a place like this," he said, nodding toward Pete's Pets. "I might even make a sign that says 'Need money for dog food.' That gets 'em every time."

Note to self: Never believe what you read on signs.

"But I'm going to get something cute, little, and floppy eared," he continued. "You know, some mutt that'll attract kids and chicks. I'm certainly not going to get a monster that looks like an overgrown wolf and acts like a wolverine. Everyone said George was crazy to keep that dog."

"So you knew George?"

"*Dollars for Change* isn't exactly a huge corporation, lady. Everyone pretty much knows everyone else." He shrugged. "We weren't friends or anything."

"Do you know if he had any enemies?"

"Not that I know of, but like I said, we weren't friends." He looked at me suspiciously. "Why are you asking about George's enemies, anyway? Are you seriously going to give his dog to someone he hated? That's cold, lady."

My Miss Marple routine needed some work. I changed the subject before he stopped talking to me altogether.

"Honestly, I'm just curious. I found his body."

My Surfer Dude friend shook his head, looked at the ground, and sighed. "That sucks, man. That really sucks."

Not very eloquent, but accurate nonetheless.

"Yes, and it's got me a little freaked out. I guess I'm searching for a reason—you know—a reason why this happened to George and not me."

"It's all about karma, lady. Payback. You can't avoid it if you try."

Adrenaline surged from my fingertips to my toes. Now I was getting somewhere. Only twenty dollars and ten minutes into my investigation, and I was about to uncover a crucial clue. Not bad for a newbie.

"Payback?" I said, edging closer. "Did George do something bad? Something worth getting killed over?"

Surfer Dude frowned. "Nah, you're not listening. I already told you, I didn't know the dude. I have no idea why someone offed him. I'm talking about *karma*. Universal. Life. Karma." He pointed toward the studio. "Since you work at the yoga place, you should know all about it. The crap that happens to us in this life is payback for all the stupid stuff we did last time. George must have been really bad in one of his past lives to get himself killed this go-around. Maybe he was a vicious dictator or a serial killer… Heck, maybe he was even a Republican.

"But it doesn't matter, lady. You can't stop karma. You can only ride the wave and hope for a better trip next time."

I ignored my new friend's flawed interpretation of Eastern philosophy. If Surfer Dude didn't know anything about George's death, maybe he could connect me with someone who did.

"You're probably right," I said, pretending to be relieved. "I'll stop worrying about it." I held up the second ten-dollar bill. "But back to my original question, do you know any of George's friends? I still need to find someone who'll take this dog off my hands."

"Sorry, lady, like I said, I didn't really know him. But if I were you, I'd go to the paper's main office and ask around there. It's not like they keep a lot of records or anything, but someone there might at least know if George had family."

"Thanks, I will." I handed him the money and walked away.

———

Before heading back to the studio, I stopped at the car to check on Bella. One look at me and she started to whine, squirm, and moan, acting like she'd been stuck in the car for a thousand years. That girl needed a walk, and she needed it bad.

The day was gorgeous: The kind of day we don't often get in Seattle—the kind that proves the sky actually *is* blue, not steel gray. On days like this, Seattle residents emerge from their caves, hang up their umbrellas, and gravitate toward the sun's golden rays en masse. The local parks would be packed with sun-starved Seattleites and their canine companions. Unless I wanted to burn off my breakfast running away from off-leash dogs and their oblivious owners, I needed to find some place less crowded.

We drove fifteen minutes south to Fremont and a little-used section of the Burke-Gilman Trail. Nestled between the University of Washington and the Ballard Locks, this sweet little waterfront path had the city-meets-nature feel so typical of Seattle. Separate bike and pedestrian trails meant Bella and I were less likely to get run over by a speeding bicycle commuter—always a plus.

Even better, the trail nestled up against a steep embankment overlooking the Lake Washington Ship Canal—a river-like body of water that connected Lake Washington to Puget Sound. The beauty of this cliff was more than cosmetic. The cliff prevented dogs and people from approaching us from the south. One less thing to worry about.

I enjoyed breathing the fresh air and watching boats make their way to the Ballard Locks. Bella enjoyed tracking the assorted critters that had traveled the path before her. The sun's warm rays baked my shoulders. Seattle's version of Heaven.

I daydreamed about Michael's and my next date. And the next. And the next. Before I knew it, my mind had created an entire life for us: gorgeous white wedding dress, beautiful house, two perfect kids. I had to laugh at that one. I didn't even like kids. But I sure could daydream about making those kids ...

I should have known better than to let my attention wander. But in my defense, it wasn't a dog or even a bearded man this time, and I couldn't be prepared for everything. Right in front of us, slightly to the right, waddled a male mallard duck. Evidently, in Bella-speak, the word "duck" meant *delicious*.

Bella roared with delight. She went after that mischievous mallard like a cheetah after a gazelle, completely forgetting she had a human deadweight attached to her leash.

I wasn't a very effective anchor. Dogs can pull two-and-a-half times their weight. So, at eighty pounds, Bella could easily pull 200 pounds of yoga teacher. Chunky thighs or not, I was nowhere near that weight. And Bella had an advantage—she was pulling me off the cliff.

Off we went, after that damned duck, over the embankment. I slid, bumping along the ground, hanging on to Bella's leash with all my strength. One large crashing "oomph!" into the dirt, and I lost hold. Bella took off running, much faster now that she didn't have to drag her 130-pound burden. I continued rolling down the hill, straight toward the water below.

I felt each and every bruise assault my body and prayed no bones were breaking. A few feet from water's edge I came to a sudden stop—by smashing into a tree. An insane thought whipped through my mind right before impact. *Isn't this how Sonny Bono died?*

Stunned, I lay there, afraid to move. Part of me wanted Bella to keep running and never come back. Part of me wanted to catch her so I could strangle her. Then, the logical, responsible part of me realized what I'd done. *I'd dropped the leash.* Bella was out there on her own, without anyone to protect her from herself. What if she went after another dog? What if she got hit by a car? What if she saw Santa again?

The first step in finding her was getting up. Easier said than done. I slowly wiggled my toes and began the other small movements typically suggested at the end of yoga class. I rolled my shoulders, turned my head, and moved my legs. Nothing seemed broken—so far.

A blond, twenty-something biker called to me from the trail. "Oh my God! Do you need help? Should I call an ambulance?"

The answer was yes. Of course I needed help. As for the ambulance, it could whisk me off to the insane asylum, which was exactly where I belonged for agreeing to care for this hound-from-Hell.

"I'm OK, but thanks. Did you see where the dog went?"

He looked around. "No, sorry. Hang on. I'll come down and help you get up."

Over my "I-wish-I-were-dead" body.

I was beyond embarrassed, and I wanted to lick my ego's wounds in private. I certainly didn't want that cute biker to see me flat on my back—at least not this way. What if my hair was messed up?

What if I had mud on my face? What if the butt was ripped out of my jeans?

"I'm fine, but thanks. You can go. I appreciate your help."

My Good Samaritan looked unconvinced, but he climbed back on his bike and rode away. Now for the real challenge. How *was* I going to get up? And if I did, how on earth would I find Bella? I groaned and covered my face with my hands. Even if I made it back to the trail, Santa would just sue me for Bella's soon-to-be dog mauling. I lay back down with a heavy sigh, closed my eyes, and resolved to let nature take its course.

A creature the size of a water buffalo came crashing through the brush, skidded to a stop next to me, and shook itself dry. Water flew through the air like a sprinkler system on high. Bella looked incredibly, insanely proud of herself. She danced, wiggled, pranced, and play-bowed, ears cocked forward with a huge doggy grin on her face.

Did you see me? Did you see me? She looked like a kid on a bike yelling, "Look, Ma, no hands!"

She suddenly stopped, staring at me curiously and cocking her head to the side. The look on her face clearly asked: *Why in the heck are you lying here on the ground?*

I wanted to yell at her. I wanted to shake her. In fact, I think it's fair to say I wanted to kill her. But my sense of relief was too profound. Instead, I wrapped my arms around her neck, hugged her with all my might, and sobbed into her wet fur. "Thank God you came back, Bella. *Goooood* girl."

Slowly, tentatively, painfully, I made my way back up the embankment, a completely self-satisfied Bella walking calmly by my side. That damned duck swam slightly offshore, watching our slow progression and mocking me.

Once we arrived on the trail, I took inventory of my injuries. Not nearly as bad as I'd feared—just a couple of scrapes and a few bruises. My back felt tight, but I could take care of that with some yoga poses later. The only things really damaged in the incident were my clothes, which were shredded and filthy, and my pride, which was much more bruised than my body.

I drove home to change clothes. Now that I had the luxury of perspective, I had to chuckle. "What a sight we must have been, Bella: careening downhill, chasing after that wily waterfowl. I'll bet that biker tells that story for weeks!"

I hobbled back into the studio at five-fifteen—forty-five minutes before my Yoga for Healthy Backs class was scheduled to start. My mind told me to spend those few precious minutes returning the day's neglected phone messages, but my body disagreed. My low back had tightened up considerably on the drive back to the studio. If I wasn't careful, it would go into a full-blown spasm. I rubbed the aching muscles along my spine and considered my options.

Option one was by far the most appealing: drive back home, soak in a hot bath, and self-medicate with a huge glass of Merlot. I closed my eyes and mentally traveled to my cherished jetted tub. In my imagination, eucalyptus-scented bubbles eased the aches from my body. The wine's soft hints of black cherry, cedar, and currant teased my tongue.

Meanwhile back at the studio, fifteen angry, abandoned students pounded on the studio's door.

No deal.

Option two was to ice the injured area. But somehow I doubted that my Yoga for Healthy Backs students would be impressed if I limped through class wearing an ice pack—even if I decorated it with OM stickers.

The obvious solution was option three: ease away my body's aches with over-the-counter pain relievers and a short dose of yoga. I scrounged around in the bottom of my purse until I found an ancient bottle of Advil, popped two of the candy-coated pills into my mouth, and rolled out a mat.

With less than thirty minutes to practice, I had to make every pose count. I deepened my breath, and my tightened muscles relaxed in an almost Pavlovian response. I inhaled and swept my arms out to the side and up, then laced my fingers together overhead and lifted my ribs, feeling my chest open. As I exhaled, I swept my arms down and gently lowered my chin to stretch the back of my neck.

So far so good.

From there I performed several kneeling poses designed to gently warm my body and stretch my low back. I groaned in delicious agony as I transitioned to my belly and did several repetitions of Cobra Pose, using my back muscles to lift my head, collarbones, and rib cage away from the floor. At first my back threatened to spasm in a show of not-so-passive resistance, but by the third repetition, even it decided to relax and join the party.

A few minutes later, I moved to standing. My legs felt stable and strong as my heart opened in Warrior I. Sweat beaded the back of my neck when I moved sideways for Warrior II. My whole body trembled with effort as I lowered my hips halfway to the floor in several Half Squats.

But the true test of my body's forgiveness came ten minutes later. I lay down on my back, drew my knees toward my chest, and placed my arms out in a low T. As I exhaled, I pulled in my belly and twisted, bringing my knees to the floor on the right and turning my face to the left. I heard a delicious pop-pop-pop as vertebra all up and down my spine moved back into place. No wonder this pose was often called the Chiropractor's Stretch.

After two more gentle poses, I stood up from my practice, spine now completely pain-free. I greeted my students with a bright smile and renewed confidence that yoga did, indeed, work. Two classes later, I was ready for my well-deserved bubble bath, not to mention the large glass of wine. Heck, I might even finish the bottle. I'd had a very long day.

I almost made it.

Bella and I were halfway out the door when the phone rang. I debated letting the call go to voice mail, but I hoped it was Michael. Maybe he wanted to get together for a drink, or dinner, or to snuggle or …

In the end, curiosity won. I should have remembered what it did to the cat.

"Serenity Yoga, this is Kate. How can I help you?"

"I hear you have my dog."

SIXTEEN

THE DRIVE TO FEDERAL Way took forty-five minutes in good traffic, and Tuesday morning's traffic was terrible. You'd think Seattleites would be wet-weather driving experts, but it never fails. Whenever there's a significant rainstorm, we drive like we've never seen the stuff. The ninety-minute trip in the dark, dank weather matched my mood perfectly. Even Bella seemed uncharacteristically subdued as she rested in the back seat.

I should have been happy to take Bella back to her original home—ecstatic, even. Soon I'd be rid of my unwanted burden. I could go back to the orderly, focused life I craved. I could concentrate on feeding my new relationship with Michael and building my struggling business. But the story of Bella's early life haunted me. I tried to convince myself that Betty was right; that George had lied to me about Bella's origins. I tried to imagine happy reunion scenes, complete with misty-eyed adults and joyful children, screaming as they reunited with their long-lost friend.

I failed.

Each daydream was interrupted by visions of a lonely, howling puppy being violently kicked by a sociopath. My phone conversation with Bella's prior owner did nothing to allay my fears. He didn't seem concerned in the slightest about his missing pet. He didn't ask about Bella, thank me for taking care of her, or even tell me his name. He just called, gave his address, and ordered me to return his dog. I hoped he made a better impression in person.

I turned off the car's ignition and confirmed the address. Bella's Dash Point home was, as George described it, gorgeous. Most of my Ballard bungalow would easily fit in its three-car garage. The front of the house faced a large, open yard, and its abundant west-facing windows opened to a stunning Puget Sound view. For a moment, I allowed myself to rekindle a spark of hope. Maybe Betty was right; maybe Bella belonged here. I got out of the car and prepared to put on Bella's leash.

A low, menacing rumble froze me in my tracks. I noticed the stake first, then ran my eyes up the chain. It ended in the spiked leather collar of a large, muscle-bound rottweiler. A rottweiler with big teeth. Big, pointy teeth. The kind of teeth that would thoroughly enjoy sharpening themselves on the femur bone of a trespassing yoga teacher. The term "junkyard dog" suddenly sounded cute and cuddly. Somehow I doubted Bella would like her new brother.

"Wait here, Bella. I'll be right back."

Bella cowered, hiding in the back seat's far corner. Frankly, I wished I could hide back there with her. Instead, I stood frozen in the driveway, debating the wisdom of entering that Rottie's coveted yard.

Finally, the front door opened, and a short, dark-haired man swaggered out, closely followed by a timid-looking blonde. He wore black ostrich skin cowboy boots and the facial expression of a mean-spirited long-haul trucker. She wore a tentative smile and expertly applied makeup that couldn't completely hide the greenish-yellow bruise underneath her right eye. I had a terrible feeling that Bella wasn't the only one this Trucker Man liked to kick around. My earlier spark of hope fizzled, replaced by a slow, burning rage.

Trucker Man turned to the woman. "Go back inside. I'll take care of this." He scowled as the door closed softly behind her. "You the woman who stole my dog?"

I glared right back at him. "I told you on the phone last night. I didn't steal her. I've just been taking care of her since my friend passed away." I nodded toward the still-growling Rottie. "I see you've already got another dog."

"Yeah, a good one this time."

"I don't think you should take the shepherd back then. She doesn't like other dogs."

"That's none of your concern. Give me the dog and get on your way."

I stood there a full minute, staring him down, willing my eyes to turn him to stone. I didn't want to give Bella back to this jerk. In fact, I would have preferred to dance barefoot through a football field covered in broken glass. But Betty's orders were unequivocal: unless I had proof of abuse, I had to surrender Bella to her original owner, no matter how odious he might be. So I forced myself back to the car, hooked on Bella's lead, and tried to coax her out of the back seat.

Tried, to no avail. Bella dug her paws into the upholstery and leaned away from me, transforming herself from an eighteen-month-old dog to a stubborn eighty-pound pack mule. I pulled with all my might. She refused to budge.

"Come on, Bella! You're home now. Everything's going to be fine." She looked at me with large, frightened eyes. We both knew I was lying.

"Bella, please," I whispered. "There's nothing I can do." I finally enticed her out of the car with a handful of treats and a battery of empty promises. I coaxed her toward the house as she cowered, trembling behind my legs.

"Oh for God's sake," Trucker Man grumbled. He stomped down the stairs, reached over Bella's head, and snatched her leash out of my hands. "Get over here, you stupid mutt." He gave the leash, and Bella's neck, a good hard jerk.

Bella erupted like Mount St. Helens. She let out a deep roar and leaped forward, planting her paws on her prior owner's chest and knocking him into the mud. He hit the ground hard, swore like the trucker he resembled, and dropped the leash. Bella wasted no time. She bolted back to the car and scratched frantically at the door, begging to be let back in.

Trucker Man looked like a cross between Big Foot and the Loch Ness Monster—only meaner. "That's it," he yelled, jumping to his feet and roughly grabbing my arm. "Wait 'til I catch that no-good flea bag. I'll kick that bark right out of her."

"You'll do no such thing," I yelled back, yanking my arm free. I imagine I looked like a monster myself. I shoved my palm directly in his face, feeling a good foot taller and at least 100 pounds more muscular than my 130-pound frame. "Stay here. Don't you *dare* move an inch. If you touch that dog, I swear I'll kill you."

I ran to the car and flung open the door. Bella scrambled in, whining, and tried desperately to crawl underneath the seat. I stood with her for several moments, consciously slowing my breath, willing each inhale and exhale to calm my frenzied emotions. So far, this boxing match wasn't going well. Round one had gone to Bella and me, but no matter how tough I felt, Trucker Man was tougher. I had to come up with a better strategy than beating the crap out of him.

The authorities would be of no help. In the eyes of the law, Bella was nothing more than a piece of stolen property that should be returned to its rightful owner. I considered fleeing, but since Trucker Man knew where to find me, making a run for it didn't seem like a good plan, either.

Diplomacy was my only option. I waited until my heart rate slowed to normal, then I returned to the mud-covered jerk and tried to reason with him.

"Look, I'm sorry," I said. "We've obviously gotten off on the wrong foot here. Why don't you let me take Bella back to Seattle? You've already got the rottweiler, and you don't seem to like Bella very much. Frankly, she's not fond of you, either. I can't believe you really want her back."

"You're damn right I don't want that dog back," he spat. "Any guard dog stupid enough to get himself stolen from his own yard is of no use to me."

She wasn't stolen, I thought. *She was rescued.*

But I didn't say that. Instead, I said, "You know this dog's a *she*, not a *he*, don't you?"

Trucker Man responded with a scornful laugh. "Of course I do. That's part of the trouble. I should have known better than to expect a *bitch* to do a man's job."

Bitch is, of course, a commonly used term for female dog. And, as Dad used to say, if you think that's what he meant, I have some swampland in Arizona to sell you. I wanted to come up with a scathing reply, but I couldn't. I just stood there with my mouth hanging open.

"Listen, lady," he growled. "I paid good money for that dog, and I intend to get it back. I'm selling her."

"To whom?" I asked, incredulous. "She doesn't like other dogs, and she's not healthy. Didn't you notice how skinny she is? She needs expensive medication."

Trucker Man's upper lip lifted, exposing a cruel-looking grin. "Guess that drunken bum didn't get much of a deal when he stole that worthless mutt, now did he? He should have stuck to raiding garbage cans and selling newspapers."

My fists clenched so hard that my fingernails practically drew blood from my palms. If I'd been a cartoon, steam would have poured from my ears. How could this cretin talk about George that way?

"Listen, you son of a bi—"

I stopped mid-sentence, frozen.

Did he say drunken bum?

How did Trucker Man know about George? I thought he had no idea who took his dog. My mind raced, searching for answers. I hadn't told him about George, that much was certain. But maybe I didn't have to. Maybe George hadn't been as invisible as he thought. Maybe Trucker Man knew about George all along…

I took a step back, feeling suddenly vulnerable. Could Trucker Man be George's killer?

Trucker Man's eyes narrowed; his lips barely moved. "What did you call me?"

Prickly uneasiness tingled down my spine. *Time to get the heck out of Dodge.* I fingered my keys and cautiously backed away. I'd just ease on over to the car, hightail it back to Seattle, and call Detective Johnson. He could deal with this cowboy-booted psychopath. I hadn't come here to face off with a killer, anyway. All I wanted was to get rid of a dog. Like I'd already told Betty…

Then it hit me. Of course. Betty.

Betty and I had discussed Bella's history that night at the rescue. She must have told Trucker Man about George, though I was surprised he gave her the chance; he didn't strike me as much of a conversationalist. I glanced up at my would-be assailant. Trucker Man glowered and grumbled under his breath, but he made no move to attack. Frankly, I couldn't blame him for being angry. I'd be grumpy, too, if a stranger showed up on my doorstep and started calling me names. *Give it a break, Kate. Not everyone who pisses you off is a killer.*

I took a deep breath, relaxed my hands, and consciously let go of my keys. Trucker Man was obviously a jerk; he might even be a wife beater. But that didn't make him a murderer. My overactive imagination was getting the best of me again—or at least I hoped so. In any case, I'd have plenty of time to puzzle this through later. Bella was my priority now.

I held up my hands, hoping to mollify him. "I'm sorry. I shouldn't have said that."

He didn't reply.

"My point is, you can't sell this dog. Nobody in their right mind is going to buy her. And if they do, they'll bring her back as soon they take her to a vet. You'll end up right back where you started—with a sick dog and no money. You'll either have to spend a fortune on Bella's treatment or put her down. And I'd hate to see her put down."

Trucker Man smiled in a "gotcha" sort of way. "Well, then," he said in a low, threatening tone, "at least I'll get the pleasure of shooting her." He looked pointedly at his truck. The gun rack mounted on top couldn't have been more ominous. My entire body flashed hot, then cold as I imagined Bella cowering in front of one of those awful hunting rifles.

I desperately wanted to hold my ground. I wanted to show that sociopath that he couldn't get away with bullying women and defenseless animals. I wanted to prove I was more of a "man" than he'd ever be. But I couldn't help myself. I flinched and took several steps back.

"You wouldn't—"

"Unless, that is, *you're* interested in buying her. You seem mighty attached to that mongrel."

I swallowed hard. "How much do you want?"

"I paid $800 for her."

I had the money. It was a significant part of my dwindling savings, but I had it. I seriously considered calling his bluff. No one would have blamed me. The money I had left in savings was my only emergency cushion, and it was already worn dangerously thin.

We're trained, in our culture, to take care of ourselves first. Even flight attendants tell you to put on your own oxygen mask before helping those around you. But they never tell you what happens afterward. How do you live with yourself if you survive and the person next to you doesn't?

I could never leave Bella here. I'd never forgive myself.

"Fine. Eight hundred it is. Let me get my checkbook." I turned toward my car.

He stepped in front of me, blocking the way. "Not so fast, pretty lady. I also fed this mutt for three months. I figure that's worth at least another few hundred."

"Are you kidding me? There's no way—"

"Don't test me," he snapped, raising a fist.

I flinched, waiting for impact. Trucker Man froze. We locked eyes for several uncomfortable seconds. Finally he lowered his arm and smiled disingenuously. "But since I'm in a generous mood, I'll let her go for an even grand. That seems like a pretty good deal if you ask me."

"You win." Trembling with an odd mixture of fear, frustration, and disgust, I grabbed my purse, ripped out the check, and slapped it in his hand.

"This had better not bounce," he snarled.

"It won't." I jumped into the car before he raised the price again. "Bella, we're out of here." I peeled away from the curb, wishing I could splash that creep in even more slime. I settled for giving him a nasty look and mentally showing him the finger.

I whispered a prayer to the universe as Bella and I drove away. "Please don't let him cash that check today." Until I got money transferred from savings, it would bounce to high heaven. But I wasn't about to stiff this guy on purpose. My arm still throbbed where he grabbed it; it would be black-and-blue there tomorrow.

I'd been threatened and bruised, and my only crime was buying a dog he didn't even want. I couldn't help but wonder: What would Trucker Man do if someone stole from him? Would he be capable of worse violence—even murder? A stray thought nibbled at the edges of my subconscious—a detail just out of my grasp. But I was too full of angst and adrenaline to puzzle it out then. My only goal in that moment was to escape. I pressed down on the accelerator and sped back toward Seattle, where Bella and I would presumably be safe.

SEVENTEEN

Twenty-four hours later, I still felt oddly elated—especially since I'd just spent a thousand dollars I couldn't afford to buy a dog I had no intention of keeping. Still, we take our victories where we can, right? On to my next contest. Mocha Mia was my battlefield. My target, Rene. I fired off my first verbal volley before her plate hit the table. I didn't even give her a chance to complain about her "World's Best Grandma" coffee mug.

"I can't *believe* you went and schemed with Michael behind my back. I feel like a call girl, and *you*, well, you may as well be my pimp."

Rene didn't even pretend to look guilty as she snarfed down her salted caramel brownie. For a moment, I considered a trade: forgiveness for a bite of sweet, salty, chocolate-laced decadence. Rene read my mind and pulled her plate closer. The word *share* was not part of her vocabulary.

"What did you expect me to do?" she said between mouthfuls. "Leave the evening up to you? Without my help, you never would have figured out that this guy is perfect for you."

"What do you mean, 'perfect for me'? I barely know the guy! And you know him even less. Unless, that is, you two traitors have been conspiring even more than I realize." I sternly shook my finger. "If so, you'd better fess up now."

My fictional hissy-fit had no effect. Rene stared back, completely relaxed and self-satisfied, as she licked the last crumbs of brownie off her fingertips. I exacted revenge by not pointing out the smear of caramel hanging off her chin.

I wasn't sure I wanted to know, but I asked anyway. "Tell me the truth, Rene. Did you tell Michael to shave off his beard?"

"Well, I may have mentioned that you had a thing about facial hair, but he was planning to shave it off anyway—for Bella. He really has a thing for that dog, which proves he's *almost* crazy enough for you. How does he look without it?"

"Gorgeous." I sighed. "Simply gorgeous."

Rene's lascivious grin spread ear to ear. "Ha! I knew it! So spill. Tell me every last disgusting detail. Now that I'm an old married hag, I have to get my kicks vicariously. Your sputtering love life will have to do."

"Spare me. You and Sam will still be making out like newlyweds when you're old and toothless, feeding each other butterscotch pudding in a nursing home." I paused and tried to look bashful. "Besides, a nice girl like me doesn't kiss and tell."

"But there was a lot of kissing, right? And maybe a little—"

"You're right, he *is* perfect for me," I interrupted, hoping to change the subject. "He's broke, he works too hard, and"—I looked at her pointedly—"he obviously shares my terrible taste in friends." I smiled in spite of myself. "But you're right. I do like him. A lot."

Rene leaned back in her chair, looking positively pleased with herself. "Now all I have to do is keep you from discovering his faults before the infatuation phase is over." She rested her chin in her hand and tapped an index finger against her lips. "Hmm … perhaps another visit to the pet store is in order …"

"You wouldn't dare."

"You know me better than that—of course I would!"

I threw my wadded-up napkin and hit her square on the nose. "That's five points for accuracy." I smirked.

Rene smiled back. "I do love you, you know. I only want you to be happy."

I took a deep drink of my triple cappuccino and sighed. "Honestly, Rene, what would make me happiest right now is having my life back. And that means getting Bella out of my house and figuring out what happened to George. I can't shake the feeling that there's more to his murder than the police realize." I idly drew shapes in the coffee's foam swirl. "The answer has to lie in those ten days George and Bella were gone. I can't stop thinking about it. Where did he go, and who did he spend that time with? Bella's test results took three days, and I'm sure it took George a couple of days to get to Sarah's and back. But that still leaves almost five days unaccounted for. I can't help but think the answer lies in that missing time."

"Have you gone to that place he worked yet?"

"The *Dollars for Change* office? No, but I will. First I have to come up with a good cover story. The 'I need to find a home for the poor lost dog' routine only gets me so far. The minute I start asking questions, people know I'm up to something. I'm not exactly Nancy Drew."

Rene perked up. She looked like a toy poodle begging for a cookie. "That's because you need a partner! Ooh, ooh, ooh! Take me with you, please? We'll have so much fun!"

I gaped at her incredulously.

"Don't you ever read mystery novels?" she continued, brimming with excitement. "You can't snoop alone. There's always a sidekick!"

"No. Freaking. Way," I replied. "I haven't forgiven you for meddling in my date with Michael yet. I absolutely will not, under any circumstances, encourage you to snoop around in something else."

"Please, please, please? I'll be good, I promise!" She practically started drooling.

"What makes you think you'll be so much help, anyway?"

"Come on, Kate, be real. You're cute and all, and women like to confide in you—probably because of all that woo-woo yoga energy. But when it comes to men, straight-up sex appeal does it every time. And I've got you beat in that department, hands down." She batted her eyelashes. "One little wiggle of my derriere, and the guys in that office will spill all of their deep, dark secrets. They won't be able to help themselves. You, on the other hand, will have to talk to the women. I don't know why, but women don't seem to trust me."

I sure didn't. But Rene had a point. Double-teaming seemed to work in all of my favorite police dramas. Maybe it was that whole good-cop, bad-cop routine.

"Well, I suppose I could use the company. But if you misbehave, I swear I'll—"

"We're outta here!" she said, jumping up. "Put that coffee in a to-go cup. We girls are going on an adventure!"

I paused before opening the door. "Rene, are you sure Sam will be OK with this?"

"Honey, what Sam doesn't know won't hurt him one little bit. Besides, how much trouble can we get into, anyway?"

———

While I drove to the Georgetown office of *Dollars for Change*, Rene prepared for her role. She unbuttoned the top buttons of her blouse, freshened her lipstick, and brushed out her hair. After wiping the caramel off her chin, she gave herself a final come-hither look in the mirror, removed her wedding ring, and placed it in the glove box. She clearly planned to take no prisoners.

We walked into the tiny, clean, and basically deserted office a little after eleven. A busy-looking receptionist typed at a computer, while a balding, ponytailed man with a scruffy blond beard poured burnt-smelling coffee into a Styrofoam cup. After adding two sugars and a hit of nondairy creamer, he meandered to a makeshift cubicle created from a single partition and two short filing cabinets.

Rene whispered in my ear. "You take her. I've got handsome back there." She ambled around the room, pretending to examine the assorted newspaper clippings tacked along the wall. She eventually arrived at the coffee area, where she stopped to pour a glass of water.

"Good morning, can I help you two?" asked the friendly-looking receptionist. She wore red oval-shaped glasses. They perfectly matched the heart trapped in the center of her spider web tattoo. Her name plate read Tali Rodriguez.

"Hi. I'm Kate, and I sure hope so. This is kind of awkward, but I was hoping to talk to someone in your Human Resources department."

"You're looking at it. We all pretty much do everything around here." She took off her glasses, seemingly confused. "Are you here for a job? You don't seem like one of our typical vendors."

"Oh, no, sorry, I'm not. Actually, I'm a friend of one of your vendors, or at least I used to be. He died recently. I'm trying to locate his family, and I thought you might have his emergency contact information."

I launched into Bella's story. I basically stuck to the truth, though I may have exaggerated about the direness of her circumstances. I might have even hinted that she only had a day or two left before she'd be sent to the great doggy playground in the sky. I certainly didn't divulge the fact that I had already spoken to George's daughter.

As Tali and I talked, I surreptitiously monitored Rene's progress. She continued to wander around the room, pretending to be engrossed in the posted articles. She made her way to the ponytailed man's makeshift office, leaned against one of the file cabinets, and started whispering. Not long after, I heard girlish giggles and the deeper voice of an appreciative male.

Did he seriously offer her a cigarette? And did she take it? I couldn't help but be amused at the thought of Rene, a militant nonsmoker, trying to look sexy while gagging on a menthol light. She leaned in closer, suggestively touching her hair and playfully punching her new friend in the arm. *Pulllease*. Sidekick indeed. All she would get from this sort of behavior were the guy's phone number and an embarrassing outbreak of some social disease.

Rene was useless. Our sleuthing success would be solely up to me. I flashed a winning smile, fully expecting Tali to give me everything I requested.

She responded by shaking her head. "I'm afraid I can't help you. We don't keep many records here. Frankly, some of our folks have disappeared from their families for good reason. They'd just as soon stay lost, if you know what I mean."

"Maybe you could connect me to some of George's friends, then. Did he hang out with any of the other vendors?"

Tali's reply was firm. "I'm sorry. We don't give out any information about our staff members. These folks lead difficult lives. Many of them have been traumatized—abused even. I understand your dilemma, but our vendors are finally taking steps to improve their situations. We won't do anything that could jeopardize that. Unless you have a court order, my hands are tied."

"But the dog—"

Tali's courteous tone vanished.

"The dog is irrelevant. Society may not treat these people much better than animals, but they are certainly more important than some dog. Now, I'm busy, so if you don't mind—" She put her glasses back on and resumed typing.

I was completely out of cash, and I suspected bribery wouldn't work with Tali anyway. I was about to give begging a try when Rene sidled up beside me and whispered, "I've got it. Let's go."

Her ponytailed friend stood up in his cubical. "See you at seven, Suzie! I'm looking forward to our date!" Rene grabbed my hand and practically dragged me to the door.

"Suzie?" I asked as we bolted for the car.

"Well you didn't expect me to give him my real name, did you? I'm a married woman! Now hop in, we're off to the U district!"

———

"What's at the U district?" I asked as we pulled onto West Marginal Way.

Rene smiled in triumph. "While you were trying to defrost the ice queen at the front desk, I was busy making friends with Ralphie."

"Ralphie?"

"His real name is Ralph, but I call him Ralphie. Men love it when you give them cute little nicknames." She scowled. "But that's beside the point. Are you going to listen to my story, or not?"

I nodded for her to continue.

"Well, when Ralphie asked me what we were doing at the office, I told him about George and how sorry I was that he couldn't fulfill his last wish."

"And what, may I ask, was George's last wish?"

"To tell his best friend how much he loved her."

"Where in the world did you come up with that?" Rene was obviously a much more accomplished fibber than even I realized.

"Isn't that what people always wish on their deathbeds? That they'd spent more time with the people they loved?" Rene took her wedding ring out of the glove box and slipped it back on her finger. "Ralphie was real sympathetic. I told him you found George right before he died. I even got a little teary-eyed when I told him George's dying words: 'Tell her I love her.'"

She rebuttoned her blouse. "I begged Ralphie for help. I told him you were desperate to find George's lost love so you could relay the message. One look in my sad, smoky-blue eyes, and he poured out everything he knew."

I could only hope "Ralphie" and Tali didn't compare notes. And I *really* hoped Ralphie realized that Rene had been kidding about that date.

"So what's in the U District?" I asked again.

"Turns out, one of the vendors is quite a character. She calls herself Momma Bird. According to Ralphie, she has sharp eyes, a big mouth, and she knows everything about everyone. If anyone knows who old George was hanging out with, it's her."

"Not bad, Rene, not bad at all." I had to admit, I was impressed. A little distressed at her methods, but impressed nonetheless.

"I know." Rene replied, "I *am* that good. Now step on it. Momma Bird works until five, but all this sleuthing has made me hungry.

Next stop: The Thai Dive. This momma needs some shrimp pad thai. And some coconut ice cream with hot fudge sauce doesn't sound half bad, either."

EIGHTEEN

"How can I possibly be Super Sleuth's sidekick when I'm stuffed full of noodles and ice cream? All the blood's gone straight to my stomach!" Rene practically waddled as we walked from The Thai Dive to the University Bookstore.

"Nobody told you to eat the whole thing, Miss Piggy. And asking for seconds on the ice cream was simply gluttonous. Not even you can do enough Sun Salutes to burn off all those calories."

"I know. Whatever was I thinking?" She twisted to look at her backside. "Does my butt look big? I think it's already grown two sizes from that fudge sauce."

Ever the obliging friend, I looked at her rear. Size three as always. "You know, I think it *does* look bigger." Even the most enlightened yoga master couldn't have resisted torturing Rene—especially when she so clearly deserved it.

"That's it," Rene replied, sulking. "We're in training. Frankly, your derriere doesn't look so tiny itself. As of this moment, I formally decree: we are both running the Seattle marathon this year. That should get our bulging booties back in line." Her sadistic eyes sparkled with visions of torture. "We'll start training today with a six-mile run. That's only twice around Greenlake. Even you should be able to do that much."

Great. Now I'd unleashed a whole new side to the monster masquerading as my best friend. And what did she mean, six miles? The last time I tried jogging, I practically passed out after six blocks. "I was kidding, Rene. You look great as always. But can you pick up the pace a little? I'd like to get there before midnight."

Calling the University Bookstore a mere bookstore would have been a colossal understatement. It was, indeed, a massive bookstore selling everything from romance novels to texts on advanced surgical techniques. But it also boasted a variety of other departments specializing in a wide array of non-literary products, ranging from office supplies and high tech toys to clothing and designer makeup. I had no idea how we'd find the woman we were looking for.

I needn't have worried.

Momma Bird loitered inside the main entrance, near a busy espresso cart. She held a stack of papers in one hand and swigged a large cup of inky black coffee from the other. Wearing pink Crocs, a neon green muumuu and a hat shaped like a pink flamingo, she definitely stood out from the crowd. I had no doubt this woman could talk, but could she tell fantasy from reality?

I skipped the small talk and got right to the point.

"I understand you knew the vendor who was killed a few days ago in Greenwood."

"Sure, I knew George. But then again, I know almost everyone around here." She paused and looked at me suspiciously. "But what business is that of yours?"

Up close, Momma Bird didn't look the slightest bit delusional. Her unusual outfit may have fooled me at first, but as soon as I looked into her sharp blue eyes I could tell: she might be a tad eccentric, but she was nobody's fool. She'd never buy into some lame story about a poor, abandoned dog. If I wanted her help, I'd need to drop my Bella ruse and use a different approach. So I decided to try something unique. An option I had considered before, but discarded as amateurish and completely ineffective.

I told her the truth.

"I'm investigating George's murder."

Momma Bird didn't look surprised, but she didn't reply, either. She set down the papers, finished her coffee, and tossed the cup in the trash. She scrutinized me through wary eyes. "You don't look like no cop. What are you, some kind of private eye?"

"No, I'm just George's friend. Or at least I was."

She frowned and turned back to pick up the papers. "I ain't got no time to sit around here talking to amateurs, honey. Best keep your nose out of things that don't concern you. I don't know who sent you, but they wasted your time." She pointed to the door. "Head on home now."

Momma Bird clearly thought I was a nincompoop. Frankly, the way my investigation had gone so far, I couldn't disagree with her. But that was immaterial. She knew something about George, and she was going to tell me. I simply had to convince her that talking with me wouldn't be a waste of her time. But how could I convince a total stranger I was competent when I barely believed it myself?

I'd opened with the truth, so I might as well keep going. "You're right. I'm a complete amateur, and honestly, I have no idea what I'm doing here. I'd like nothing better than to let the police handle the investigation, but they're looking for the wrong person. I cared about George. I can't sit back and let his killer go free."

"What makes you think the cops are after the wrong guy?"

"They're convinced George was killed in some sort of drunken fight."

"And you know better?" She sounded more than a little skeptical.

"Not always, but in this case, yes. The detectives are wrong. I can feel it."

She snorted derisively. "Oh, you can *feel* it, can you? That's a new one." She mumbled under her breath and walked away, abandoning our conversation. She approached the espresso line newcomers. "Care to buy a *Dollars for Change* today?"

Acid boiled up from the bottom of my stomach. Ralphie had been right. Momma Bird *did* know something. She was my best lead, and I was blowing it. I followed her and kept talking.

"You have to help me!"

No response.

I may have upped the volume a tiny bit louder than necessary. I certainly stopped using my yoga voice. "The detectives on this case are idiots! Why can't anyone see that but me!"

The would-be coffee purchasers shuffled uncomfortably and murmured among themselves. Rene traitorously wandered to a magazine rack and acted like she didn't know me. Momma Bird, on the other hand, simply pretended to be deaf.

My frustration peaked, and the now burning, gurgling stomach acid splashed up into my esophagus. I truly regretted the spicy Thai chili sauce I'd poured all over my lunchtime curry. My throat burned with chili paste and indignation. "Why won't anyone listen? George was not murdered in some random street fight." I stepped directly in front of Momma Bird and grabbed her arm. "I know it, and frankly, I think you know it too. No one but me may give a rip, but I promise you, I'm not going to stop looking until I figure out who killed him and why." I pressed my face close to hers and shouted. "Now are you going to help me or not?"

The people in the coffee line stopped murmuring and stared at us in stunned silence. The young, blonde barista stepped behind the espresso machine and pulled out a cell phone, presumably to dial 911. I suddenly had a feeling that yelling that the police were idiots might not have been such a smart move.

Momma Bird, on the other hand, finally acknowledged me.

"Let. Go. Of. My. Arm."

I unhanded her and stepped back, face red-hot with embarrassment. Momma Bird gathered her papers and walked away, I assumed to put as much distance between us as possible. I stood there, watching her leave and feeling like an idiot. When I screwed up, I did it royally.

After a few steps, she looked back and gestured to a bench. "Are you coming or what?"

Sensing the drama was over, the caffeine seekers resumed their conversations. The barista laid down her phone. Rene, once again the loyal sidekick, wandered back next to me.

Momma Bird sat heavily on the bench. "I'll say this for you, honey. You've got spunk. And amateur or not, you might be onto something." She patted the seat next to her. I quickly sat down before she changed her mind. "George was a nice guy and all, but he was up to no good at the end. No good at all. If you ask me, that's how he up and got himself killed."

"What do you mean, 'He was up to no good'? Was George in some kind of trouble?"

Momma Bird looked at a nonexistent watch on her wrist. "Look, hon, you seem sincere enough, and I'd like to help you, but this is valuable selling time. I got no time to sit around chattin' my fool head off. Unless, that is, you're thinking about making me a donation..."

Didn't anybody talk for free anymore? I'd already spent the cable money bribing my Surfer Dude friend. I looked at Rene for guidance. She shrugged and pointed to my purse. The good news was I'd had the foresight to visit a cash machine after lunch. The bad news was it only gave out twenties. Silently swearing, I pulled one out and handed it to Momma Bird.

"You know, for another twenty, I could have a nice warm bed to sleep in tonight, maybe even a nutritious meal."

Forget shutting off the cable. If all of my sources were this expensive, I'd have to start shopping for groceries at the Ballard Food Bank. I pulled out my one remaining twenty and handed it to Momma Bird, hoping it would be enough.

"That's it. Bank's closed. Now talk."

"Well," she began, "I saw George the day before he was killed. He was all uptight over some plan of his. Seems old George had the goods on someone, and he thought they'd pay a pretty penny to keep him quiet. I figure that's what he was doing when he got himself killed—meeting with the money tree, if you know what I mean. Only he got himself stumped for his trouble." She laughed, obviously amused at her own joke.

Could George have been involved in blackmail? My heart broke at the very idea. The man I knew had made some mistakes, sure, but he had never deliberately harmed anyone. Not for money. I didn't want to know the answer, but I asked anyway.

"George was blackmailing someone?"

"You can call it that if you want. I like to think of it more like he was getting paid to do a job. Only in this case, his job was keeping his mouth shut."

I had at least a thousand questions, but two were most important. "Who was he blackmailing? What did he know that was worth killing over?"

Momma Bird shook her head. "I don't poke my nose in other people's business. He didn't say, and I didn't ask. Sometimes in my world, the less you know the better." She leaned down and picked up her stack of newspapers. "Now unless you got another twenty in that purse of yours, it's time for me to get back to work. These papers don't sell themselves."

I walked to the car feeling unaccountably depressed. For once, even Rene sensed my dark mood and allowed me to sulk in silence. I should have been pleased, or at least self-satisfied. After all, I'd found the information I was looking for, and I was ostensibly one step closer to solving George's murder. Even so, a part of me hoped Momma Bird had been lying. The George I knew wouldn't resort to something slimy like blackmail. The George I knew was a good man. The George I knew had honor.

In the end, all I felt was a sense of deep betrayal. Blackmail might not be up there with armed robbery and murder, but it was still a crime. In spite of all of my protestations to the contrary, it looked like George had been a common criminal, after all. How could I have been so wrong?

———

I called Sarah as soon as I got home. No doubt about it, I was still upset about George. But criminal or not, George deserved justice, and this extortion theory was my best lead so far. Maybe Sarah could tell me who he might have been blackmailing and why.

I'd barely said hello when she interrupted.

"I told you, I'm not taking that frigging dog. If you call here again, I'll block your number and charge you with harassment."

"I'm not calling about Bella. Hear me out for a minute, please."

Nothing but silence. I hoped that meant she was listening, not that she'd hung up.

"I'm sorry I misled you before, but I need your help. I've been looking into your father's murder, and one of his co-workers told me something interesting. Your father started blackmailing someone shortly before he was killed."

I waited for a response. Still silence, but no dial tone. I took that as a good sign and continued. "Do you have any idea who that might be? Blackmail would be a pretty powerful motive for murder."

When Sarah finally replied, her tone was so bitter I could almost taste it. "Co-workers, huh? Is that what you call them? I'd call them beggars and bums. Asking strangers for money is hardly a legitimate career. And why should I care what he did? He certainly didn't care about me."

Trying to justify George's actions would only further irritate Sarah. "I know you're angry at your father, and you have every right to be. But he didn't deserve to die. Not like that. Not beaten like an animal and left to die in a parking lot. Please try to think. You might know something that can help me find his killer."

"Like what?" Sarah asked, clearly annoyed. "What exactly do you think I know?"

"Your husband said George made some enemies when his business went under..."

"Of course he had enemies," she snapped. "He bankrupted his business, drank himself into a stupor, and dropped off the face of the earth. I'm sure his investors weren't too happy—neither was Mom's side of the family, for that matter. But that was years ago. If anyone was going to kill him over that, they would have done it back then."

I slowly exhaled, hoping the soothing rhythm of my breath would calm her. "You're probably right. But extortion has a way of reopening old wounds. Shortly before he was killed, George mentioned to me that someone 'owed' him. Does that mean anything to you?"

She answered automatically, without reflection. "No, nothing."

"Please think about it for a minute, Sarah. Did someone harm your father or your family? Someone he might have resented enough to blackmail?"

"I already told you, we weren't close. And extortion isn't exactly the subject of intimate father-daughter chats." She paused, as if carefully considering what she should say next.

"Look. My dad was a lowlife. He walked out on us when I was thirteen, and he never looked back. He left Mom and me completely on our own. Sure, my grandparents had money, so we didn't starve or anything, but what we really wanted was him." Her voice cracked. "But he didn't care about that. He didn't care about us. He only looked out for himself."

I wanted to tell Sarah I knew how she felt, but truth be told, I didn't. No matter how tough life got, no matter how bad we fought, Dad was always there for me; his support was a given. A life without him never even occurred to me.

I couldn't imagine the agony Sarah must have felt when George abandoned her, especially at that vulnerable age. The yogi in me—the human in me—wanted to acknowledge her suffering and leave her alone. But I couldn't.

I felt like a bully, but I ignored her pain and pressed forward anyway.

"You're only remembering that time from your point of view. Try remembering that time from your father's perspective. Was he angry with anyone—someone from his old company, perhaps?"

Sarah laughed derisively. "You are truly unbelievable. You don't give up, do you? You've got it the wrong way. My father was the bad guy. He may have been self-centered, but he wasn't delusional. He was the one who messed up, and he knew it. Why do you think he started drinking? I can imagine lots of people who might have wanted to get back at him, but not the other way around."

I toyed with the phone cord, thinking. "What about his business partner? Could he have done something to make your father hold a grudge?"

"No way," Sarah replied quickly—too quickly. "My father might have resented the way things turned out, but he wouldn't have *dared* pulling anything on Robert."

The hair on the back of my arms stood up. "What do you mean?"

I waited several seconds for Sarah's reply. "Never mind. I misspoke. Robert and my father were fine." I felt, rather than heard, the door close on our conversation.

Sarah was hiding something, but pressing her now would be useless. I decided to try a different approach. "I'd like to talk to Robert. Do you know how I can get in contact with him?"

There was a long pause, punctuated only by the sound of Sarah's breathing. I was about to ask again, when I heard her clipped reply. "I have no idea. I'm done talking with you. Don't ever call here again."

The dial tone left no room for doubt. Sarah had hung up. I loathed the thought of calling her back, but I needed one final piece of information: her mother's phone number. If Sarah wouldn't help me, perhaps George's ex-wife would. I redialed, held my breath, and steeled myself for what was sure to be an unpleasant conversation.

An automated message answered my call. "We're sorry. The number you have dialed does not accept calls from this number. If you believe you have received this message in error, please hang up and dial again."

NINETEEN

WEDNESDAY NIGHT PASSED BRUTALLY slowly, in an insomnia-laden, tossing and turning nightmare. All of my breath practices, all of my meditations, failed me. I obsessed about George and his alleged crimes, haunted by an odd sense of betrayal. I had believed in George. I knew he wasn't perfect, but blackmail? If he was capable of blackmail, what else had he done?

I staggered out of the house at seven-fifteen and propped myself up with caffeine. Sleep or no sleep, I had a business to run. I arrived at the studio a full two hours before the first class, locked the door securely behind me, and tackled the monthly bookkeeping. I was drinking my third fully caffeinated triple macchiato when the phone rang.

"I hear you've been harassing the victim's family now."

Fueled by a mind in caffeine-induced hyperdrive, my words tumbled out at twice their normal speed. "Detective Martinez, I'm so glad you called. Did you know that George was blackmailing someone? That's probably who killed him. And that daughter of his is hiding something, I know it. But don't worry, I'll figure it out. All

I need is for you to connect me with George's ex-wife. I'll talk to her and—"

"Slow down, Kate," Martinez interrupted. "Take a breath. You're not talking to anyone."

"But something's obviously going on in that family," I continued, talking even faster. "And I can get George's ex-wife to open up, easy. I'm good at getting people to talk."

Martinez's voice dripped with sarcasm. "You could have fooled me." So far, all you've been good at is pissing people off and dodging harassment charges. It took me thirty minutes to calm that Crawford woman down. She was determined to take out a no-contact order."

I took another long swig of coffee. "Doesn't that make you suspicious? There's no way she'd be that upset if she weren't trying to hide something. Maybe she killed George!"

I heard a telltale squeak as Martinez sat heavily in her chair. "Kate, I know you mean well, but you're not helping. You may think Henderson and I are incompetent fools, but we know what we're doing. And your friend O'Connell has been harassing us on your behalf. Believe me, no one's skating on this."

"But George's daughter—"

Martinez didn't disguise her impatience. "I checked out the daughter's alibi days ago. She was at home from nine-fifteen until well after ten last Tuesday night. Her phone records verify it. She's not the killer."

"Well then, couldn't her husband have done it? They weren't both on the phone."

"Likely not, but they verify each others' alibis."

How could she be so gullible? "Of course they do. But do you really think that's credible? I'll bet they're in on the murder together."

"Kate, just because someone *could* have been the killer doesn't mean he *was*. Where's the motive?"

My head throbbed and my shoulders knotted in frustration. "I don't know," I admitted. "At least not yet. But Sarah was furious—out of control, even—when George asked her for money. And she flat-out told me that she'd kill George before she let him get near her son."

"That's merely an expression, Kate."

"I know, but it shows how upset she was, even days later. Who knows what she might do in a rage? And Rick obviously loves his family. He might have killed George to protect Sarah and Davie in some twisted way."

"Seems pretty flimsy to me."

I picked up my coffee cup—empty. Nine shots was a new record, even for me. I didn't dare go for ten. Frustrated, I slammed the empty cup down on the desk.

"Fine. What about George's old business partner, Robert, then? He blamed George for ruining their business. He has motive!"

"We looked into all that, too, Kate. That business dissolved over ten years ago. A decade seemed like an awfully long time to hold a grudge, but we checked him out anyway. He was at Tech Life Expo in New York City the night of the murder."

"So he says. Anyone can sign up for a conference. It doesn't mean he actually went."

Martinez was firm. "In this case, it does. Robert was one of the presenters. Over 300 attendees can verify his alibi. Which puts us right back where we started: a mugging or a garden-variety street crime." She softened her tone. "I know you don't want to hear this, Kate, but your friend's murder may go unsolved."

"There has to be something else we can do. We can't let George's murderer go free!"

Martinez spoke slowly and deliberately. "There is no *we* in this, Kate. You are not a member of the police force. Henderson and I are already doing everything that can be done. Nobody needs your help."

Fueled by an overdose of espresso and muddled by lack of sleep, I opened my mouth and inserted my Birkenstock-clad foot. "That's not true. If George weren't indigent, you'd be working this case a lot harder and you know it. You two may not think George's life was worth much, but I do. If you're too apathetic to do your job, I'll have to do it for you!"

As soon as the words tumbled out, I wished I could take them back. Martinez was the one ally I had on the case. At least she used to be.

"Pay attention, Kate, and pay attention closely," she warned. "You are not a part of solving this case. I've put my neck on the line telling you this much. The last thing we need is an untrained civilian messing up the investigation. Now back off. You're doing way more harm than good."

"But—"

"I mean it! *Back the hell off.* If you harass even one more person about this case, including me, I'll arrest you myself!"

For the second time in less than twenty-four hours, I heard nothing but dial tone. Martinez had hung up.

Muttering phrases that should never pass the lips of a yoga teacher, I slammed down the phone, picked up my coffee cup, and threw it. It sailed across the room and smashed into the wall, barely missing the forehead of an elderly woman.

Where had she come from?

"Oh, my!" she gasped, bringing her hand to her mouth and dropping the flyer she'd been reading. She turned and scurried out the obviously *not* securely locked front door. Why, oh why, hadn't I called a locksmith?

I picked up the flyer dropped by my not-in-this-lifetime student. "Yoga for Inner Peace." Perfect. Just perfect.

I felt bad about frightening her. I felt worse about insulting Detective Martinez. But I hadn't gotten much sleep, no one appreciated my efforts, and the person I was trying to help had likely been a thug. I had every right to be a little grouchy.

———

This had better work, I thought, as Bella and I headed north on I-5 to Snohomish. Less than five hours after what would forever be known as "the coffee cup incident," I was in no mood for another failure. Traffic slowed to a crawl. Why hadn't I chosen a dog trainer near Greenwood? Bella settled in for the long drive and fell fast asleep. I settled in and tried to stay awake. Her snoring taunted me.

Forty-five minutes later, we pulled into a long, gravel driveway and stopped at an automatic gate. I opened the car door to complete silence. Not a single bark? In a dog training center? Maybe we had the place to ourselves.

As I neared the building, a single warning bark pierced the air, followed by a strict, staccato "Shush!" Silence again. Impressive.

A tall, well-built man dressed in impeccably tailored clothes emerged from the building. He grabbed my hand. "Hi, I'm Jim," he said, crushing my fingers. "You must be Kate. Come with me." He turned on his heels and marched back to the building, not showing a single doubt that I would follow.

I followed.

Compared to Betty's office at the rescue, this place was a castle. Clean, sanitary, large and bright, Jim's office had a huge desk, state-of-the-art computer system, and ample space for several guest chairs. I glanced around. Trophies lined the shelves, and framed photos of ribbon-bearing dogs adorned the walls.

Jim sat behind the desk and got straight to business. "Now tell me more about this dog of yours."

"She's not my dog," I replied automatically. "She's just staying with me until I can find her a new home. But she doesn't like other dogs, and she's not very fond of some people, either."

Jim leaned forward. "What makes you think that?"

I laughed. "Well, it's pretty obvious. When she sees another dog she goes crazy—kind of like the canine version of *Jaws*. But as soon as they're out of sight, she calms right back down."

"She's a German shepherd, right?"

"Yes."

He looked at me appraisingly. "What do you weigh? 115, 120?"

"About that." I wasn't about to admit those extra ten pounds.

"And you're a yoga teacher?"

"Right ..."

"And I'll bet you're one of those vegetarian types too, aren't you?"

"Uh-huh ..." Where was this going?

Jim interlaced his perfectly manicured fingers. "I hate to tell you this, but *you're* the problem. You're too nice to own a German shepherd."

"Too nice?" He had to be kidding, right?

"German shepherds need a strong hand. If you're weak, they'll run all over you. But don't feel bad. Most of my clients with 'problem' dogs have this same issue. Generally speaking, the *dog* isn't the problem. The *people* are. They treat their dogs like human children, and it just doesn't work."

"Huh?" Not very eloquent, but I was flabbergasted. I was *not* the problem, Bella was. As for treating her like a child, I hadn't exactly dressed her up in a tutu and enrolled her in nursery school.

Jim stared directly into my eyes, without flinching. "Let me make it simple for you. Your dog thinks you're a wimp. She doesn't respect you. She's the alpha, and she wants to keep it that way. So she fights with other dogs to establish her dominance over them. If you want to control her, you'll have to become the alpha—the human pack leader. But that takes a strong hand and a confident demeanor." He smiled, displaying teeth too perfectly straight to be real. "Cute little thing like you probably doesn't have it in her."

"I may be little, but I'm scrappy," I replied, a little insulted. "Besides, Bella had this same problem with her previous owner. I'll admit that she's worse with men than she used to be, but she's always hated other dogs."

"She was probably alpha over her prior owner, too. Your dog obviously needs a very strong hand." He stood up. "Come with me. I'll show you what I'm talking about."

I followed him into a large, cavernous space. A gorgeous red Doberman stood caged in the back. "That's my dog, Duke," he said. "He'll be our bait dog."

"Bait dog?" That didn't sound good.

"Some trainers call them neutral dogs," Jim replied. "But I believe in calling a spade a spade. I work with lots of dominant dogs like yours. Duke here helps me teach them their place." He opened the cage and snapped a leash on the gorgeous animal. Duke quietly followed him to the back of the room.

"Duke. Down," Jim commanded. "Stay."

"What's that thing around his neck?"

"Oh, that's a training collar. It's a very useful tool. It allows me to gently shock Duke if he misbehaves."

I'd never experienced anything I would describe as a "gentle" shock, but I didn't volunteer that information. While Jim continued extolling the virtues of "training collars," I watched Duke.

I had to admit that Duke acted like a paragon of proper doggy behavior. He lay on the floor, stone still. He didn't so much as twitch while his owner and I chatted. After about ten minutes, Jim left and returned with a timid-looking husky. It wore a choke collar tight and high on its throat.

"This guy's been with me a little over three weeks," Jim said. "When he first arrived, he couldn't be within fifty yards of another dog without going berserk."

Jim walked the husky progressively closer to Duke. It averted its gaze, panting and trembling. About two feet away, the husky locked eyes with Duke and froze. I steeled myself, mentally preparing for Dog Fight Central.

Jim snapped the collar, and hissed a loud "eh!" The husky turned his head and kept walking. Duke still hadn't moved an inch. I was impressed.

Jim smiled and looked at me confidently. "Now, as you can see, we're not quite there yet with this one, but he'll be perfect by the time his owners come and get him next week."

"The dogs you train stay here?"

"Ideally, yes. I like to keep my canines-in-training away from their owners' bad influences. That way I can have complete control over them."

"Sounds expensive."

"Not when you consider what you get. It's only $5,000. And of course, we accept all major credit cards."

Five thousand dollars? I'd have to rob a bank. "There's no way I can do that."

Jim hesitated. "Well, you *could* work at home with your dog, but I can't guarantee the results..." He paused, as if thinking.

"Tell you what. Let me show you another dog that recently started my program. Once you see the beginning stages of this work, I'm sure you'll understand why you should leave it to a professional."

He left the room, taking the husky with him. He returned with a strong, powerful-looking brown and white dog. "This fellow's an akita," he said. "Akitas are one of the most willful breeds. They'll take any opportunity to become pack leader. He's only been with me for three days."

Jim walked the akita back and forth, ever closer to the still motionless Duke. About twenty feet away, the akita bared his teeth and lunged. Jim leapt into action. He jerked on the lead, tightened the choke collar, and lifted the akita off the ground, hanging it by its neck. The dog fiercely struggled, spinning and snapping, until Jim slammed it to the ground and pinned it under his legs. "This is called an alpha roll," he said, breathlessly.

The akita lay on the ground, motionless, as urine pooled on the floor. I suspected it didn't come from Jim. "Ah, submission. Exactly what I was looking for. Now he knows who's boss."

Jim stood up and recommenced walking the now trembling akita back and forth in front of Duke. The dog held his head down, averted his gaze, and pretended Duke didn't exist. Jim smiled, obviously pleased at his training accomplishment.

"Well, now you can see for yourself how effective good training can be. But do you really think a cute little thing like you can do it? You'd be much better off investing some money and leaving this work to the pros."

I stared at Jim, speechless. He smiled, looking positive that he'd convinced me. "Think about it for a minute. I'll put this guy back in his pen. Then we can talk." Jim left with the akita. Duke remained lying on the floor, motionless.

I had a long, hard conversation with myself while Jim was gone. The yoga teachings were very clear on the subject of violence. Yogis must live by the principle of ahimsa, or non-harming, in all situations. Still, I lived in the real world. And in the real world, violence was sometimes a necessary evil. In some situations, the results of using force outweighed the costs.

In the end, I decided this wasn't one of them.

Instead, I applied a different teaching, even though it was significantly more challenging. I chose to be neutral toward evil. I summoned every single ounce of my willpower. I used every element of self-control that my yoga practice had taught me.

To my surprise, it worked. I successfully refrained from punching that sadistic SOB in the nose before I marched out the door.

———

"Positive his methods work, indeed," I mumbled.

"Macho jerk. I can think of a place or two I'd like to put that shock collar…"

Bella was quiet on the subject, but I could tell she agreed completely.

As I raced away from Jim's obviously *not* positive training center, I couldn't quite let go of my outrage. I couldn't shake an image of Bella being hung by her neck or reeling in pain from some medieval torture-like collar.

My emotions surprised me. I was embarrassingly familiar with anger; the morning's coffee-cup incident demonstrated that perfectly.

But this feeling was different. It was an intense, almost uncontrollable energy, vibrating from deep in my core. *Protect, protect, protect. I must protect.*

I finally understood why Dad acted so overbearing sometimes. Granted, I'd been almost thirty, but when you loved something and thought it was in danger, you—

Oh, no.

Anxiety fluttered underneath my sternum. I pulled to the side of the road and took several deep, gulping breaths. This was bad. I couldn't kid myself anymore. I wasn't helping Bella because I owed it to George—I was starting to care about her. If I wasn't careful, I'd soon fall in love. I needed to find her a new home, before it was too late.

TWENTY

"IMAGINE THAT YOUR BODY is light—as light as a helium balloon, floating away from the earth."

My students all lay on the floor, completely still, covered up with warm blankets. I fought the urge to lie down and join them. Several hours after my visit to what I now called Jim's Den of Dog Abuse, I led—or more accurately, sleep-talked—several students through the practice of Yoga Nidra: an ancient meditation technique designed to relax and refresh.

I stifled a yawn and continued speaking in low, soft tones, as if wrapping my students in a verbal cocoon. "Pretend you're lying on a warm beach, soaking up the summer sun. Allow the sun's warmth to spread throughout your entire body." My own body swayed. A soft snore fell from my lips.

Get it together, Kate. This is ridiculous.

Yoga Nidra might be called "the divine sleep," but I was practically comatose. I stood up, glanced around the room to make sure no one was looking, and took a deep drink of the quadruple Americano I'd hidden behind the flowers.

I tried to stay upright as I continued. "Feel the right side of your body, and imagine light pouring through it, all the way down through your fingers and toes…"

Thirty interminable minutes later, my students folded their blankets and prepared to leave. I hoped they felt significantly more rejuvenated than I did. Only one thought kept me upright as I ushered them to the door: If I worked quickly, I could clean up and be on my way home in ten minutes. A first-time student browsed through the retail area until everyone left, then approached me, smiling.

"What a perfect way to end the day. I've never felt more rested."

That makes one of us.

I walked him toward the door, counting the seconds until I could go home.

One thousand one, one thousand two, one thousand—

"Do you have a second? I'd like to ask you a quick question."

Ugh. I pasted on a fake smile and said yes.

At least twenty questions and forty-seven minutes later, I locked the door behind him.

Ten-seventeen. I wanted desperately to go home and crawl into bed, but first I had to prepare the studio for the next day's classes. I considered leaving Bella in the car, but the thought of her sad, lonely eyes guilt-tripped me into bringing her inside. She pulled me into the studio and enthusiastically sniffed around, before quickly deciding that nothing interesting had happened since the evening before. Apparently bored again, she curled up in a corner to watch me clean.

"You know, I go through a lot of trouble for you, Missy Dog," I grumbled. "You could at least learn to push the dust mop."

Bella had no janitorial aspirations. She had a more important responsibility: self-appointed head of security. She sprang to her feet and roared, jumbo-sized claws scratching into the hardwood floor. *Intruder alert! Intruder alert! Guard dog on the job!*

What was she all riled up about now?

Bella charged to the lobby and hurled herself at the door, or more accurately at Jake, who stood behind it, knocking and waving. "What are you doing here?" I yelled through the window. "We're closed!"

"I know, but Alicia told me you're having trouble with the lights. I'm here to take a look at them."

"Now's not a good time. The dog will never let you in."

"Now is the *only* time if you want them fixed this week. Put the dog away and let me in! I'm tired of standing out here shouting."

I should have known I wouldn't get off that easily. "Hang on," I said, resigned to an even later night. "I'll take her out back and lock her in the car. I'll be right back."

I dragged the snarling monster-beast outside and shoved her in the car, so exhausted I felt like weeping. A thousand dollars for an electrician suddenly felt like nothing. I'd have traded the winning Lotto ticket to go home and collapse in my comfy warm bed.

I forced myself back to the studio, one heavy step at a time. When I opened the door, Jake sat comfortably in my chair with his feet on the desk, jangling a huge set of keys. "I have the master key, so I let myself in."

I looked pointedly at his boots. "I'm glad you made yourself at home."

"I figured there was no need to stand outside in the cold," he replied, ignoring my sarcasm. "I would have come in before, but I was afraid that dog would eat me." He shuddered. "God, I hate that thing. I told Alicia you were crazy to keep it."

"I'm not keeping—oh, never mind." I sighed.

Jake swung his legs off the desk and planted his boots on the floor. He looked from my eyes to my feet and back again. "You're looking really good, by the way. Is that a new haircut?"

I looked like a zombie, and I hadn't changed my hairstyle in months. I took several steps back, suddenly wishing my new student hadn't left so quickly. "Jake, it's late. What are you doing here after ten at night, anyway?"

"I've been around the complex a lot lately. People are all riled up about that murder." He frowned. "You know, it's bad enough that we have to let those bums hawk their stupid paper on our property. Couldn't they at least have the courtesy to get themselves killed in their own part of town?"

"Your empathy and dedication astound me."

Jake stood up and angled closer. "Yeah, well, we can't have you lady folk all in a tizzy. Someone's got to make you feel safe at night."

Did he really think I'd paid him a compliment? I tried changing the subject. "Let me show you what's going on with the lights."

Jake followed me into the yoga room. "I heard you found the body. What was that like?"

"It was horrible." I reached for the light switch. "Now, the flickering doesn't always happen, but when it does—"

"Aren't you scared to walk through the parking lot by yourself now? Half the ladies in the apartments are scared out of their wits. They want extra security lights, neighborhood patrols, better locks—their demands have been driving me crazy. They act like we're made of money."

I could have argued that he was, indeed, rich, but I doubted it would make any difference. "No, Jake, I'm not scared. The neighborhood is as safe as it ever was. George was targeted deliberately."

Jake stepped back, looking surprised. "What makes you say that? The cops are convinced the guy was killed in some drunken fight. Not that I wouldn't like a different explanation, but aren't you letting your imagination get the best of you?"

Exhaustion left me cranky. "Believe me, Jake, I know what the police think. I've talked to them, too. But I knew George, and he had a routine. He never stayed in Greenwood after seven."

"Come on, Kate. You can't possibly know—"

"And he hated leaving Bella alone. He wouldn't have locked her up unless he had a compelling reason." I crossed my arms, defiant. "No matter what the police think—no matter what *you* think, for that matter—whoever killed George knew him. His murder was premeditated."

Jake's mouth fell open. "You think someone *planned* to kill him? That's ridiculous! Look, I'll be the first to admit that those street bums can be annoying as hell. But the guy who was killed seemed essentially harmless. Who'd hate him enough to commit premeditated murder? Sorry, Kate, but the police's theory makes a lot more sense."

"You're wrong, Jake," I replied. "I've been looking into this on my own, and I know something that you don't. George was blackmailing someone. That's who killed him."

Jake flinched, as if startled. "Be serious, Kate. Who would he blackmail, the local street preacher?"

That, of course, was the critical question. And I still didn't have an answer.

"Maybe he was blackmailing you!" Jake teased. "I hear you yoga people are into some pretty weird stuff. Wasn't the *Kama Sutra* a yoga text? Maybe you've got something going on here that I don't know about." He elbowed my ribs, grinning. "A little 'happy ending' yoga, perhaps?" He wiggled his eyebrows suggestively.

I ground my teeth together. I knew Jake was kidding, but I still felt like slugging him. "Look, Jake. I don't have all the answers yet, but I'm not going to stop looking until I figure it out. Now, can we change the subject, please? I thought you wanted to look at the lights."

We spent the next twenty minutes playing with those blasted lights. I turned them on and off. I dimmed them. I put them on full strength. I tried every possible setting. They'd acted up all week but now that I wanted them to misbehave, they were in perfect working condition.

"I swear, Kate. Sometimes I think you make up excuses to spend time with me. These lights are fine." He eased closer. "But feel free to call if you want me to come back. Maybe we can figure out a creative way to break them." He paused meaningfully. "Only leave the dog at home."

He walked half out the door then turned back. "Kate, I still think you're wrong, but you might want to stay out of this murder business, just in case. Messing around in murder sounds like a good way to get hurt. I'd hate to see that pretty rear of yours in trouble."

He'd been gone almost ten minutes before I realized I'd forgotten to tell him about the broken door.

TWENTY-ONE

I AWOKE THE NEXT morning to the steady drip, drip, drip of Chinese water torture. Fluid fell from above, landing squarely between my eyebrows. Was this the universe's newest prank—a roof leak? I slowly cracked open one eye, terrified of what I might find. I came face-to-face, or rather nose-to-drippy-nose, with a bored-looking German shepherd. Bella towered over me, willing me to awaken. Drool fell drop by drop from her lower lip, splashing into an ever-expanding pool of saliva on my forehead. "Gross! Knock it off!" I yelled, sitting up and vigorously wiping my face. "Can't you at least close your mouth?"

Bella leaped off the bed and began her morning barking ritual. *Listen up!* she announced. *It's breakfast time!* I jumped up and joined her, determined to make today a better day. After all, we create our own destinies, right? I prepared Bella's food and set the timer. The pulverized, moistened, medicated kibble needed at least twenty minutes to incubate before Bella could consume it. I decided to spend that time nourishing my own body with a revitalizing yoga practice.

I started the same way ancient yogis began their morning practices over a thousand years ago. I faced my mat east— to honor the morning's sunrise—and began the first of twelve Sun Salutations. The strong flow sequence warmed my muscles and revitalized my mind. A delicious burning sensation spread across my arms and shoulders, then down my belly and legs, as I floated through each repetition. Rivulets of sweat dripped down my back, but my breath continued to be long, smooth, strong, and deep—evidence that I worked effectively without overexerting.

Bella watched my movements curiously, as if trying to decipher the point of this strange human game. At first she tried to join in by licking my face each time I lowered my body to the floor. When that didn't work, she nudged my hands as I returned to standing, either looking for treats or hoping for neck scratches. She eventually gave up and wandered to the corner, where she lay down and watched me, her expression a mixture of confused boredom.

"Sorry, pup. You wouldn't understand."

By the time I finished practicing forty-five minutes later, my mind buzzed with the energy of a caffeine addict after a triple shot of espresso—but without the annoying jitters. A delicious tingling energized my fingers and toes; a sensation of warmth spread across my shoulders, back, and thighs. My body rested heavily on the mat, as if rooted to the earth, but my heart seemed open and light, as if connected to that universal spirit of joy the ancient yogis called ananda —unending bliss.

I luxuriated on the floor for several more minutes, daydreaming about Michael's and my first night together. I closed my eyes and smiled, remembering his touch. The tingling sensation in my toes quickly moved up to my root chakra, if you know what I mean.

This would never do. I shook my hands and feet, forcing myself back to reality. I arose from my mat and cooked a quick-but-delicious bowl of Scottish oatmeal heavily garnished with dates, raisins, almonds, and brown sugar. As Bella and I slurped down our breakfasts together, I planned the rest of my day.

I looked at the clock. Sixty minutes until my first private client. How should I spend that time? I *could* spend it cleaning my fur-covered house. I *could* spend it finishing the studio's bookkeeping. Or I could spend it contemplating nature's finest artwork—Michael's gorgeous face. My tingling netherpart chakras left me no choice.

"C'mon, Miss Bella, we're going for a visit."

I put on Bella's collar, threw a few treats in my pocket, and set off for Pete's Pets. Five days had passed since my first date with Michael, and we had yet to set up a second. Although we had traded several longing glances through our respective storefront windows, thus far the universe—in the form of ill-timed customers, mismatched schedules, and way too much dog walking—had conspired to keep us apart. Five traded voice mail messages later, it was time to take matters into my own hands.

The parking lot was gloriously deserted. No stray dogs wandered about; no bearded men lurked in the shadows. I decided to take a risk and bring Bella into the pet store. The sign on the door said "Well Behaved Pets Welcome!" That certainly applied to us. Bella would be an angel. After all, she loved her Cookie Man!

We walked up to the door to survey our territory. Damn. Tiffany sat behind the counter, looking bored. Michael was probably doing inventory in the back. Time for Plan B. I tried to take Bella back to the car. Tried, to no avail. She sniffed the air, smelling the enticing aroma of dog treats. She wanted those treats. She *needed* those treats. And to get them, she had to go into that *fascinating* room. She glued her butt to the ground and refused to move, no matter how hard I pulled.

"OK, Bella, you win," I said to the obstinate mule-dog. "But first we need to make sure there aren't any other dogs inside."

I opened the door and glanced around the room. "Hey, Tiffany. Are there any dogs in there?"

"What do you mean?" she replied in a bored tone.

"I need to know for Bella here." I said, pointing at the treat-seeking-missile pulling on my arm. "She doesn't get along with other dogs. Are there any dogs in the store right now?"

"No." Tiffany sighed. She pulled a nail file out of her purse and started working on an imaginary hangnail.

Evidently she wasn't big on small talk.

"OK, girl, let's go in." Bella's eyes got twice their normal size. I could practically read her mind. This place was doggy heaven. She could smell treats—lots and lots of treats. They were right there, right on that counter. The woman sitting behind it was obviously the treat dispenser.

Bella walked up to Tiffany, sat down, and stared. She gave Tiffany her most adorable look. She even offered her paw. Tiffany continued to gaze down at her nails, ignoring her. Bella leaned back, furrowed her brow, and let out a low, disappointed moan. The human treat dispenser was broken.

"Bark!" said Bella.

Tiffany gave no response.

"Um, Tiffany, I think she wants you to give her a treat."

Tiffany looked at me drolly.

Bella barked again.

I reached into my pocket. "Here, I'll even provide the treat. Would you please give it to her?"

I handed Tiffany one of the cookies I'd thrown in my pocket for just such an emergency. With an air that the action was somehow beneath her, Tiffany handed the treat to Bella, then wiped her hands disgustedly on her pants.

Bella didn't look at all satisfied. And who could blame her? She had given Tiffany her most beguiling cute-dog behavior, and the response had been entirely inadequate. She let out a series of six sharp barks, clearly voicing her opinion of Tiffany's poor customer service.

Tiffany sighed as if Bella and I were both insane, then turned her back to us. Man, was she ever in the wrong profession.

"Come on Bella. Let's get some dog food."

We were three aisles back when Jake ambled in. I was in luck, or at least I thought so. Jake was here to flirt with Tiffany, not to harass me. If I was clever, I could forget about the dog food and sneak out unnoticed.

Jake sauntered up to the desk. Tiffany flashed him a sexy smile, no longer seeming bored in the slightest. She leaned toward Jake and giggled, touching him in a manner a little too familiar for strangers in a pet store.

"Hey, gorgeous. How's that new water heater working out for you?" Jake eased around the counter, wearing a broad grin.

I'm sure they were about to engage in scintillating conversation, but those were the only words Jake got out before Bella got a good look at him. One glance at that nasty goatee and she roared toward him in a flurry of teeth, fur, and noise the likes of which I'd never seen. I held on to Bella's leash as tightly as I could, but to no avail. It was like trying to restrain a canine freight train.

Bella dove through a stack of wet dog food, scattering cans in every direction. Distracted by the noise, she veered left and knocked over a display of sale-priced cat litter, ripping open several bags in the process. I slid on the pelletized pine and grabbed a shelf for balance, only to pull down a box of individually priced dog cookies. Broken cookies littered the ground in a six-foot radius. By the time I got Bella under control again, one thing was abundantly clear: Hurricane Bella had been a Category Five.

Jake hid behind the desk and yelled, "Get your crazy dog out of here! Lord, I hate that thing!"

"I told you, she's not my dog!" I shouted back. *But frankly, we're not too fond of you, either.*

Michael rushed out to see what was causing all the commotion. One look at the mess and his face turned as red as Rene's nail polish. Steam practically poured from his scalp.

"Kate, what were you thinking? You know better than to bring Bella in here!" He turned to the desk where Jake still hid, crouching behind a chair. "I'm sorry, Jake. For some reason, this dog doesn't like beards. This won't happen again."

"See that it doesn't," Jake replied, still shielding himself with the chair. Evidently Tiffany would have to protect herself.

Michael's look invited no argument. "Kate, get Bella out of here."

His stern tone took me by surprise. Michael was supposed to be on *our* side. My feelings were hurt, but I'd never show that. Instead, I pretended to be angry. "Bella, let's go. We're not welcome here."

I marched toward the door imperiously. Six steps later, I jerked to a stop. I'd finally hit the end of my rope, or rather the end of my leash. Bella planted her feet, glaring at me accusingly. How could she possibly leave now, when she still had dozens of broken cookies left to eat?

"Don't even think about it," I hissed. I summoned superhuman strength and dragged the struggling beast toward the door, past a still-cowering Jake, a smirking Tiffany, and a now-laughing Michael, who had evidently rediscovered his sense of humor.

"I'll come over later," Michael said, flashing a crooked smile.

"Don't bother," I grumped. "We're not interested."

I stomped out the door, pulling Bella behind me. "So much for that relationship, Bella," I said as the door closed behind me. "Anyone who takes Jake's side over ours is history."

———

I shoved Bella in the car and skulked back to the studio, determined not to cry. How could Michael choose Jake over me? The Yoga Over Fifty class was still leaving, so I hid in the bathroom and tried to pull myself together before Alicia's appointment. I adored Alicia, but she was the last person I wanted to see. Lord only knew what I'd say if she started mooning over Jake.

The prior class's instructor yelled through the door. "I'm on my way home. Talk to you later, Kate!" I looked at my watch. Almost eleven o'clock. I couldn't hide in here much longer; Alicia would arrive in five minutes.

I willed myself to let the past hour fade away. Rationally, I knew the morning's events had nothing to do with Alicia, and my rational mind would prevail. I would be calm, balanced, and strong. My professional behavior would be an example to yoga teachers everywhere. A couple of deep breaths, and I was ready.

I took one look at Alicia and burst into tears.

"That odious girl was at the front desk. And then Bella tried to attack Jake … never wanted a stupid dog anyway … and Michael's a big jerk, no better than the rest of them … but now I'll never go out with him again. And George really *was* a criminal … and—"

Alicia wrapped me in a great big hug. "Whoa, Kate, hold on there! I've never seen you like this! Slow down now." She stepped back and gazed in my eyes, as if hypnotizing me into a greater state of calm. "Slow down your breathing, like you've taught me to do." I swallowed hard and tried to stop sobbing. "That's it," Alicia continued, "take a nice, deep inhale and feel peaceful energy enter your system. Exhale, and let all of your frustrations go."

I was horrified. I'd never broken down this way in front of a client. I swallowed back the rest of my tears in several uneven, hiccupping gulps. "Oh my God, Alicia. I'm so very sorry. How completely unprofessional." I wiped the tears off my chin.

"Truly, it's OK." Alicia handed me a tissue. "Just goes to show that you're human like the rest of us."

"This all happened so recently, but I'm supposed to be more professional than that." I groaned. "And on top of it all, Jake's your husband. Please, *please* forgive me. I'm exhausted, but that's no excuse. This session is on me. Maybe I should even pay you. I'm so embarrassed."

"Don't worry about it," Alicia interrupted. "Haven't you told me at least a dozen times that I need to let my emotions out every now and then? You're no different. You've been a rock for me these last few months; maybe it's time to return the favor." She gestured to the lobby. "Let's sit down and talk."

Alicia poured me a glass of water. I gratefully gulped it down, allowing the cool liquid to soothe my aching throat.

"First of all," Alicia began, "forget about Jake. He's terrified of dogs, so I'm sure he was upset, but he'll get over it." She sat down beside me. "There was no harm done, so what's he going to do anyway? Sue you for scaring away his manhood? He's probably already forgotten about the incident, so let it go. It's over and done with."

I sincerely doubted Jake had forgotten anything, but Alicia had a point. Bella had created a scene, but she only damaged Michael's displays, Jake's ego, and my pride. All could theoretically be repaired.

"Second, so what if you and your new beau had a tiff? You know the best thing about fights between lovers? Making up is so very much fun." She grinned. "Put your silly pride behind you, give him a call, and apologize."

"But it's not my fault that Bella—"

She held up a stern hand. "Hush, Kate. I'm talking now. You're listening." She smiled to take the sting out of her words. "Who cares who's at fault? Call up your guy and make nice. By tomorrow, all of this will be behind you.

"Third," she continued, "you're a saint for taking in that dog. But even saints have their limits. You have to do something about her."

"But there's nothing I *can* do!" I argued. "No one else will take her."

"That may be true, but you don't have to put up with her erratic behavior, either. Hire a trainer."

I vigorously shook my head. "I already tried that. Too violent."

"Come on, Kate, you're smarter than that. Is all yoga the same?"

"No, of course not, but—"

"Well, neither are dog trainers. Their methods vary as much, if not more, than yoga teachers." Alicia opened her purse and pulled out a cell phone. "One of my Magnolia tenants trains dogs. I've seen her in action, and her methods are far from violent." She wrote down the number. "Her name's Melissa. Tell her Alicia from The Cedars sent you. She books pretty far in advance, but maybe I can pull some strings and get her to squeeze you in."

"Thanks, but—"

"Shush," she interrupted. The sound reminded me of Jim, that odious trainer, and the sound he used to quiet his barking dogs. It was surprisingly effective. I shushed.

"You'll call Melissa today, correct?"

I nodded my head yes.

"Good. Finally, and this is important. It's time for you to forget about that murder. The police are completely capable of handling a murder investigation, and frankly, playing amateur detective is driving you crazy. I know the victim was your friend and all, but do you honestly think you're better equipped to solve a murder than the entire Seattle Police Department?"

"Maybe not, but—"

"Let the murder go, Kate," Alicia said emphatically. "Stick with what you're good at—yoga. If your new relationship is supposed to work out, it will. If not, you'll move on. The rest is simply a distraction." She stood up. "You always say I should focus on my most important priorities. Well, Kate, it's time to practice what you preach. I'll focus on beating my disease. You focus on getting your life back together. That's an order."

I stared off into space for a moment, thinking. Now that I'd had a good cry, I felt better. And I had to admit that Alicia was right—at least for the most part. I stood up, smiled at her, and threw my tear-stained tissue in the trash. "Understood."

Alicia had given me four pieces of advice: forget about Jake, make up with Michael, call her trainer friend, and drop the investigation.

I figured listening to three out of four wasn't bad.

———

I called Melissa later that afternoon. Alicia made good on her promise and pulled those magic strings. Although Melissa normally had

198

a month-long waiting list, she agreed to squeeze in an appointment for Bella the following weekend. Even better, she insisted that we meet at my house, so she could interact with Bella in her normal environment.

Score! No forty-five-minute commute! Things were definitely looking up. And they got better. Around three o'clock, Michael appeared at my door.

"Hey, I'm sorry about getting so angry earlier," he said as he sheepishly entered the lobby. "I got caught off-guard. First I was shocked at the mess; then I saw Jake hiding behind the desk. I can't afford to make him mad. Jake hates dogs, and he'd love to find an excuse to kick Pete's Pets out of the complex. When I saw him cowering behind the chair, I overreacted."

"I'm sorry, too." I smiled. "That whole catastrophe was my fault. I really should have known better than to take Bella in with me." I picked up my billfold. "How much do I owe you for the damage?"

"Forget about it." Michael replied, smiling. "That's the least of my worries. Tell you what. Let's make it up to each other over drinks tonight. How about nine-thirty?"

I felt a familiar flutter low in my belly—and a few other body parts I don't care to mention. "Sounds perfect. It's a date!"

I spent the rest of the day literally whistling while I worked. I took Bella home during my dinner break and freshened up. Today was going to be a great day. It was *Kate's* day. If I was lucky, Kate's *night* would involve an overnight guest.

Michael arrived at nine-thirty on the dot.

"Hey there," I said. "Ready for our hot date?"

"You bet!" He raised his eyebrows and grinned. The Cheshire Cat couldn't have been cuter.

"Give me a second to lock up," I said, grabbing my keys. "There's a new wine bar in Ballard I've been dying to try. Do you mind if I drive?"

I didn't really lie. True, I'd been to that wine bar twice before, but never on a Friday. And the fact that it was within walking distance of my house was simply a bonus. No self-respecting yoga teacher would ask a guy to spend the night on the second date, but she could always stack the deck in her favor, couldn't she?

We headed out to the parking lot, hand in hand. I walked Michael to the passenger side of my car. "Allow me to get the door for you, sir," I said, bowing and using my most chivalrous voice.

Michael pulled me close.

"Uh, Kate, hang on a second. Do you see that?"

Unfortunately, I did. *So much for Kate's night.*

My driver's side window was shattered. I carefully opened the door, picked up the rock on the seat, and read the attached note.

"Stay out of it. Or you'll be next."

TWENTY-TWO

"THIS CAN'T BE HAPPENING again," I moaned into my hands. The patrol car's pulsating lights shattered the darkness, like flashes of memory best left forgotten. I spoke with detectives Martinez and Henderson through a PTSD-like haze.

"Thank you for coming. I asked the officer to call so you could see for yourself. You may not have believed me before, but this note proves I'm right. I'm getting close."

Martinez looked at me warily. "Close to what?"

"Close to solving George's murder."

Henderson frowned. "It's just a broken window, ma'am, not a professional hit." He handed the note to Martinez. "But you're right about one thing: it does look like someone isn't too happy with you. Any idea who that might be?"

"Of course not," I snapped. "If I knew who did this, I would have told you already." I immediately regretted my tone; arguing would get me nowhere. I took a deep breath and ratcheted my attitude back a notch. "But it has to be George's murderer, or at least someone involved with his death."

"That's quite a stretch, ma'am," Henderson replied. "Vandalism like this happens all the time. Probably some kids having their version of a fun night out on the town."

"But you *will* take a closer look at George's murder, won't you?" I turned to Martinez. "Here, look at this. While I was waiting for you, I wrote down everyone I've questioned about the case so far. The answer is bound to be in there somewhere."

She scanned the paper, frowning. "I'll add this information to the murder book, but we've already talked to most of these people—although this 'Momma Bird' character doesn't sound familiar." She folded the list and placed it in her notebook. "Look, Kate," she said soberly. "I'll admit that this vandalism is suspicious, but the note isn't exactly specific. Detective Henderson is right. It was probably some kids getting their kicks."

"Why would kids leave a note like that?"

She shrugged. "Who knows why teenagers do half the things they do?"

"You can't ignore—"

"Kate," she interrupted sharply, "I promise we'll look into this." The two detectives exchanged a knowing look. "But don't get your hopes up."

"But you have to—"

She held up her hand in the universal stop sign. "I *said* I'll look into it."

I didn't respond—at least not verbally. Martinez and I faced each other in mutual aggravation, our prickly silence so charged a stray spark would have ignited it.

"In the meantime," she continued, "my advice is to go home, call your insurance company, and get some sleep." She pointed at the broken glass littering my Honda's interior. "Do you need a ride home, or can your friend here take you?"

"Don't worry, I've got her," Michael replied.

The patrol car drove off twenty minutes later, leaving Michael and me to sweep up the glass and cover my missing window. An hour ago I'd been excited about the evening ahead. Now I wanted to crawl into bed, pull the sheets over my head, and forget the entire day ever happened. I collapsed in the passenger seat of Michael's Explorer, so weary my bones ached. "Not exactly the hot date we had planned, was it?"

"Not exactly," he said soberly. "But at least now maybe you'll see reason."

Uh-oh. My stomach tightened.

"What do you mean?"

"Maybe now you'll take everyone's advice and stay out of this murder investigation."

Adrenaline flooded my system, replacing exhaustion with agitation. "Are you kidding? Martinez was the closest thing to an ally I had on George's case. If she's convinced the note was left by some prankster teen, then my car was damaged for nothing! You all may think I'm delusional, but that note proves I'm not. I'm getting close, and someone doesn't like it."

Concern and irritation vied for dominance on Michael's face. "So what if you *are* getting close? George's killer obviously isn't afraid to use violence. What do you hope to accomplish by provoking him? Do you want to get yourself hurt—or worse?"

"No, but—"

"You're out of your league here, Kate. At best, you're making a fool of yourself. At worst, you're risking your life. I know it's not your strong suit, but see reason for once."

I went from agitated to furious in three seconds flat. Michael didn't know it, but he had just declared war. "Reason's not my strong suit, huh?" I hissed. "Well, evidently not. If I were *reasonable* I'd never have agreed to go out with *you*."

Michael winced, surprised by my outburst. "Come on, don't be that way. I'm trying to protect you."

The last person who'd tried to protect me was my father. I didn't appreciate it from him then, and I liked it even less from Michael now. In a weird flash of insight, I remembered my Aunt Rita. She used to refer to her monthly cycle as "the curse." Now, glowering at Michael, I knew she was wrong. If God cursed woman, it was by forcing her to live with the testosterone-driven beast called man.

It was high time woman fought back.

My words spewed out like venom. "I've lived without you and your big, strong, manly presence for thirty-two years, and I've managed to survive just fine." I crossed my arms and glared, daring Michael to reply.

He answered with echoing silence. He set his jaw, stared straight ahead, and drove. We both quietly seethed for the ten-minute drive home. After what felt like ten hours, he pulled into my driveway, parked the car, and turned to face me.

Michael spoke slowly and sternly, as if scolding an obstinate child. "Kate, let me be very clear about this. You will not continue this murder investigation, under any circumstances. I forbid it." Michael's words were unequivocal, not to be challenged. He was man. He was in charge. He expected no argument.

He was an idiot.

"You *forbid* it?" I shouted. "What are you, a Neanderthal? What next? Are you going to hit me over the head and drag me off to your cave?"

Michael opened his mouth, but remained speechless. That was fine by me—I wasn't finished. "If you think you can waltz into my life and start giving me orders, you are sorely mistaken."

I jumped out of the car, then leaned back in to give Michael one final message. "Take your big, macho self and your jumbo-sized ego and drive on out of here, mister. No one tells me what to do." I slammed the door and stomped away.

Michael followed, practically chasing me to the house. "Kate, wait," he yelled to my back. "I'm sorry. That came out horribly wrong. I'm just worried about you!" He grabbed my arm. I yanked it back and kept walking.

"Slow down!" he pleaded. "You can't march off in a huff every time we disagree. Let's talk this through."

I spun around to face him with a defiant grin. "That's the beauty of being single, Michael. I can do anything I want. Now get off my property before I call the police for the second time tonight."

I stomped into the house and slammed the door. The deadbolt turned with a satisfying click. "Bella, I'm home!" I yelled in a voice loud enough to be heard by Michael or anyone else stupid enough to still be standing on my porch. "We were wrong. This one's a dud like all the rest. *Too bossy.*"

I turned off the exterior lights. If Michael was still out there, he could *feel* his way back to the car. I completed my diatribe by releasing Bella from her crate, marching upstairs, and flopping on the bed. Bella jumped up after me, looking concerned. I lay there for several minutes, congratulating myself on my clear victory.

At least, that is, until my adrenaline levels returned to normal and my rational mind reengaged. I looked at Bella, read the confusion on her face, and realized what I'd done. I'd lost my temper and lashed out exactly like I had that night with my father. No matter how much I wanted to, I'd never change.

All the emotions I'd fought to suppress for the past two years came flooding back. My body felt heavy—so heavy I could barely lift my head. This was exactly what I'd been afraid of. I'd deluded myself into thinking I could open up again, but I'd been wrong. I didn't *want* a relationship. I didn't *deserve* a relationship. Michael was better off without me. I was better off alone.

Bella whined, clearly uncomfortable with my pain. She lay down beside me and licked at my tears. I hugged her back and sobbed, rocking slowly back and forth.

"I know girl, I know. We're on our own again."

———

I gave up on sleep at five-thirty the next morning, crawled out of bed, and shook off the fog of depression threatening to envelop me. Ten days had passed since George's murder, and the police still didn't have any viable suspects. If my conversation with Martinez and Henderson was any indication, they weren't even actively working the case. Well, police be damned. Michael be damned. Now that I was single again, no one would stop me. I would get to the bottom of George's death, even if it killed me.

But how? I'd obviously stirred someone up, but I had no idea who, how, or why. I considered interviewing every *Dollars for Change* vendor in the greater Seattle area, but how many papers could one girl buy, anyway? My best bet was to go back to the source.

I didn't want to stir up trouble; in fact, the last thing my heart could take was more conflict. But depression's cold tongue licked at my heels. If I didn't force myself to take action soon, I would give into it entirely. So I rented a car and drove, solo this time, to *Dollars for Change*. I walked into the office with my head held high, praying that Ralphie and Tali hadn't compared notes.

"You again. You lied to us!" Tali hissed. "If you're going to make fools of us, you and your friend should at least get your stories straight. Poor Ralph was heartbroken. He waited for Suzie for over two hours."

"I'm so sorry," I replied. "I had no idea she was going to set him up like that. But we meant well." I spoke loud enough to be heard throughout the entire office. "I'm investigating George Levin's murder, and I need information."

A small crowd gathered around the desk. Even Ralph emerged from his cubicle to see who was causing all the commotion. This time, we weren't alone. At nine o'clock in the morning, dozens of *Dollars for Change* vendors of assorted ages, ethnicities, shapes, and sizes loitered about the office, waiting to pick up the daily edition.

I turned to face them. "Hi, everyone," I said feigning significantly more confidence than I felt. "My name is Kate Davidson. I knew George, the vendor who was killed in Greenwood, and I'm looking into his death. Who here has information that can help me?"

The crowd murmured and shuffled, but no one shouted, "I did it!" or volunteered any other useful information. Tali stormed out from behind her desk and roughly grabbed my shoulder. "Get out of my office."

I threw off her hand and shouted, "A man was murdered! Why doesn't anyone besides me care about that?"

Tali was firm. Not the slightest bit friendly. "I said get out. *Now*."

I had no intention of leaving until I got my information. Tali may have been a few pounds heavier than me, but I was tougher. I planted my feet, placing my hands on my hips.

"No. I'm not going," I said belligerently. "You'll have to make me."

Big mistake.

A huge man with multiple tattoos, a pierced ear, and more than a little body fat stepped between us. He looked like a cross between a sumo wrestler and a strip club bouncer. I looked up—way up—to his face, seeking eye contact. His deep voice boomed. "I believe the lady asked you to leave."

He left me with one intelligent option. Retreat. I said I'd solve George's murder even if it killed me, but I didn't mean *literally*.

"Fine. I'm going."

I made one last-ditch effort to get my message out to the crowd. I yelled over my shoulder as the sumo-bouncer pulled me to the door. "I'll be waiting out in the parking lot, and I work at Serenity Yoga. Find me if you know something. I'll pay one hundred dollars for any information that helps solve the case!"

I waited by my car for forty-five minutes, until every vendor had left the building. Most studiously avoided my gaze, quickening their pace as they passed. Two stopped to see if I wanted a paper. Only one brave soul offered any information about George's murder. Momma Bird marched straight up, frowning. With a look of apparent disbelief, she said, "What are you, stupid? I told you already. George was blackmailing someone. That's who killed him." She turned and walked away, shaking her head in disgust.

TWENTY-THREE

I spent the next few days locked in mortal combat with my most feared adversaries—guilt and depression. Getting out of bed each morning was a major victory. Summoning the energy to teach, nothing short of a miracle. Interacting with the steady stream of newcomers to the studio, well, that almost killed me.

No, I didn't finally obtain my much-needed flood of new students. Each visiting stranger had one goal only: to walk away a hundred dollars richer. As I'd hoped, word of my reward traveled far beyond *Dollars for Change*. In fact, most of Seattle's homeless seemed ready to take me up on my offer. While a hundred dollars felt like a lot of money to me, to the desperate people lined up outside my door, it was a fortune—a fortune worth waiting for, a fortune worth lying for. I began to think the police might be right. For some, a hundred dollars might even be a fortune worth killing for.

By Wednesday, I had interviewed a dozen "witnesses." By and large, their stories were obvious works of fiction. A few were simply heart-wrenching delusions ranging from CIA cover-ups to alien abductions. Although I gave away several small bills to my most desperate visitors, no one received the magic c-note. After three days of dodging unbathed con men and trying to reason with well-meaning schizophrenics, I was ready to throw in the towel. My visit to *Dollars for Change* had been a waste of time.

The thirteenth visitor changed my mind.

I was hiding in the studio's storage room, ostensibly taking inventory while the studio's most valiant teacher—the instructor of the Mommy and Me yoga class—wrapped up her weekly hour of self-torture. From what I could hear, the theme of today's class was cultivating inner peace in the midst of screaming. I peeked around the door. The intrepid instructor sat on a large green yoga ball bouncing two red-faced, screaming infants—one on each knee. They obviously weren't doing Happy Baby Pose. The tiny humans' red, wrinkly, puffy faces were covered in tears; fluid I didn't wish to identify dripped from their nostrils and flowed from their gaping mouths; the scalp of the child on the right sported unruly, horn-like spikes of dark brown hair.

No doubt about it. These were the spawn of Satan.

The words "Thank God it's not me ... Thank God it's not me ..." pounded through my head, keeping rhythm with the unhappy cries. I glanced around the room, wondering if I should intervene somehow.

No one other than me seemed to notice the clamor.

Eight resting moms lay flat on their backs, legs draped over cylindrical bolsters. Their eyes were closed, their jaw muscles relaxed, and they wore slight smiles on their faces. The six babies not being bounced, rocked, and cooed to by the grinning yoga teacher were self-entertained by a variety of activities, from playing with plush, animal-shaped toys, to crawling around on brightly striped yoga blankets, to sleeping in car seats. I could only assume that the sleeping children were deaf.

I closed the door again, cursing myself for not selecting a hide-out with a back exit. I pretended to count yoga mats, paper cups, and toilet paper rolls while I waited for the eight yogi supermoms to gather their progeny and move to the lobby. The screaming quieted to a dull roar. If I was lucky, I could hide out in here until everyone left. If I was lucky—

The Mommy and Me teacher opened the door midway through my thought, hitting me squarely on the butt and knocking me to the ground. She didn't appear happy. "Sorry about that, Kate, but you need to come out here. There's another creepy guy hanging around by the front entrance. He's freaking out my moms."

I sighed and grabbed my jacket. "I'll talk to him."

When I entered the lobby, the eight formerly blissful new moms stared worriedly out the window, clutching their babies to their chests. Their instructor gave me a grumpy look, then smiled at them confidently. "Everything's okay, ladies. Why don't you leave from the back door today."

They murmured agreement and gathered their various baby-centered belongings—blankets, diaper bags, toys, car seats, and strollers—before moving en masse to the yoga room door. They stopped at the doorway, staring at my "No Shoes Allowed" sign. The first few moms in line turned back and frowned.

I smiled in return. "Go ahead and keep your shoes on. And don't worry," I said, hoping I wasn't about to lie. "I'll make sure this gentleman doesn't bother you next week."

Seemingly satisfied, the caravan of sixteen humans and all of their earthly belongings stomped through the studio and out the back door, leaving a trail of dirt, scuff marks, and dropped toys behind them. Sighing, I slipped on my coat and prepared to perform my thirteenth waste-of-time interview.

The man on the other side of door didn't quite look at me as he shifted left and right. "You the woman giving out a hundred dollars?"

I took a step back and swallowed the acid taste of my morning coffee. It was Charlie, the man I'd seen talking with George the day of his murder. He stood in front of the studio, leaning on his bag-laden bicycle and wearing that same filthy camouflage jacket.

"Um ... well, um ... I'm looking into George Levin's murder. Do you have information that can help me?"

He nudged the ground with his boot. "Maybe. I have his stuff."

I snapped to attention, captivated by those two short sentences. *George's gym bag.* As far as I knew, the police had never found it. The bag could contain important clues—incriminating receipts, perhaps a calendar, maybe even a Post-it note brazenly displaying the killer's identity. Excitement overcame my apprehension. I had no idea what might lie among George's possessions, but I had to find out.

I glanced at the bike. "Can I take a look?"

"I don't have it here. It's hidden. You'll have to come with me."

A hollow sensation tugged at the pit of my stomach. "Go with you? Where?"

He frowned. "To where I hid it." He didn't volunteer any additional information, but his look spoke volumes: clearly yoga teachers didn't have to be very bright.

"Tell you what," I replied. "Why don't you go get George's belongings and bring them back here. I'll wait for you."

Charlie looked at me, frowning slightly. "I already went out of my way to come to you once. If you want George's stuff, you'll come with me." He shrugged. "If not, so be it."

He must have mistaken my silence for assent. He looked me up and down blatantly, assessing my outfit. My light jacket and leggings were perfectly suited for the unseasonably cold morning—as long as

I spent it inside a toasty-warm yoga studio. Only five minutes outside, and I was already freezing. "We should drive," he muttered.

Dad's scolding voice rang through my head. *Do not get into a car with this man.* But my own trickster mind was far more persuasive. After all, it reasoned, I had Bella. She'd never let anyone hurt me. Besides, George had assured me that Charlie was harmless—that the two of them were friends. He would have warned me if Charlie were dangerous, right?

I grabbed my purse, told the instructor I was leaving, and led Charlie to my car, nervously filling our walk with mindless chatter.

I didn't even consider how Bella would react to his beard.

Bella awoke as my key turned in the passenger side lock. She took one look at the grizzly-man standing behind me and roared, clawing and snapping at the partially opened window.

I shrieked in surprise and stumbled away, startled by her outburst. Charlie, on the other hand, didn't even flinch. He just stared, deadpan, at Bella and the trail of saliva dripping down my car's interior.

"Guess we'll walk," he said. He picked up his bike and ambled off in the opposite direction.

I didn't want to follow. What if George had been wrong? What if Charlie was the killer? Without Bella, I'd be defenseless. I'd be crazy to wander off with Charlie—crazier than Rene, Momma Bird, and all of my schizophrenic sources combined. But I couldn't *not* go, either. If I let him leave, I'd never get a chance to look through George's possessions.

Charlie obviously didn't share my ambivalence. He didn't even look back to make sure I was following. He just kept walking.

My trickster mind taunted me again. *What are you afraid of, Kate? It's broad daylight.* I felt the weight of my purse against my hip. *And you do have the pepper spray...*

I started after Charlie, but immediately stopped, ashamed of myself. I relocked the car, took two steps back toward the studio, and froze. No matter how hard I tried, I couldn't take the third. Curiosity pulled me toward Charlie like a magnet. I opened my purse, took the pepper spray off safety, and tucked it in the palm of my hand.

"Hey, wait up! I'm coming!"

I caught up with Charlie a half block later. We walked together in silence for a good ten minutes before turning right on Aurora Avenue N. "Where are we going?"

No response. Nothing but the sounds of cars zooming by on the busy roadway.

Maybe this wasn't such a great idea. I shivered under my rain-soaked jacket, kicking myself and feeling like an idiot. But my feet kept on walking. I'd made it this far. Why turn back now?

When we reached Woodland Park twenty minutes later, my mind finally caught up with what my intuition had known all along. Coming here with Charlie had been a terrible mistake. As we entered the ninety acres of mostly deserted forest, I understood why he chose this location. With nothing in view but pine trees, squirrels, and the occasional abandoned bunny, the park was the perfect place to hide your most prized possessions—or the body of a newly slaughtered yoga teacher. Aurora's traffic sounds no longer gave me much comfort. Even if someone heard me scream, they'd be too far away to help.

Depressed or not, I wasn't yet suicidal. It was time to cut and run—literally. Straight down the hill to Greenlake, where there would be dozens, if not hundreds, of people to witness my execution. I slowly, tentatively backed away as Charlie continued forward. I glanced left and right, searching for a path not covered with fallen branches. The trail on the left looked promising, but I'd have to be careful. Stumbling would cost me precious seconds; a broken ankle would seal my fate. I just needed a head start—enough time to get to the road.

Wait for it … Wait for it …

"In here."

I gasped at the unexpected sound. "Here" was a fully fenced grassy area containing over a dozen sand-filled horseshoe pits. It seemed oddly out of place and yet fully at home in the deserted park—a reminder, somehow, of more innocent times. The fenced area contained multiple benches and was covered by two partial roofs, providing both protection from rainfall and the illusion of gated safety. Empty bottles littered one corner; a transistor radio sat in the other. Charlie closed the gate, leaned his bike against the fence, and turned on the radio. We'd arrived at his home.

"Sit," he muttered, pointing to the nearest bench. He stood on another bench and dug in the rafters, sorting through coats, blankets, and even more duffel bags. He finally found George's black bag and handed it to me.

It felt light, insubstantial. "Is this everything?" How could something so small hold a man's entire legacy?

"'Cept a blanket. I already told George. That's mine now."

I didn't argue. I reached to undo the zipper, but stopped, conflicted. This small bag contained everything George held precious. Snooping through it seemed wrong somehow—an invasion of George's privacy, even in death. And yet the act also felt important, as if I'd been gifted one final, completely honest conversation with my friend. I paused, closed my eyes, and asked George for forgiveness. Then I slowly, reverently opened the zipper.

A pair of pants, pockets empty. Two worn shirts, two pairs of socks, two pairs of underwear, another shirt…

The green flannel shirt was wrapped around something—a flat, rigid object with sharp corners. I laid the bundle on my lap and carefully opened it.

The photo sheltered inside delivered a blow so powerful it felt physical. A young, vital-looking George stood next to a tall wooden sailor painted in bright reds and blues. George held a child under one arm and a pretty, dark-haired woman under the other. I opened the frame and removed the picture. Written on the back was "Sarah, Maddie and me—Cannon Beach, 1995." I gazed at George's family portrait for several minutes, lightly running my fingers across the image.

"I ain't got all day, lady."

Charlie's gruff voice brought me back to reality. I carefully put the photo back in the frame, rewrapped the bundle, and kept looking. Only two items remained—a small collar and George's most valuable possession: Bella's $200 bottle of medicine. No zippered pockets or hidden compartments. No notebooks, receipts, or damning Post-it notes.

This was it? I'd wandered off with a stranger for this?

Heavy with disappointment, I returned the contents to the bag, closed the zipper, and stood up, placing the bag over my shoulder for the long walk home.

"Where's my money?" Charlie asked.

My earlier uneasiness returned. "I appreciate your help, but I don't see anything in here that will help solve George's murder. I'm sorry, but I can't pay you the reward."

Charlie's eyes turned cold. He moved closer, clenching and un-clenching his fists. The fence surrounding us suddenly felt like a prison; Charlie, a not-quite-sane cellmate. I clutched George's gym bag to my chest and slowly backed away.

"Where do you think you're going?" he growled.

The hair on my arms vibrated. Every nerve ending screamed re-treat! I grabbed for the pepper spray but couldn't find it. I glanced around, terrified. Where had it gone?

Charlie leaned toward me, and I panicked. I turned to run, but tripped and tumbled face-first into the sand. I pulled myself up and tried to scramble away, but my feet slipped on the wet ground. My eyes locked on Charlie's enraged face and I knew: this man intended to kill me. *Or worse.*

"I *said*, where's my money?"

My mind screamed run but my legs refused to obey. Why couldn't I move? Sour breath flooded my nostrils as Charlie pushed me deeper into the sand. I squeezed my eyes shut and tensed my muscles in horrified anticipation. One final thought tortured me. *Who'll take care of Bella now?*

Time seemed to stand still. My life flashed by in a series of dis-connected still-frames, but I felt no regrets. In fact, I felt—nothing. No pressure restraining me, no hands on my windpipe, no painful abuse. Nothing but the deep, ragged gulps of my own desperate breath.

One breath became two, became three. After what felt like an eternity, I relaxed my muscles and cautiously opened my eyes. Char-lie stood several feet away, glowering and holding the bag he had ripped from my shoulder. Once he made sure I was watching, he conspicuously leaned down, picked the vial of pepper spray off the bench where I'd dropped it, and tossed it in George's bag.

"When I get my money, you'll get your stuff."

I practically wept with gratitude. *Money.* He only wanted money. The math was easy. One hundred dollars wouldn't buy me any information about George's murder, but I *would* net a two-hundred-dollar bottle of Bella's medicine. And my life, well, that was priceless.

A quick stop at the nearest cash machine secured my freedom. Charlie put the five crisp, new twenty-dollar bills in his pocket, handed me George's bag, and shuffled off, pushing his loaded-down bicycle.

My teeth still chattered hours later, long after I'd peeled off my wet clothes and scrubbed my skin raw in a scalding shower. I tried to tell myself that I'd never been in any real danger—that my terror was the product of an overactive imagination. But deep inside, I knew better. Charlie only backed down because he got what he wanted. George had been wrong; the man was insane. What if I had refused?

I knew I should file a police report, but I was still too shaken, so I called John O'Connell instead. I didn't have a chance to tell him what happened in Woodland Park. In fact, I'd barely started telling him about my visit to *Dollars for Change,* when he exploded.

"You did *what?*"

"I was desperate, John. I'm not making any progress, no one else seems to care, and—"

"Of all the *stupid, reckless, irresponsible—*"

This time I pre-empted the inevitable dial tone by hanging up first. I avoided further conflict by leaving the bag and a detailed letter on John's front porch. I knew John would be furious, but I asked him to deliver George's belongings to Detective Martinez anyway. Well, at least most of George's belongings. I told myself it wasn't really stealing. After all, I paid a hundred dollars for that bag. Sarah might want the photo someday, but she'd never miss the enzymes or Bella's puppy collar. Those I kept for myself.

TWENTY-FOUR

LIFE, AS THE SAYING goes, went on, but slowly and without meaning. I functioned, but barely—heart and mind co-existing in one body, yet strangely disconnected. My heart dragged, weighted by the dual anchors of loneliness and depression, while my mind raced, running on the hamster wheel of obsession. I would have thought that facing death would reinvigorate me—make me appreciate how precious and fleeting life could be. But the effect was exactly the opposite. That day with Charlie drained every last drop of my energy, every last drop of my will. I barely muddled through each passing hour, step by agonizing step.

After two-and-a-half weeks, the chances of anyone—police officer or concerned citizen—solving George's murder were miniscule. But that didn't stop me from obsessing about it. I became consumed with solving the mystery of that note. What did I know that was worth threatening me over? My visit to *Dollars for Change* may have been reckless, but at least it had provided a welcome distraction. Once I exhausted that idea, all I had left were the endless repetitions of my own useless thoughts.

So I did everything I could to keep from thinking. I cleaned my house, cleared out the attic, landscaped the yard—and ignored Michael's phone messages. In spite of his many recorded apologies, our relationship was over. When it came to romance, Rene was right. I didn't give second chances. More importantly, I didn't *deserve* second chances.

Bella and I spent our time together avoiding fur-covered creatures of any kind, canine or human. Forcing her to live in total social isolation didn't seem fair, but I was out of ideas. I permitted one tiny spark of hope to illuminate my otherwise defeatist attitude. In spite of all evidence to the contrary, I still believed in the basic law of karma: that on balance, good things happened to good people. Bella and I had clearly experienced more than our share of hardship lately. If the universe was even slightly fair, we were due for a break. I hoped it would come on Saturday afternoon.

My phone rang Saturday at three-thirty on the dot.

"Hi, Kate, it's Melissa. I'm here for Bella's evaluation."

"Great! Come on up!" My perky confidence sounded forced, even to me.

Melissa paused. "Why don't you bring Bella outside so I can meet her on neutral ground. German shepherds can be territorial."

My stomach did flip-flops as I snapped on Bella's lead. Was Melissa's reticence a good sign or a bad one? I kneeled down, placed my hands on either side of Bella's face, and gazed into her deep brown eyes. "Please be good. You and I both need this to work."

I walked Bella outside but stopped on the porch, confused. Where was Melissa? The only person outside was a child standing next to a blue Chevy hatchback. Surely Melissa hadn't given up and left already? I scanned the horizon in search of lost dog trainers, but found no one except the child, who was now vigorously waving. My stomach stopped flopping and dropped to my toes.

Oh, no. It couldn't be.

I blinked to clear my eyes and looked again. As I'd feared, the waving munchkin wasn't a child after all; she was the world's tiniest dog trainer. Upon closer inspection, her shoulder-length brown hair was streaked with gray. But she stood less than five feet tall and weighed at most 100 pounds—if she carried a backpack full of rocks.

This woman could never handle Bella. A new headline flashed through my mind: "Pint-Sized Trainer Dragged to Death by Super-Sized Dog." I considered hiding, but that would be rude. She'd already seen us.

Melissa smiled and turned slightly sideways. "Bring Bella up, but let her decide how close she wants to come."

Bella enthusiastically pulled me up to her new best friend. "Hello, there, girl, aren't you a pretty one!" Melissa cooed, scratching Bella's throat. To me she said, "Bella's very thin. How's her appetite?"

I explained Bella's disease and what I had learned so far about managing it. "Treating EPI is expensive and lifelong, but the disease can be managed. So far, Bella's doing really well. She's gained three pounds since she's been with me, and she eats great." I ruffled Bella's ears. "In spite of her looks, there's nothing Bella likes better than food of any kind."

"That's actually great news," Melissa replied. "Food-motivated dogs are much easier to train than those who won't eat." She thought for a moment. "You know, her disease may be causing some of her issues."

"What do you mean?"

"Dogs that are sick often exhibit behavior problems."

I shook my head in dissent. "I know she's hungry, and she certainly begs, but that's far from our biggest problem. I'm worried about her aggression."

"That's exactly what I mean," Melissa said. "Think about it. How do you act when you're stressed out and hungry?"

I thought back to Martinez's call and the infamous coffee cup incident. I couldn't help but smile.

"I think you get my point," Melissa continued. "All beings are crankier when they don't feel well. Getting Bella healthy may be a huge step in managing her behavior."

We spoke outside for a few more minutes while Melissa continued to bond with Bella. Finally she said, "I think it's OK to go inside your house now. Let's sit down and talk."

Once we were seated, she asked to hold Bella's lead. "Tell me more about Bella's issues."

Melissa pulled out a clipboard and wrote down my description of Bella's behavior. Although she ostensibly listened to me, she closely observed Bella. So far, Alicia was right. Melissa was nothing like Jim, that obnoxious trainer in Snohomish.

"Has Bella ever hurt anyone?" Melissa asked.

I felt my face turn red. "What do you mean?" I knew perfectly well what she meant; I just didn't want to answer. Even hearing the question filled me with dread.

Melissa looked up from her writing. Her expression was serious. "I'm trying to understand the severity of Bella's aggression, and I need you to be honest with me. Has she bitten before? If so, how many times, and how much damage did she do?"

She was asking if Bella was dangerous. This was, of course, the core issue—one I needed to face, whether I wanted to or not. I reflected for a minute, both on my time with Bella and on the stories

George had shared. "I've only had her for a couple of weeks, but she's never bitten that I know of."

"Has she had the opportunity to bite?"

"No," I replied. "I always keep her on leash."

"That's good, but it's not what I'm asking. Has Bella ever gotten close enough to bite?"

I shuddered as I remembered our two closest calls—with Coalie and that awful Trucker Man. "Yes, but she missed. She knocked a guy down once, and I saw her jump on a dog, but she didn't actually bite it."

"Believe me," Melissa countered, "she didn't miss. If a dog wants to bite and is close enough to do so, it bites."

I took a moment to mentally replay Bella's blowups. "She certainly creates a scene, but now that you mention it, I don't think she's ever actually put her teeth on anyone."

"That's a *very* good sign," Melissa replied, smiling. "That means Bella likely hasn't *wanted* to hurt anyone. And that makes all the difference." She put down her pen. "What you've described doesn't sound like aggression to me. I'd call it reactivity."

"Reactivity?"

"Reacting to a stressful situation without trying to do harm. Essentially, Bella's trying to communicate that she's uncomfortable. She's simply doing it in a way we humans consider inappropriate." Melissa nodded her head with confidence. "We can do a lot to help reactive dogs."

My whole body sighed with relief. "You mean there's hope for her?"

"Definitely." Melissa smiled, but her eyes remained sober. "But I have to be honest with you. This is still a serious issue, especially in a dog Bella's size. It's great that she hasn't bitten so far, but that doesn't mean she couldn't be pushed to bite in the future."

I remained silent, listening intently.

"And her issues won't go away overnight. She'll need consistent work and a lifetime of management in certain situations. But with a dedicated owner like you, she *can* get better."

The familiar queasiness in my stomach returned. "She's not my dog, though. I'm just fostering her until I find her a new home."

Melissa remained silent. Her face bore no expression.

"You do think I'll be able to find Bella a new home, don't you?"

Melissa spoke slowly, as if choosing her words carefully. "Stranger things have happened. Bella's a beautiful dog and people love German shepherds." She paused. "But honestly? I don't think you'll find one any time soon."

My throat tightened. "What should I do?"

Melissa's look was grave. "I can't tell you that. You have to decide for yourself, and there's no easy answer here. I've helped lots of dogs like Bella. The process isn't difficult, but it takes time and considerable effort." She laid the clipboard on her lap. "I'm willing to help, but ultimately you have to do the work." She leaned forward. "Are you up for it?"

I considered giving up—but only for a moment. As much as I struggled, as much as I grumbled, I had committed myself to Bella the night I found her owner's body. It was much too late to give up now.

"Yes. Definitely." This time, I didn't fake my confidence.

"Awesome," Melissa replied. "Let's keep going then. As far as you know, has Bella had these issues all her life?"

"Well, yes, but they've been different lately."

"How?"

"She never got along well with other dogs, but as far as I know, she liked men with facial hair until I took her in."

Melissa's brow furrowed. "And you're sure this is new behavior?"

"Yes. At least I think so."

She looked away for a moment, absently rubbing Bella's ears. "This may seem like an odd question, but bear with me." Her eyes met mine. "How do *you* feel about bearded men?"

My expression betrayed me.

"I see." She smiled. "Dogs are incredibly intuitive, you know. Some people even believe they're psychic—that they see images we subconsciously send. I tend to be more pragmatic than that. I think dogs are simply master observers with finely tuned senses. They can smell changes in body chemistry, see slight twinges in body language— even hear subtle differences in breathing. But either way, Bella may be picking up on your feelings."

"*My* feelings?" Had Jim been right, after all? "You mean her behavior is my fault? I really *am* a bad alpha?"

"I didn't say that," Melissa replied emphatically. "And frankly, assigning blame is useless. However I am saying this: we have no way to know what Bella is thinking, but we can't discount what she intuits from you. Look at her."

I glanced at Bella. She sat, on leash, next to Melissa. But she stared intently at me.

"Look how closely she watches you. I don't believe in all that alpha nonsense, but Bella clearly looks to you for guidance. We would be naïve to underestimate the impact of your thoughts on hers."

She had to be kidding me. "Now I have to worry about sending out random psychic images?" I looked down at the floor. "This is too much. I can't do it."

Melissa tolerated no argument. "You're a yoga teacher, right? This should be easy for you. All you have to do is pay attention. Notice how you behave immediately before Bella reacts. Do you tense up? Do you tighten the leash? Perhaps you hold your breath? Whatever you notice will give useful clues.

"As you learn to change *your* reactions, Bella may well change *hers*. In the meantime, we'll practice some simple exercises to help both of you gain some confidence."

Melissa departed ninety minutes later, leaving a very happy Bella, a completely exhausted Kate, and a long list of homework assignments in her wake. Priority number one was perfecting Bella's recall—her willingness to come to me when called. According to Melissa, there was no margin for error. No matter what Bella was doing, no matter what she was after, she had to immediately stop, turn, and come running when I gave the command.

Melissa left with these words: "A solid recall may one day save Bella's life."

TWENTY-FIVE

ANOTHER WEEK PASSED AS I began to reclaim my life. Melissa's homework provided a welcome distraction—the Bella Project. Bella and I spent hours every day practicing, or in Bella-speak, playing. Our games included chicken delight—in which I rapid-fire fed Bella rotisserie chicken every time she looked at another dog—and hide-and-seek. Hide-and-seek was a slight twist on the childhood favorite. I would ask Bella to stay in one location, then I'd "hide" in another. Once in place, I'd release her by yelling, "Bella, come!"

And come she did. She ran at me, full speed, knocking me down several times in the process. Her reward? Several pieces of medium-rare flank steak. Hide-and-seek rapidly became Bella's favorite game, and I became the most popular vegetarian at PhinneyWood Market's free-range deli.

Bella trained, and I waited. I waited for the final, elusive clue that would allow me to solve George's murder. I waited for the day I'd stop missing Michael. I waited for Bella's adoption requests to start pouring in.

I waited in vain.

The three calls I did get about Bella were from crackpots. The first was Trucker Man's evil twin. He wanted an outdoor-only guard dog and hung up as soon as I told him about Bella's illness. The second was willing to overlook Bella's genetic disease—as long as he could still breed her. And although I couldn't prove it, I was pretty sure the third was looking for his next champion fighting dog.

Michael finally stopped calling. His last message couldn't have been clearer. "I guess you're not willing to work this out. Again, I'm sorry. But this is my last call. From here on out, it's up to you."

I decided avoidance was the better part of valor. Instead of returning Michael's calls, I found creative ways to get to the studio without passing by Pete's Pets. I tried and tried again to get my head on straight—to forget about Michael and concentrate on yoga. My teaching was less than inspired. After one particularly lifeless attempt, I overheard a longtime student tell her friend, "Her classes are usually much better than that. Why don't we try the Tuesday instructor instead." I should have been mortified, but honestly, I just didn't care.

Rene finally talked me into meeting her at Mocha Mia, only to harass me mercilessly. I tried to ignore her by inhaling the sweet, steamy aroma of my hazelnut mocha. When that didn't work I stared down at the table, pretending to be mesmerized by the cartoon "coffee buzz" bumblebee printed on my coffee mug. Earplugs would have been much more effective.

"You're being pig-headed, even for you! And don't give me any of that 'What if he dies?' bull crap. That may be true for Bella, but Michael will likely outlive us both." She leaned back and glared, so intent on browbeating me that she hadn't touched her dessert. "Frankly, you're acting like a commitment-phobic little girl, scared of rejection. The first time in years you find a guy who's completely compatible with you, and you bolt at the first tiff."

"Officially, it was our second tiff—and after one date. Not great odds for the future, if you ask me. Why should I waste my time with someone who will inevitably try to control me?" I tried to distract her by threatening her food. "Now, shut up and give me a bite of that brownie."

Rene stopped talking and uncharacteristically pushed over her plate. Her mouth remained blissfully silent, but her eyes practically screamed with concern. At first I ignored her. I chewed and stared hollowly off into space, not even tasting that delicious concoction of chocolate, butter, and confectioner's sugar. I felt strangely disconnected from everything, including myself. My body may have sat next to Rene, but my mind was off wandering, lost in a fog.

But only at first.

As the minutes passed, the fog began to dissipate; shapes became clearer; my heart and my mind reconnected. By the time I pushed away Rene's empty plate, something deep inside me had shifted.

Who knows why? Maybe I was finally ready. Maybe I was moved by Rene's unusual patience. Maybe she laced that chocolate fudge brownie with truth serum. Whatever the reason, when my mind returned, it brought with it unusual clarity. The time had come: I needed to share my secret.

I looked up and met my friend's worried gaze. "We fought the last time I saw him, you know."

"You and Michael? Of course you did. I know that. But what couple doesn't fight? If I had a dollar for every time Sam and I got into an argument—"

"No. I mean Dad and me."

Rene looked confused. "You lost me. I thought we were talking about Michael."

"*You* were," I replied. "I stopped listening twenty minutes ago."

She gave me her trademarked "wounded Rene" look, but remained silent.

Beads of sweat dotted my hairline; my heart raced erratically; for a moment, I even forgot to breathe. I never felt more vulnerable.

Here goes…

Everything.

"Two nights before Dad's heart attack, we had a fight. I'd been dating Jason for about a month—"

"*That* creep. That's one even *I* thought you should dump."

"I know. Everyone saw through him but me. I fell head over heels." I smiled ruefully. "Dad was the worst, though. He loathed Jason, and he made no secret of it. That was bad enough, but he finally went too far. He ran a background check."

"Uh-oh."

"Doing that was over the top, even for Dad. I was beyond furious. Even worse, he was right. Turned out Jason had a record. Nothing violent, just slimy: a conviction for check fraud and a DUI. The kicker, though, was that Jason was dumb enough to get arrested not once, but twice for soliciting a prostitute—once while he and I were dating."

Rene shuddered and pretended to gag.

"I should have been mad at Jason for being such a pig or even at myself for being so stupid. But I wasn't. I was *furious* at Dad for meddling in my life." My throat tightened. "It certainly wasn't the first time Dad and I fought, but it was the last."

Rene grabbed my hand. "I'm so sorry, sweetie."

"Yeah, me too. The kicker was that I calmed down a couple of days later. I was planning to apologize. But before I could, I got the call from the hospital—"

"Oh, Kate, honey, you can't possibly think you caused that heart attack."

I shook my head. "No, a blood clot in Dad's coronary artery did that. I'm sure the stress of our fight didn't help any, but it wasn't the cause."

Rene looked confused. "Then what? What aren't you saying?"

I held back a guilt-ridden, terrified sob. Rene was my best friend—in many ways, my only *true* friend. What if she hated me after I told her? What would I do if she left me too?

"You don't know how bad it was, Rene. How bad *I* was. Dad and I fought a lot, but never like this. Right before I stormed out the door, I told him to get out of my life—and to stay out for good." Tears threatened my eyes. "And I never got a chance to take it back. I never told him what a great father he was. I never even told him how much I loved him. His last image of me was my butt with a door slamming behind it." I finally broke down, quietly sobbing.

Rene grabbed my shoulders and forced me to look at her. I'd never seen her so earnest. "Kate, you listen to me, and you listen good. Your father knew how you felt. You two fought all the time, but it always blew over. You adored him, and everyone, including your father, knew it. Don't you *ever* doubt that." She pointed to the ceiling. "If there's a heaven up there, your father is looking down at us right now, and he's furious at you for wasting even one single second on this guilt trip."

I hesitated, afraid to ask. "So you don't think I'm a horrible person?"

Rene's shocked expression admonished me. "Don't be ridiculous, Kate. Of course not. And neither did your father. If he were here, he'd say, 'Kate-girl, you knock off that pity-party this instant. I didn't raise some guilt-ridden Catholic school girl. I raised an intelligent, confident, resilient woman. Now act like one!'"

I could almost hear my father in Rene's voice. For the first time in two years, I even sensed his presence. I felt lighter, brighter somehow, as if a leaden trench coat had been lifted from my shoulders. And suddenly I knew: my father's spirit had never truly left me. I'd simply been too ashamed to let him in.

Confessing my guilt somehow extinguished its power. I was like a child who'd finally shone a flashlight under her bed, only to discover that the scary monster had been just a big dust bunny all along. For the first time since my father's death, I found my missing piece. For the first time in two years, I felt—whole.

I dabbed the napkin at my eyes. "That does sound like one of his tirades."

"You bet it does. I didn't spend every Saturday at your house and not pick up on a thing or two." She paused. "Is this why you've been obsessing about your friend's murder? Are you trying to make up for some overblown mishap with your father?"

I'd wondered that myself but had no answers. "Honestly, Rene, I don't know. In some ways, this situation feels so familiar. In others, it's completely different. But I can't stop thinking about George's death. I have to know what happened."

Rene squeezed my hands. "Kate, you know I'd do anything for you. All you have to do is ask."

I had no qualms about taking Rene up on her offer; I just didn't know how she could help. My head swam, and it had been swimming for days. The answer was there, hovering barely out of reach. It was like having all the pieces of a jigsaw puzzle, but no photo or form to guide its construction. I needed context. I needed perspective.

Perhaps she could help after all.

"Can you come over tonight?"

We agreed to meet at my house at seven o'clock. Before then, I had one more task. Even Nancy Drew needed a sidekick, right? And the past few weeks proved one thing for certain: I was no Nancy Drew.

I needed two.

The phone rang three times. I was about to hang up when I heard a welcome voice on the line. "Pete's Pets, how can I help you?"

"Michael, it's Kate. I need your help."

TWENTY-SIX

At seven o'clock I was nervous. By seven-fifteen I was two minutes away from a full-blown panic attack. Butterflies didn't just flutter in my stomach, they did the mambo. Even Bella looked concerned. I hadn't seen Michael in almost two weeks. What if he'd gotten over me? What if he was dating Tiffany? What if he'd grown back that god-awful beard? Rene plied me with alcohol and tried to bolster my confidence.

The doorbell finally rang at seven-twenty. "Hi, stranger," I said, not quite meeting Michael's gaze.

"Hi yourself," he replied. His tone was civil but distant. No mischievous wrinkles softened his eyes. Michael and I may have negotiated a temporary cease-fire, but a permanent peace treaty was far from certain.

We walked into the living room. "I'd introduce you, but I think you two have already met," I said, smirking at Rene.

I should have known better than to tease her. In Rene's world, I had just declared war. She ignored my sarcasm and greeted Michael with a great big hug. Her eyes sparkled with good-natured malice as she looked him up and down, appraisingly. "Kate's right, you know. You look *gorgeous* without that beard." She cemented her victory by claiming the room's only chair.

Michael and I sat on opposite ends of the couch, leaving a full cushion's width between us. I hid my tomato-red face by pretending to study the bottom of my wine glass—not that anyone noticed. Michael and Rene were too busy teasing each other about facial hair, fake cats, and early morning wake-up calls to pay attention to me. Bella, the traitor, joyfully alternated between begging Michael for treats and rubbing fur all over Rene's tights.

At least someone was having a good time.

In spite of my grumpy embarrassment, I couldn't help but smile. I'd lived in that house for most of my life, but it had never felt more like home. I sipped my wine and watched them playfully banter away the room's tension. Several drinks and a few dog cookies later, we all sat together in companionable silence.

I wanted to repair my rift with Michael, but that would have to wait. Instead, I jumped into the evening's stated agenda. "I can't figure out where I'm going wrong. Someone obviously thinks I'm close to solving George's murder, but I have no idea why. As far as I can tell, everything I've come up with so far has been a dead end."

"Maybe brainstorming a list of suspects would help," Rene offered.

I pulled out a notebook. "It certainly can't hurt. Let's start with the obvious. The murderer could have been someone from George's past. The police say George's old business partner, Robert, has an alibi, but he could have hired a hit man."

"I doubt it," Michael replied. "What kind of hit man bashes his target over the head? Besides, a professional killer wouldn't waste time threatening you, Kate. He'd either get out of town or make you his next victim."

"You have a point," I conceded. "But Robert might have involved someone who wasn't a professional. He still has motive. We simply don't know the means or opportunity yet."

"But what's his connection to you?" Rene asked.

"What do you mean?"

"You've never met this guy. You don't even know his last name. So why would he leave you that note?"

I thought for a moment. "Sarah could have told him about me. She got pretty cagey when I asked about him."

Rene disagreed. "Sounds too convoluted to me. According to that theory, at least three people were involved in George's death—Sarah, Robert, and the murderer." She shook her head. "You're reaching, Kate."

She was right. "OK, scratch Robert." I drew a line through his name. "How about someone George knew through *Dollars for Change*? Tali was furious that day I went back to the office."

Rene absently rubbed Bella's ears. "Well, you *did* lie to her. I'd be angry too. Besides, what motive would Tali have?"

"Just because we don't know the motive doesn't mean there isn't one. I think Tali should stay on the list." I put a question mark next to her name. "She's local, she knew I was asking questions about George, and I told her where I work. She's at least good for the rock through my window." I took a sip of wine. "For that matter, lots of people at *Dollars for Change* know I've been looking into this. I haven't exactly kept it a secret. What about that Surfer-Dude guy?"

Michael frowned. "I'm sure dozens of people knew George. But we won't get anywhere if we list every homeless person in Seattle. Did anyone you interviewed stand out?"

My stomach dropped to my knees. "No, no one," I quickly replied. I had no intention of telling Michael about Charlie's and my trip to Woodland Park, especially since it ended up being a dead end. Michael had barely gotten over the rock through my window. If I told him about my close call with Charlie, his head might explode.

I avoided eye contact and pretended to think. My quiet subterfuge didn't fool anyone—least of all Michael. His facial expression morphed through multiple emotions, from suspicion, to anger, to worry, to frustration. It finally settled on resignation.

"Fine," he said drolly. "Have it your way. No one stood out. But then what about you, Kate?"

"What about me?"

"If we're going to suspect everyone George knew, you should be at the top of the list. After all, we *know* you have a violent temper."

I leaned over and punched him in the arm. "Keep it up, funny man." I reluctantly crossed out Tali's name. "You do have a point, though. Most people would never kill without a compelling reason. A killer has to be either highly motivated or insane, especially if the murder is premeditated. Tali and Surfer Dude didn't seem either." I paused a moment, thinking. "But Bella's old owner might be. I think we should add him to the list."

"Why him?" asked Rene.

"He's obviously violent; my arm had the bruises to prove it. And his wife's face looked like a punching bag. I may not be able to *prove* that Trucker Man beat her, but I'd be willing to bet the rest of my savings on it."

Rene looked skeptical. "But what motive would he have to kill George? Did he even know him?"

"I didn't think so at first, but I'm beginning to wonder. When I took Bella to Trucker Man's house, he mentioned that the "bum" who stole her should have stuck to selling newspapers. At the time, I assumed Betty had told him about George, but now I'm not so sure."

Rene leaned forward. "Why not? Betty must have spoken with him. After all, she gave him your phone number."

"Yes, but I was deliberately vague with Betty about Bella's history. I know I told her George was homeless, but I don't think I said anything about *Dollars for Change*. So how did Trucker Man know George sold newspapers?

I looked at Bella's puppy collar lying on the mantle. "And the whole blackmail angle has always bothered me. I couldn't believe George would do something so cruel. But George was fiercely protective of Bella. I never understood how he felt until I met with that awful trainer, Jim." I suppressed a shudder. "I almost electrocuted Jim with his own shock collar, and he never even touched Bella. Can you imagine what George must have wanted to do to Trucker man? He would have felt justified, righteous even, extorting money from that monster."

"Maybe, but—" Rene tried to interrupt, but I was on a roll.

"And my Trucker Man theory explains George's missing time. Trucker man lives thirty miles from Seattle and almost forty miles from Sarah. Traveling that distance without a car can't be simple, especially with a dog as scary-looking as Bella. George could easily have spent several days getting back and forth."

Michael took over Rene's role as devil's advocate. "But what about the note in your car?"

"Trucker Man could have thrown that rock. Betty told him where I worked, and he knew my car. I drove it to his house."

"When was the last time you talked to this guy?" Michael asked.

I didn't have to look at my calendar; that morning was indelibly printed on my memory. "Over two weeks ago. The Tuesday after our date."

"Did you talk about George's murder?"

I hesitated. "Well, no, we were focused on Bella."

"That's what I thought. But then, why would he feel threatened enough to risk vandalizing your car?"

Damn. The familiar dull throbbing behind my eyes returned. "You're right." I sighed. "The problem is *nothing* makes sense. I've been thinking about this for weeks now, but I keep spinning in circles." I tossed my notebook on the coffee table in frustration.

Rene stood up and handed it right back to me. "Don't give up so easily, we're just getting started." She refilled her wine glass. "What about George's daughter?"

I hesitated. "I'm conflicted about her."

"How?"

"Well, Sarah hated her father, and both she and her husband seemed capable of violence, given the right provocation. Plus, I'm not fully convinced of their joint alibi the night of the murder." I shook my head, frowning. "But they don't feel right to me."

Rene looked at me, puzzled. "They have motive, means, and opportunity. What am I missing?"

"George felt horrible about how he hurt his family. He never would have blackmailed Sarah."

"What if you've got the whole blackmail angle wrong?" Michael interjected. "You're putting a lot of weight on that one woman's word. And even if George was blackmailing someone, that person isn't necessarily the killer. Let's set extortion aside for a moment. Who else has motive?"

We all three stared at each other in silence.

Finally, Rene spoke. "You know, even without blackmail, money may still be involved. We know George asked his daughter for money. What if he asked his ex-wife as well? Can you imagine how angry she would have been? If Sam ever deserted me, I wouldn't even wait for him to ask for a handout. I'd kill him on the spot."

"Perhaps at the time, but several years later?"

"Even then. Some wounds cut too deep."

I sighed in frustration. "To tell you the truth, Rene, I'd love to question George's ex-wife, but I have no idea how to reach her. George told me she moved to Denver, but I don't know when. She might not even live there anymore." I shrugged. "Besides, I don't know her name. George's last name was Levin, but I doubt she kept it after the divorce."

"Think, Kate," Rene said. "Did George tell you anything else about her?"

I thought for a moment, but came up blank. "Other than that she divorced him and moved to Denver, nothing. George was a talker, but he didn't share much about his family." I flashed on the family picture in George's gym bag. "I suppose thinking about them made him too sad."

In my mind, I turned the photo over and examined George's careful handwriting. "Sarah, Maddie, and me—Cannon Beach, 1995."

I shrugged. "I don't know if this helps or not, but his wife might go by Maddie."

Michael perked up. "Of course that helps. That's all we need!"

Rene and I stared at him, bewildered.

"Seriously. Haven't you two ever heard of the Internet?"

The three of us moved to my office, Bella trailing close behind. Rene and I huddled behind Michael as he tapped at the keyboard. "How do you spell George's last name?"

"L-e-v-i-n, but that won't help. His wife has remarried."

"Doesn't matter. It gives us a start." He typed it in. "And you say she goes by Maddie?"

I envisioned the picture again. "I think so, yes."

"Let's hope we get lucky." Michael stared at the screen. "OK. I see a few Levins here with the first initial M." He ran the cursor down the screen as he continued reading. "Here's a possibility: a Madeleine Levin who has lived in both Seattle and Denver."

Perhaps my trip to Woodland Park hadn't been so worthless, after all. I pointed to the screen. "That must be her! What's her phone number?"

"Sorry, Kate, this site only lists names."

My heart sank. "How does that help us, then? I doubt her last name is Levin anymore."

"Maybe not," Michael replied, "but the site lists all of her legal names. According to this, she's used two last names: Levin and Yeates."

"Wouldn't Yeates be her maiden name?"

"I don't think this database goes back that far. I'm not positive, of course, but chances are good that Yeates is her new last name." He clicked the mouse and leaned back in his chair. "Do you want me to order a full background check?"

I wavered, suddenly feeling unclean. I'd been furious with my father for checking up on Jason—livid even. And like me, Dad had the best of intentions. I flashed on an image of my mug shot with the word "HYPOCRITE" stamped diagonally across it in bold red letters.

"I don't know. Ordering a background check seems pretty invasive."

"Well, if all you want is a phone number, we can try something else first." Michael typed some more, then tapped the screen with his fingertip, smiling. "We might be in luck. There are only seven listings with the last name of Yeates in Denver. None of them may be her, but we can at least try." He cracked his knuckles. "Shall we get started?"

I looked at the clock. Almost nine o'clock. I was exhausted, and I still had one very important conversation ahead of me. "Not yet. I need to come up with a cover story. We've done enough for tonight." While Michael printed out the list of phone numbers, I handed Rene her coat. "Weren't you just leaving?"

"How's that for gratitude?" Rene took her jacket and walked to the front door—alone. Michael and I stood frozen in place. "Don't worry," she quipped. "I'll see myself out. But you two had better make up, or you'll have me to contend with." She paused, then ran back, gave me a hug, and whispered, "Don't worry, you'll be fine."

I hoped she was right.

Michael and I sat on opposite ends of the couch again, oddly uncomfortable now that Rene was gone.

"So," I began.

"So," he replied.

More silence. Michael stuck by his final phone message. Throwing out the first olive branch would be up to me. I hugged a throw pillow to my chest, as if holding it could somehow make me less vulnerable.

"I'm sorry, Michael. I know I overreacted. Truth is, I've never been very good at taking orders. That's not a good excuse, but it's an honest one. I know we can't pretend the last two weeks didn't happen, but can we at least give our relationship another try?"

Michael's face turned serious. "To be honest, I don't blame you for getting angry. I was out of line. But I *do* blame you for not returning my calls. I tried to apologize for days, and you ignored me.

You acted like I was disposable. That was beyond anger, Kate. It was selfish and insensitive."

His words hit me like a punch in the gut, even more painful because they were true.

"We'll have fights," Michael continued. "Every couple fights. But if you're going to cut and run every time we disagree, we don't stand a chance."

For once, I didn't argue. I stared down at my hands, trying to scrape together the courage to reply. My words, when I found them, sounded inadequate. "I don't even know what to say, Michael. You're right. I behaved terribly." I looked up to meet his eyes. "I had reasons, but they weren't very good ones, and I'm not sure they even matter anymore. But I will say this: You are not disposable, and I won't shut you out again. I'm a slow learner, but I promise you, I do learn."

Michael looked skeptical, so I pulled out my secret weapon. "Besides, look at Bella. Don't we owe it to her to try again?" Bella sat between us, obviously concerned about the rift in her pack. She closely monitored our conversation, peering left and right, as if watching a tennis ball in the championship match at Wimbledon.

Michael burst out laughing. "Come here, girl." Bella broke her stare and moved next to him. He leaned down and affectionately scratched her throat. "So you think I should give this spitfire another chance, do you?"

Bella remained silent, but her eyes clearly said yes. Michael looked up and grinned. "How can anyone say no to a creature this beautiful?"

"Do you mean me or the dog?"

"On that, my love, I plead the fifth." Michael ducked just in time. My pillow barely missed his head. They don't call them "throw pillows" for nothing. "Yes, I'd like to try again," he said. "You know I would."

Michael stood, melting me with those smoldering blue-green eyes. I closed my eyes and waited, fully expecting him to close the distance between us, draw me into his arms, and start the "oh so fun" make-up process Alicia had promised.

The sound of rustling fabric and an opening zipper caught my attention—from across the room. I opened my eyes again, confused. Michael stood near the door, holding his jacket. Was he leaving? Admittedly, Alicia hadn't been specific. But somehow I didn't think waving goodbye was the fun between lovers she'd had in mind.

He pulled a thick white envelope from his pocket. "I have something for you."

The envelope was full of cash. Fives, tens, twenties, even a couple of fifties.

"What's this?"

"If you'd come by the store in the last two weeks you'd know. We started a collection for Bella. My customers were really moved by her story—especially how you basically paid ransom to keep her away from that abusive jerk. There's over $850 in there. I know it doesn't cover everything you've spent so far, but it's a start."

I didn't want to cry, but I felt a lump in my throat all the same. "You did this for me, even though I refused to speak with you?"

"For you and for Bella."

"Why?"

"In spite of your recent experiences, dog owners are usually pretty decent people. So are pet store owners. So, I have heard, are yoga teachers." He paused a beat. "But the jury's still out on that one." He smiled.

I smiled back. I didn't feel like crying anymore. I crooked my finger, beckoning him closer. "Come here, boy. You've been *very* good. And you deserve a treat."

Bella sighed as I stood and wrapped my arms around Michael's neck. All three of us knew she'd be sleeping on the floor again that night.

TWENTY-SEVEN

"I've missed our sessions," Alicia said as we walked into the studio the next morning. She looked good—better than she'd looked in a long time. Rosy cheeks, sparkling eyes, animated step. Something definitely agreed with her.

"I've missed you, too, Alicia. I have to say, though, you look great!"

"I'm done with this round of chemo, and I'm starting to feel like myself again—for now, anyway." She rolled out her mat and sat on the floor. "I'm scheduled for another set of scans next week, but hopefully the new protocol worked and I'll be in remission." She knocked on the hardwood floor. "Until then, I'm footloose and fancy-free."

I smiled and sat next to her.

"But how are you doing, Miss Kate? I've been worried about you. You were so upset at our last appointment—then you disappeared."

I'd canceled our appointments during my two-week funk. At the time, I couldn't face Alicia's inevitable questions about Michael, but now I owed her an explanation. A two-week break might not have been long with an ordinary client, but in Alicia's circumstances, every day was precious.

"I'm so sorry," I said. "I've been having some personal issues lately, and I wasn't much good to anyone, including myself. But canceling that way was selfish. I won't do it again."

Alicia smiled. "Well, you're certainly allowed to take a day off every now and again. But honestly, Jake and I were getting worried. We both thought you were too caught up in that murder investigation. I'm so glad you've dropped that now."

I didn't contradict her. Instead, I asked her to close her eyes and settle into her practice.

"Notice where your body touches the earth, and imagine that you are rooted through that connection. As you inhale, expand your ribs and extend the crown of your head toward the sky. As you exhale—"

Alicia's eyes popped open.

"Hey, whatever happened with your boyfriend?"

I laughed at the sudden change of topic. If nothing else, my sessions with Alicia were consistently unpredictable.

"We're doing much better now, thanks. You were right, by the way. Michael and I kissed and made up." I felt myself blush. "I'm kind of embarrassed, though. I never thought some silly argument —with a boy of all things—could affect me so much."

Alicia grinned. "I know what you mean. Jake and I have certainly had our share of fights. We even considered separating for a while. But luckily, those days are long behind us." She looked away for a moment, idly playing with her wedding ring. When she looked back, her eyes held back tears. "To be honest, I don't know what I'd do without Jake. He's been so wonderful since I got sick. This may sound odd, but in a way my illness has been a gift. Learning that I might die was a real wake-up call for Jake. He's kinder now, more considerate. More willing to work on our relationship."

That didn't sound like the Jake I knew. Perhaps I had misjudged him.

Alicia continued, "Our marriage vows said 'for better or worse.' Poor Jake definitely got the worse." Her expression turned wistful. "I just wish he could spend more time at home. I hardly ever see him anymore."

I wondered how much time Jake spent flirting with his female tenants, but I kept that thought to myself.

Alicia playfully shook her finger at me. "As for you, young lady, it's about time you got your priorities in order. Relationships are important. Playing amateur detective is not. I'm so glad you took my advice and gave up trying to solve that murder."

I didn't want to quarrel, but I couldn't continue deceiving her. "I haven't given up, Alicia. If anything, I'm reinvigorated."

Alicia's expression turned uncharacteristically cross. "Oh, Kate, whatever are you thinking? You're normally so level-headed. This nonsense is completely unlike you!"

"But I know I'm on to something! I have to be close. Someone even left me a threatening note!" I raised my voice, as if speaking louder would make my words more compelling. "And you know me; I'm stubborn as a mule. Once I get my mind set on something, I don't give up until it's done."

Alicia's cheeks changed from light pink to red—blood red. She stood up from her mat and clenched her jaw. "Kate, let me be frank," she said, sternly crossing her arms. "You're acting like a fool."

I winced, but gave no other reply. I just stared up at her, stunned. In the two years I'd known Alicia, I'd never seen her get angry. At least not until today.

Time seemed to stand still as Alicia towered over me, right eyelid twitching involuntarily. I leaned back and braced myself, waiting for her to explode.

Finally, she blinked, as if coming out of a trance. The color left her cheeks as rapidly as it had come. "I'm so sorry," she said, softening her tone. "But I'm really worried about you." She kneeled next to me and pleaded. "Please, *please* let this go. It won't end well; it *can't* end well. At best, you're wrong, and you're wasting time and energy you can't afford. At worst, you're right. Then you might get hurt, or worse. And for what? No matter what you do, no matter how hard you try, you won't bring your friend back."

Her reaction surprised me. The Alicia I knew had never walked away from a challenge. But then again, who was I to judge? Each day she fought a battle more terrifying than anything I'd faced in my entire life. Maybe solving the riddle of another man's death seemed inconsequential when you were trying so desperately to prevent your own. Maybe in the process of dying, she had learned some lesson on life balance I had yet to understand.

Then again, maybe she was pissed at me for canceling her last two appointments.

In that moment, I understood my mistake. I had blurred the student-teacher boundary with Alicia yet again. Our time together was supposed to be about her, not me.

"I'm sorry, Alicia. You're probably right. And in any case, we're not here to talk about me." I looked at my watch. "Let's start your practice. Do you want to work more strongly today?"

Alicia didn't want to change the subject, but she acquiesced. When we finished our gentle flow sequence, her breath sounded strong, vital, and deep. She finished sitting upright, to maintain the energy she'd worked so hard to build.

I rang the chimes, indicating it was time to come out of meditation. She sighed, smiled, and opened her eyes. But instead of finishing with our normal "Namaste," she placed her hand on my arm. "Kate, I'm sorry for being so short with you earlier. I don't know what came over me. I *am* concerned about you, but that's no reason to get angry. I must be more worried about those scans next week than I thought."

I smiled. "Don't worry about it. You may well be right."

"So you'll drop the case?"

I didn't answer right away. Lying to her would be wrong, but refueling her irritation would be worse. In the end, I compromised. "I'll think about it, I promise."

I didn't break that promise, I swear. I took a full thirty seconds to carefully consider Alicia's advice.

Then I chose to completely ignore it.

TWENTY-EIGHT

I CLOSED THE DOOR behind Alicia, double-checked the lock, then moved to the desk to review my notes and gather my wits.

Whose crazy idea was this, anyway?

Playing the role of "Kate, the yoga teacher" was hard enough. Pretending to be someone else seemed virtually impossible. If I thought about my planned deception too much, I'd freeze with stage fright. So I didn't give myself time to think. I wiped my sweat-drenched palms on my pants, picked up the phone, and started dialing. The first two calls went to voice mail. The third was a wrong number; the fourth, disconnected. On the fifth, I got lucky.

"Hello, may I speak to Madeleine Yeates?"

"Who am I speaking with?" Her voice sounded slightly irritated, like someone about to hang up on a telemarketer.

I smiled and hoped my voice was engaging. "My name's Jessica Oppenheimer. But don't worry, I'm not trying to sell you anything. I'm a writer for *Seattle Life Magazine*."

"I'm Madeleine. What can I do for you?" She still sounded suspicious.

"Are you the Madeleine Yeates that was married to George Levin?"

"Yes, but we divorced years ago. What's that got to do with a magazine?"

My pretend smile morphed into a huge, excited grin. I'd found her! I held back a one-sided high five and forced my voice to stay calm.

"I'm writing a human interest story on the ups and downs of the Seattle high-tech industry. Sort of a 'rags to riches, riches to rags' piece. I'm particularly interested in telling Mr. Levin's story, since it ended so tragically." I lowered my voice and whispered, as if telling a secret. "Are you aware that he was recently killed?"

"Yes," she said warily, "but I'm not sure I want to talk about that, especially with a reporter. This has been a very hard time for my family."

"I understand, and I promise to only take a few minutes of your time. In fact, we don't need to talk about your husband's death at all. I'd actually like to learn more about his life—specifically about the company he formed while you were married."

"That's *ex-husband*. We were divorced, remember?" She didn't wait for a reply. "I don't think I can help you. I wasn't involved in the day-to-day operations."

"I don't need specific details about how he ran the business, Mrs. Yeates," I assured her. "I'm more interested in the human aspect of Mr. Levin's story. How a man who was focused, intelligent, and dedicated enough to build a company from scratch ended up living on the street. I hope my story will illustrate how quickly life can change. One spate of bad luck, one uninsured illness, one accident—poverty and homelessness could happen to any of us."

After several seconds of silence, I heard the click of a lighter and Madeleine's deep inhale. "The human aspect, you say." Her tone softened. I felt her resistance dissipate, dissolving like the curly wisps of smoke from her cigarette. "Well, here's something you can put in your article. George was a good man, with a good heart. He'd been on the street for a long time, but he was about to turn his life around. If he hadn't been killed, things might have ended very differently for him."

I sat up straight, paying close attention. "You'd spoken to him recently?"

"Yes, twice, actually. The first time was the Friday before his death. He told me he'd just come off a three-day bender, but that it would be his last." She paused. "And you know what? I believed him."

George's missing days. That's how he spent them—drunk in an alley somewhere. I didn't know which to feel: elated that I'd finally solved that part of the puzzle or heartbroken that George's last actions had been so predictably self-destructive.

Madeleine's voice grew pensive. "George wanted to get in touch with our daughter. In hindsight, I never should have told him where she lived. It was unfair of him to just show up on her doorstep after all that time…"

"How long had it been?"

"Years. George left when Sarah was thirteen. It scarred her, in so many ways. I've tried to get her into counseling, but she's as stubborn as her father." Madeleine took another long drag on her cigarette. "I hoped that if George apologized and came back into her life, Sarah could finally heal."

I didn't know what to say, so I remained silent. At least five awkward seconds passed before she continued.

"I don't know why I'm telling you all this. You're a complete stranger—a reporter, no less."

"Don't worry, Mrs. Yeates. I won't print anything about you or your daughter." I smiled at the irony. In the midst of my subterfuge, I could still offer one piece of truth.

"Thank you." Her voice sounded sad. "Honestly, I feel a little guilty. I had no idea George was looking for money. If I'd known, I would have given it to him myself—anything to keep Sarah from getting hurt again. But he never asked. I suppose he didn't want to make waves with my husband."

"You said he contacted you again?"

"Yes, two days later, shortly after he saw Sarah. Their meeting didn't go well. Sarah's reaction was a real wake-up call for George. He called to say he was sorry for all of the heartache he'd caused, for both of us. He said he'd make it up to us one day..." Her voice trailed off.

Make it up to them? Could George have been trying to reconcile? "Sounds like maybe he wanted to get back together."

"It's a little late for that now. I'm remarried."

I thought of the happy-looking family in George's photo. "That wouldn't necessarily keep him from trying."

"A different man maybe, but not George. George wasn't exactly a fighter." Madeleine paused. "I think he wanted forgiveness—to know that I didn't hate him."

"I'm so sorry." The words weren't enough, but they were all that I had.

"Me too. I'm just grateful that I had a chance to give it to him."

Madeleine wasn't exactly the raving lunatic I'd hoped for in a murder suspect. She still cared about George—too much to have hurt him. Our conversation was one more dead end in a series of failures. I should have been disappointed, but honestly, I felt relieved. Before he died, George had made peace with at least one of his loved ones. That had to count for something.

"Do you know if Mr. Levin contacted anyone else?"

"I'm sorry. Other than Sarah and me, I have no idea."

That wasn't the answer I wanted. "Perhaps someone who wasn't as compassionate as you? Maybe an investor or partner who was still angry about the business?"

"I don't think you understand," Madeleine replied. "The only person still upset about that business was George. He took that failure harder than anyone. I don't know if you were around Seattle back then, but dot coms started and folded all the time. Investing in one was like buying a lottery ticket. You crossed your fingers and hoped to win big. And a very few people did—make it big, that is. Most, however, were lucky to get part of their original investment back. George's investors knew the risks. They only gambled with money they could afford to lose."

I stood up and paced, nervously playing with the phone cord. I had to be missing something. "What about his employees?"

Madeleine laughed, but without humor. "Sure, they were upset at first, but then they moved on to the next big idea. Everybody moved on but George. He blamed himself way too much. That's probably why he turned to alcohol in the first place. He couldn't take the weight of all that responsibility anymore."

I could practically feel my last lead slip through my fingers. Out of sheer desperation, I tried one final maneuver. "That's very understanding of you. But I'm betting not everyone felt the same way. One of my sources said that George's business partner was pretty upset at the time. I know I'd have a hard time letting go if someone betrayed me that way."

Madeleine's friendly tone vanished. "Don't be ridiculous. No one betrayed anyone. And what's that got to do with your story, anyway?"

I backpedaled quickly, hoping to avoid yet another dial tone. "I'm sorry if I've upset you, Mrs. Yeates. I'm just trying to understand the pressures George faced—pressures that may have ultimately led to his demise."

"Well, scratch Robert off your list. I don't think George felt too badly about him, in the end. Robert may have lost money, but he ultimately got what he wanted."

"What was that?"

"Me. Robert is my second husband."

———

We spoke for about ten more minutes, but the conversation felt more and more like a dead end. Madeleine wasn't my killer, and try as I might, I couldn't get her to name any other suspects. She promised to have Robert give me a call, but I suspected my conversation with him would be equally fruitless. Robert had an alibi. Unless he had an accomplice, he couldn't have committed murder from nearly a half continent away. George's life story was certainly tragic, but it didn't contain any rage-filled enemies lying in wait for the opportunity to strike.

I felt more frustrated than ever. Almost four weeks had passed since George's death, and I wasn't any closer to solving the mystery than when I started. No matter who I questioned, no matter how hard I thought, I still ended up in the same place. Nowhere.

So I decided to stop thinking and clear my mind. My yoga practice was slow and gentle, focused on linking movement and breath. Forty-five minutes later, I rested in Savasana, hoping meditation would quiet my chatterbox brain. It worked, to a point. My mind was quiet, but definitely not still. Instead of listening to a barrage of random thoughts, I was besieged by a dizzying tornado of interconnected images.

First I saw Sarah's beet-red angry face, then mud splashed in all directions as Bella knocked Trucker Man to the ground. Detective Henderson arrived next—the saliva in his beard reflecting the police car's flashing lights, followed by George's broken skull lying in an ever-expanding pool of blood. Rene's Ralphie appeared, complete with his ridiculous ponytail, right before I saw Tiffany and her too-tight jeans, Charlie's beard, and George's gym bag. Next were my broken car window and Jake angrily hiding under the desk at Pete's Pets. I even saw Momma Bird's crazy pink flamingo hat.

The murderer had to be someone I'd spoken with. Someone George would meet in that parking lot. Someone who knew enough about me to know that I posed a threat. Someone who—

I sat straight up and opened my eyes. I knew exactly who'd killed George. I even thought I knew why. I'd figure out how to prove it later, but first I had a more important priority. My prenatal class started in fifteen minutes, so I pulled out a phone book and dialed the first listing.

"AAA Lock and Key. How can I help you?"

TWENTY-NINE

I SCHEDULED A LOCKSMITH for early the next morning. Sixty minutes later, my prenatal students lifted their hips to the sky while pressing hands and heels to the ground in a final Downward Dog.

"This feels delicious," one of them groaned. Downward Dog was always a favorite of the prenatal crowd. The inverted position stretched the backs of mom's legs, released baby's weight from her back, and gave her a few treasured, ache-free moments.

"Can't we stay here all night?" another interjected.

I smiled. Yoga is ideally practiced in silence, but this group of future moms liked to chat: before, after, and especially *during* class.

After resting on their sides in a modified Savasana, the moms-to-be slowly lumbered to their feet and began putting away the myriad of yoga props needed to support pregnant bodies: blocks, straps, blankets, bolsters, and yoga mats.

"Great class tonight, Kate."

"My back feels so much better."

"I think my ankles are even less swollen."

Jenny gave me a big hug. "See you next week, Kate. You know, I might survive this pregnancy yet."

I ushered the final straggling students out the front door, double-checked the lock, and grabbed Bella's leash for our evening cleanup ritual. Three steps into the yoga room, I saw it: Jenny's purse, sitting on top of the yoga mats. I couldn't help but chuckle. If Jenny *did* survive the pregnancy, I'd have to keep a close eye on her in Mommy and Me. She might forget the baby.

Still laughing, I slipped on my shoes and went out the back door to get Bella from the car. I snapped on her leash. "Come on, pup. You've been stuck in here long enough."

Bella and I opened the back entrance to the sound of knocking at the front. *At least Jenny didn't get all the way home this time.*

Bella burst into action, barking and lunging, faithfully protecting her studio from evil yoga student intruders. "Hang on a second, Jenny!" I yelled. "I'll put the dog away and be right there!" I slipped off my shoes again, dragged the scratching, snarling dog to the bathroom, and jogged back to grab Jenny's purse.

I should have listened to Bella.

By the time I reached the lobby, Jake stood inside, smiling and jangling his keys. I pasted on a fake smile.

"Hi, Jake. What are you doing here?"

"I thought I'd stop by to check on the lights."

My stomach dropped to my toes. I hadn't complained about the lights in over two weeks. My words sounded forced, even to me. "Oh, well, you know…I think they're fixed now. Really…they haven't given me any trouble in days."

Timing is everything. As if on cue, those bulbs started flickering like bizarre strobe lights. From light to black and back again, freezing every movement in an erratic series of freeze frames.

Jake's eyes locked with mine in sudden understanding. His right upper lip lifted in an evil grin as he reached back and easily locked my finicky door—the same door I'd been struggling with for weeks. As for that damned pepper stray, it nestled next to my billfold, deep inside my purse—which was safely locked in the filing cabinet.

If there truly was a God up there watching, he had one sadistic sense of humor.

Jake pulled out a revolver and pointed it at my chest.

"Go into the yoga room, Kate. *Now.*"

I tried to obey, but my feet were frozen to the carpet.

Jake touched the gun to my sternum.

"Move."

I moved.

As we backed past the "No Shoes Allowed" sign, panic bubbled up in misplaced hysteria. I burst into giggles. "Sorry, Jake, you'll have to take off your boots."

Jake wasn't amused. "I wouldn't be laughing if I were you." He closed the yoga room door behind us. "How did you figure it out?" His face betrayed nothing more than a sense of idle curiosity.

My only hope was to keep him talking. "It was three things, really. First, I couldn't figure out who George would meet in the parking lot, of all places. George never stayed near the studio at night. The murderer had to be familiar with the area." I backed cautiously away from Jake, glancing left and right, looking for something, *anything*, to distract him.

"Second, I couldn't fathom why George would leave Bella trapped in her crate alone. Everybody else dismissed it, but I knew he locked her up for a reason. At first I thought he was protecting her. But it finally occurred to me—maybe the murderer insisted. Maybe the murderer was afraid of her."

Bella barked louder as she frantically tried to claw her way out of the bathroom.

"But ultimately, Bella convinced me. She always liked people before George was killed. I couldn't figure out why that changed. For a while I even blamed myself. But it finally clicked. She doesn't like a lot of men these days, but she *really* hates you."

"That stupid dog. As soon as I get done taking care of you, she's next."

My mouth went dry. Of course. *He'd kill Bella, too.*

Fear yanked my mind from thought to desperate thought as I tried to come up with a plan that would save us both. No one could see into the windowless yoga room, so I couldn't signal for help. I scanned the room for a weapon, only to see those useless foam yoga blocks. I couldn't even make a run for it. No matter how fast I ran, Jake's bullet would be faster. I had to buy time. If I stalled long enough, maybe someone would hear us. Maybe Jenny would come back for her purse. Maybe—

My knees buckled under a terror so white-hot it felt icy. *Oh, no. Please, God, please don't let Jenny come back. Please don't let her get hurt because of me.* Black spots danced in the periphery of my vision. I gulped in air and tried to stay upright. I couldn't pass out. Not now. I needed to think.

Somehow, I managed to keep talking. "I can't figure out why, though. Why kill him? What could George possibly have on you that would be worth killing over?"

"That lowlife scum must have been watching me. He knew I was sleeping with Tiffany."

My jaw fell open. The spots stopped dancing. My feet found solid ground. This had already been the craziest night of my life. Here I stood in my own yoga studio—a place that promoted nonviolence and inner peace—staring at a murderer's handgun. I truly thought nothing else could surprise me.

I was wrong.

Jake was a murderer; I'd already deduced that much. Jake was a cheater; well, duh.

But with *Tiffany?*

I stared at Jake, dumbfounded. "Why in the world would you cheat on *Alicia* with *Tiffany?*"

"I don't know if you've noticed," Jake replied sarcastically, "but my wife's not exactly a thing of beauty these days. There's only so much baldness and puking a guy can stand before he has to get his needs met elsewhere. And Tiffany was *oh, so happy* to oblige. Only that stupid bum figured it out somehow. I thought we were careful, but he must have seen us. Guess I should have sprung for a hotel room."

"And George blackmailed you."

"Yeah, and the idiot couldn't even do a decent job of that. He asked for $48,000. What kind of blackmailer asks for a stupid number like that?"

It seemed odd under the circumstances—I was, after all, about to be shot—but I felt relieved. I knew exactly where George had gotten that number. I'd done the calculations myself. Bella's medicine would cost $4,800 per year, and she was likely to live another ten years. Forty-eight thousand dollars would pay for Bella's medicine for the rest of her life.

I'd been right all along. George had been an honorable man. He may have committed a crime, but he wasn't a criminal—not really. He was simply a good man, desperate to save the life of the one he loved.

"Truth is," Jake sneered, "I would have given him the money, but my wife controls the bank accounts. I could never get that kind of cash without her noticing. I offered to pay him over time. I even of-fered him a bottle of booze for his troubles." Jake gripped the gun harder. "But the idiot insisted on getting it all right away. I guess he figured that once Alicia croaked, he'd never see another dime."

"But Alicia adores you! She never would have believed George. And even if she did, so what? Washington is a community property state. If Alicia divorced you, you'd still end up with half of her money. You'd be a very rich man."

"You'd think," Jake replied. "But Alicia's family attorney is a shark. He talked her into making me sign a prenup. If she divorces me, I get practically nothing." His eyes turned cold. "I couldn't risk it. Not when I'm this close. Especially not after all the work I've done to get her to trust me again. The doctors didn't expect her to last this long. With any luck, in a few short weeks she'll be dead and I'll inherit everything."

My heart broke for Alicia. Of all people, she deserved better.

Jake continued, "It's not my fault, you know. I didn't plan to kill him. But that bum made me so mad that I lost control and hit him over the head with the bottle." He grinned cruelly. "Frankly, killing him that way shouldn't even count as murder. Everyone knows these guys all eventually die by the bottle. I just sped up the process a little."

My hands trembled with anger as I bit back my response. If I told him what I really thought, he'd pull the trigger for sure.

Finally I asked, "Was Tiffany in on it?" If I was destined to die, at least something good should come out of it. Tiffany rotting in jail wearing ill-fitting prison garb might have to do.

"Are you kidding? She's a knockout, but she's so dumb she can barely tie her own shoes. Tiffany is strictly part of my junk food diet. Irrelevant and disposable."

What a scumbag. Even Tiffany deserved better.

"Now, Miss Kate, I think we've chatted enough. Time's a-wastin' and I can't be too late. Wifey Dearest might get suspicious."

Terror threatened to overwhelm me again. "Don't be stupid, Jake. You'll never get away with killing me. You should cut your losses and run. Lock me in the storage room. You can be across the Canadian border or halfway to Mexico before anyone finds me."

"Oh, I'll get away with it, all right," he said with a malicious grin. "Don't you worry about that. Everyone knows that front door of yours doesn't lock properly. I'll make it look like a robbery." He snickered softly. "Such a shame this neighborhood has become so unsafe. I may even have to sell this building."

My heart hammered in my chest. "Don't you watch television? The cops will find your fingerprints, your hair, and God knows what else. They'll know you were here!"

"Sure, they'll dust for prints and look for fibers. But people are in and out of this studio all the time. They'll find hundreds of fingerprints and God knows how many different hairs and fibers. And I own this space." He shrugged. "If they find my prints or hair among everyone else's, well that won't be surprising at all, now, will it?"

Bella hurled herself against the door, practically deafening me with her roar. I had an idea. I hated it. In fact, before that very moment, I would have sworn that I'd *never* do such a thing. That only a scumbag would take advantage of an innocent animal that way. But I was out of options—and almost out of time.

Jake's face twisted in anger. He turned toward the noise and yelled, "Shut up!"

That was my chance. I bolted toward the bathroom.

"Oh, no you don't!" Jake yelled. He tackled me a good three feet before I reached the door. Blinding pain shot up my wrist as I hit the ground. I ignored it and kept fighting, using every self-defense tool Dad taught me. I punched and kicked and screamed and poked, hoping I was hurting Jake more than myself. The gun went off in a loud bang in the struggle. I wasn't hit, but neither was Jake, and I was losing ground fast. Still holding the gun in one hand, he pinned my arms behind me with the other and dragged me to my feet. I felt a painful pop as he twisted my shoulders behind me.

Jake snarled, "I'm going to enjoy this." His upper lip twitched under that evil, disgusting, Satan-like beard.

He pointed the gun at my head, and I knew with horrible certainty: I was about to die. But unlike that afternoon with Charlie, the thought of death didn't immobilize me; it incensed me. I roared, lashing out like a rabid animal, ignoring my screaming shoulder. I wiggled free from Jake's grasp and instinctively attacked, sinking my teeth into his gun hand.

"You bit me, you bitch!"

The gun skidded across the floor. After a split second's indecision, Jake shoved me away and lunged after it. Our conversation days were over. As soon as he got to the gun, he'd shoot.

I told myself that I had no choice; that Jake was about to kill Bella, too. That by putting Bella at risk, I was actually attempting to save her life. I hope it's true. I pray it's true. In the end, it doesn't matter. I ran to the bathroom door and God forgive me—Bella forgive me—I opened it.

"Please don't let her die," I prayed.

Bella flew out of the bathroom in a rage. I swear her feet never even hit the floor. She sailed through the air and landed in the middle of Jake's chest. He went down, screaming, as the gun skidded off again. This time I got to it first. Ignoring my pain, I pointed the gun at the writhing, struggling mass that was Bella and Jake. Blood pooled on the floor. I could only imagine the damage being inflicted by Bella's powerful jaws.

Sirens wailed in the distance. At first I felt profound relief. Someone had heard the commotion and called the police. Then I froze in cold, stark terror. The cops were coming. They would be here in seconds. Martinez's words echoed through my head like an ominous death knell. "Most cops won't hesitate to shoot a dog that tries to attack them or another person. We protect human life over animal. Every time."

When the cops arrived, they wouldn't hesitate; they wouldn't ask questions. They'd shoot Bella on the spot to save Jake. And it was my fault. I'd opened that door knowing full well Bella would protect me. I put her life in jeopardy. I, and I alone, would be responsible for her death. I did the only thing I could think of at the time. I knew it was hopeless, but it was my only option.

"Bella, *come!*" I yelled, louder than I'd yelled anything in my life.

I couldn't believe it. Bella came.

THIRTY

THE POLICE BROKE DOWN that odious front door a few seconds later and found me holding a gun on Jake with one hand and gripping Bella's collar with the other, hysterically sobbing and laughing at the same time. I couldn't stop repeating, "I can't believe she came. I can't believe she came." I must have looked like a madwoman.

Jake, on the other hand, simply looked pissed. Blood poured from his nose as he cradled his purpling hand. He told the responding officers that I held him at gunpoint while my vicious dog attacked him, all for no apparent reason. "Just look at her," he said. "She's obviously nuts."

It took some explaining, but John O'Connell and Detective Martinez eventually convinced the officers not to arrest me. And when the police traced the serial number on the gun back to Jake, well, his fate was pretty much sealed. Pretty boy Jake wouldn't be seeing the outside of Monroe Correctional Facility for a very long time.

Bella survived the incident with no bites on her record. The blood covering the yoga room's floor came from Jake's shattered nose, not Bella's incisors. She must have head-butted Jake when she tackled him, or perhaps Jake smashed his face against the floor in their struggle. Either way, she never laid a tooth on him. I was obviously the biter of the family.

Ten days later, life was finally returning to normal. Alicia had replaced the studio's front door and retrofitted its electrical system. I'd started physical therapy for my shoulder and arranged for substitute instructors to cover my yoga classes. But I still had to face one final trauma—coffee break torture with Rene at Mocha Mia. She waved the week-old *Dollars for Change* through the air, smiling evilly. Her canine teeth sparkled. She was the alley cat; I was her sparrow.

She slapped the paper in front of me like a demented placemat.

"Can I get your autograph?"

I threw the infamous article back at her. "Get that thing away from me. It's not funny."

I'd finally gotten my headline: "Stray Dog Saves Mentally Ill Woman from Attack." Directly underneath it was a quarter-page photo of Bella and me posing in front of Serenity Yoga.

"I ought to sue Tali and Ralphie for defamation," I grumbled.

Rene grinned. "Come on, Kate. Where's your sense of humor? The headline's a joke, but the article's not half bad. At least they got the link for Bella's adoption page right." She paused to slurp a thick layer of whipped cream off her cinnamon-orange mocha. "Besides, after the way we tricked Ralphie and Tali, we owed them a good laugh."

"I suppose," I replied drolly. I paused a half-beat for emphasis. "That headline was right about one thing, you know."

"What's that?"

"I must be crazy. I chose you for a best friend."

Rene laughed. "Good one, Kate." She licked her finger and drew a "one" on an imaginary scoreboard.

I lifted my soy cappuccino, careful not to spill the hot, sticky liquid down the front of my shirt. For the twelfth time that morning, I wished I was left-handed. Rene pointed to my right arm, still wrapped in a sling. "How's your shoulder?"

"Not bad. I'll get out of the sling in a couple of days. The wrist is worse." I wiggled my fingers. "The doctor says I have to wear the cast at least six more weeks."

"How will you teach?"

"I won't be able to, for a while. But if I don't demonstrate poses like Downward Dog or Plank, I can try to start teaching again in a month or so."

Rene looked concerned. "A month's a long time. Are you going to be all right, moneywise? I talked it over with Sam, and we can help if you need it."

I reached across the table and squeezed her hand. "Thanks, Rene, that's really sweet of you. But I'll be OK. Alicia's paying my medical bills and covering rent for a while. I told her it wasn't necessary, but she insisted. I think she feels responsible for what Jake did to me."

"I don't blame her," Rene replied. "How could she sleep next to that cheating scumbag every night and not know he was a murderer?"

"Don't be so hard on her. In a way, she was Jake's victim, too. Alicia was blind when it came to Jake." I shrugged. "But then again, so were most women. Besides, she's getting revenge for both of us now."

"How so?"

"The scans came back; Alicia's cancer is in remission. So for now, she's taking a break from treatment. And she's using all that new-found energy to give Jake hell." I smirked. "She completely cut him off, filed for divorce, and changed her will. Jake's so broke now that he's stuck with a public defender. Alicia says making sure Jake rots in prison gives her one more reason to live."

"I'll drink to that," Rene said. We clinked our coffee mugs together.

Rene and I sat for several minutes, sipping coffee and enjoying the companionable silence. Rare Seattle sunshine warmed my shoulders as I gazed out the window at Serenity Yoga. The Ashtanga class had just finished. A group of happy-looking students chatted as they walked toward the PhinneyWood Market, yoga bags slung over their shoulders. Their instructor noticed me watching and waved before locking the studio's front door.

I turned back to Rene. "You know, I still miss George, and I wouldn't wish these last few weeks on anyone. But in a way, I've been lucky."

"How so?"

"This forced time off has been good for me. I finally had to start trusting the other instructors. And you know what? You were right. They're doing a pretty good job. I think I'll work part-time from home even after I've healed."

"Good for you," Rene said. She looked down at the table, silent.

That was it? No smart-assed remark? No "I told you so?"

Rene stared at her plate, chewing her bottom lip and breaking her peanut butter cookie into tiny pieces. When she finally spoke, her voice sounded hesitant. "Kate, I know this is a sore subject, and you can tell me to butt out if you want to. But I have to ask." Her eyes met mine. "What are you going to do about Bella?"

Ah, yes, Bella. I hadn't told her about Bella.

I gazed down at the saying on Rene's coffee mug. "A friend loves you no matter what." I thought I might cry, but I felt myself smile instead. "Michael and I interviewed the top two families last night."

"And?"

"We found the perfect home."

———

When I got back to my house, I slipped off my shoes and headed straight to the office. My conversation with Rene reminded me: I had one more task to do before Bella's adoption was official.

As it turned out, Betty, Melissa, and all the other naysayers had been wrong. It wasn't at all difficult to find a home for a special needs dog—when that dog was famous.

The day Bella's and my story was printed in *Dollars for Change*, adoption applications started pouring in. Money was an issue for some people, of course, but Michael performed more of his Internet wizardry and found a co-op that sold Bella's medicine at about one-third the cost of retail. He even found an Internet support group that offered to answer potential adopters' questions about Bella's illness.

Many of the would-be homes were as awful as the ones I'd evaluated before. But several of them were truly great families who wanted Bella with all their hearts. Some had kids; several had owned German shepherds. One was even an ex-canine handler for the Marines. After we finished interviewing the finalists, Michael and I had a long, tearful, gut-wrenching discussion. In the end, we agreed: Bella's needs had to outweigh all other considerations. We owed her that much.

It couldn't be easy for Bella to trust. Her first owner abused her. And although George rescued her from that abuse, all he had to offer her were love and a shared meal. But for Bella, that was enough. She was completely loyal to George.

Then in an instant, he was gone.

Bella must have been frightened, confused, and frustrated during our short time together. But in spite of that, she literally threw herself into danger to protect me. After living with me for less than a month, Bella risked her life to save mine. I couldn't imagine any human willing to give so much, so quickly, for so little.

Michael and I finally chose an awesome home. One in which Bella would be loved and accepted for exactly the soul she was, flaws and all. One that would spend time with her and commit to her lifelong needs for medication and training. One that knew the risks of caring for an animal with a twelve-year life span, yet would love Bella fully and unconditionally, nonetheless.

I pulled up the website for Fido's Last Chance. Bella's picture finally had the much sought-after "Adopted" banner across it. One less thing to worry about on my never-ending to-do list.

I couldn't help but smile as I reminisced about Bella's and my adventures together. But as always, time was short and my companion was impatient.

"Bark!"

Lord, did she have to do that right in my ear?

"Hey, Bella girl, is it time for your walk?"

Two more ear-splitting barks answered in the affirmative.

"All right, already, I hear you. Let's go harass Michael. I'm sure he doesn't have anything better to do anyway. And if we're lucky, we can annoy Tiffany."

I put on Bella's fancy new no-pull harness, threw some treats in my pocket, and wrapped the leash around my uninjured wrist. Bella excitedly dragged me toward the door, past the twenty-eight-pound bag of dog food sitting precariously on the counter.

"Bella, close! No pulling! Hey, slow down!"

I bumped into the counter, and the bag came crashing down. Kibble scattered all over the floor, covering every square inch of linoleum.

"Bella, stop! Hang on! We need to clean up this mess!"

She looked at me, took one quick step back, and then leaped forward, pulling on that harness with the instinct of a sled dog.

No-pull harness, my ass.

It was no use. This was one very determined canine. I gave in and trotted behind her. The mess would still be waiting when we returned. The first mess I'd clean up as Bella's official, permanent guardian.

Yes, I'd finally joined the long list of foster failures at Fido's Last Chance, and I wouldn't have had it any other way. I might not ever consider Bella my dog, but of all the people on earth, she chose me to be her guardian. I was most definitely her human.

THE END

ABOUT THE AUTHOR

Tracy Weber is a certified yoga teacher and the founder of Whole Life Yoga, an award-winning yoga studio in Seattle, where she currently lives with her husband, Marc, and German shepherd, Tasha. She loves sharing her passion for yoga and animals in any form possible. Tracy is a member of the Pacific Northwest Writers Association, Dog Writers Association of America, and Sisters in Crime. When she's not writing, she spends her time teaching yoga, walking Tasha, and sipping Blackthorn cider at her favorite ale house. *Murder Strikes a Pose* is her debut novel.

For more information, visit Tracy online at TracyWeberAuthor .com and WholeLifeYoga.com.

WWW.MIDNIGHTINKBOOKS.COM

From the gritty streets of New York City to sacred tombs in the Middle East, it's always midnight somewhere. Join us online at any hour for fresh new voices in mystery fiction.

At midnightinkbooks.com you'll also find our author blog, new and upcoming books, events, book club questions, excerpts, mystery resources, and more.

MIDNIGHT INK

MIDNIGHT INK ORDERING INFORMATION

Order Online:
• Visit our website www.midnightinkbooks.com, select your books, and order them on our secure server.

Order by Phone:
• Call toll-free within the U.S. and Canada at
  1-888-NITE-INK (1-888-648-3465)
• We accept VISA, MasterCard, and American Express

Order by Mail:
Send the full price of your order (MN residents add 6.875% sales tax) in U.S. funds, plus postage & handling to:

> Midnight Ink
> 2143 Wooddale Drive
> Woodbury, MN 55125-2989

Postage & Handling:
Standard (U.S. & Canada). If your order is:
> $25.00 and under, add $4.00
> $25.01 and over, FREE STANDARD SHIPPING

AK, HI, PR: $16.00 for one book plus $2.00 for each additional book.

International Orders (airmail only):
> $16.00 for one book plus $3.00 for each additional book

Orders are processed within 12 business days. Please allow for normal shipping time.
Postage and handling rates subject to change.